Denizens of the Holliday Beach Bookshop and Rental Library

CURIOSITY DIDN'T KILL THE CAT

M. K. Wren

BALLANTINE BOOKS • NEW YORK

Library of Congress Catalog Card Number: 73-83609

ISBN 0-345-35002-2

Manufactured in the United States of America

First Ballantine Books Edition: March 1988

FOR RDG—who sees with an unflawed lens,
past awareness to wisdom.

CHAPTER 1

" . . . according to Coast Guard spokesmen at the Holliday Bay Station, gale warnings have already been posted. Residents are warned to expect 50- to 70-mile-an-hour winds, with occasional higher gusts. High tide at 8:50 P.M. will be 8.2 feet, but onshore winds will increase the expected rise. Weather Bureau estimates place the arrival of the storm front on the central Oregon coast at approximately midnight.

"In other local news, the Holliday Beach City Council meets tonight to discuss the proposed tourist information center at the junction of Highway 101 and—"

The man in the blue Chevrolet snapped off the car radio, then leaned back again, resting one arm along the back of the seat. A middle-aged woman appeared at the door of the bookshop and hung up a CLOSED sign, but his only overt reaction was a slight narrowing of his eyes. Miss Beatrice Dobie was of little interest to him. The closing of the shop was of more concern; it meant his vigil was nearly at an end.

He briefly considered the position of his car again. He was parked less than fifty feet north of the entrance of the

1

shop, and there was some risk of recognition at that distance. Still, the object of his interest was on foot today and would be homeward bound, moving in a southerly direction—away from the car. And the approaching darkness further lowered the risk; the mercury vapor street lamps were already warming up.

He glanced up at the sky, noting the saffron glow in the dusky air, feeling the pervading tension in the atmosphere. The warnings of 70-mile-an-hour winds had caused no apparent panic among the residents, but in the last hour the little resort village had acquired the look of a ghost town. All the shops along the block were closed now, and even Highway 101, the famed Coast Highway, was empty.

He watched a miniature tornado of dust spin across the asphalt and dissipate against the closed shop fronts on the east side of the highway. Then his eyes moved back to the bookshop and idly fixed on the weatherworn sign above the doorway:

> THE HOLIDAY BEACH BOOKSHOP
> and RENTAL LIBRARY
> Conan Joseph Flagg, Proprietor
> "Consultant"

A faint sigh escaped him; the only hint of impatience in his hour-long vigil.

Consultant.

What the hell did he mean by that, he wondered—again.

The quotes around the word gave it a hint of irony, and that, coupled with the fact that it was a bookstore, made the chance of coincidence negligible. There weren't that many Conan Joseph Flaggs around. Waiting to see the man in person was only a necessary formality.

Books.

His mouth tightened, deepening the creases at the corners, as he surveyed the aging, ramshackle, shingled building. He was remembering a time when one Conan Joseph Flagg had almost blown a field assignment because he was distracted by some rare volume displayed in a German shop window.

It figured that Flagg would own this Dickensian pile.

He glanced at his watch, then reached out to the dashboard and brought a small microphone close to his lips, his eyes still focused on the entrance of the shop.

"Evans—"

After a pause, "Yes, sir. Have you had a look at Flagg yet?"

"No. Any word from Portland?"

"Yes, sir. I had a call half an hour ago. That *may* have been Harry Morton you saw coming out of the bookshop this afternoon; they haven't been able to locate him anywhere else yet. Washington's checking into it."

"I *know* it was Morton. Any hints about his recent activities?"

"No, he dropped out of sight about a year and a half ago."

"Well, I doubt he went into retirement."

"No, sir. Not Morton. You think Flagg's involved with him in something?"

"I haven't the slightest idea, but I intend to find out. We should have a preliminary report on Flagg's recent activities by tomorrow." He paused, distracted by a movement at the shop door. "I'll talk to you later, Evans." He switched off the mike and replaced it, then leaned back, his arm finding its rest on the seat.

The middle-aged woman emerged, pausing to tie a scarf over her auburn hair; then she walked quickly to the red Porsche parked south of the shop. A few seconds later, the car spun out onto the highway with a resounding drag-strip roar.

He looked at his watch, noting the time of departure out of habit: 5:04. Then his hand tightened on the steering wheel. The door was opening again.

The secret of invisibility is immobility; that attitude of stillness was as habitual to him as noting the time of even minor events. He didn't move, or even blink, his gaze intent on the man who passed through that door, then turned to lock it and give the knob a quick, testing tug.

Conan Joseph Flagg.

He allowed himself a brief sigh of satisfaction, and he was thinking that Conan Flagg hadn't changed much in the last ten years.

His vital statistics were quite familiar. Height: six feet, exactly. Weight: 170 pounds. Color of hair: black. Color of eyes: black.

And he was remembering another entry on that personnel form. Mother's maiden name: Annie Whitefeather.

The man watched as Flagg turned and surveyed the darkening sky, his face tilted up toward the street lamp.

No, he hadn't changed.

The heritage of Annie Whitefeather was written in every line of his face—the width of cheekbone; the slight epicanthal fold over his stone-black eyes; the dark skin; the straight, black hair; the high-bridged, hawk-boned nose. The Irish had lost out in Conan Flagg.

When Flagg turned and struck off southward, away from the car, the man relaxed enough to smile at a fleeting memory. The other officers in his command used to call Flagg The Great Stone Face—behind his back. Or Chief Joseph. He'd tolerated that simply because his middle name was in fact a reference to the ill-fated Nez Percé leader.

Then the smile faded. It didn't sit well, treating Conan Flagg as a potential suspect. It would seem more natural to be indulging in casual reminiscences with him over a couple of beers. But ten years was a long time. He might not have changed outwardly, but there was no way of knowing . . .

He tensed. Without a hint of warning, Flagg had turned on his heel and was walking back toward the car.

The decision not to move was made before Flagg took another three steps. Driving off suddenly would only call attention to himself and increase the chances of recognition. And the light wasn't good; and it *had* been ten years . . .

As Flagg neared the car, the man gazed absently across

the highway, but he heard the brief pause, the split-second break in pace, and out of the corner of his eye saw his head turn toward the car.

Flagg passed without further hesitation, continuing until he reached the grocery store at the corner, and only then did the man move, turning in time to see him disappear into the store.

Then he reached for the ignition switch, allowing himself no outward expression of annoyance; but the muscles of his jaw were bunched as he turned onto the highway, and his foot was a little heavier than usual on the accelerator.

This could complicate matters.

Flagg had seen him, and it was at least remotely possible that he'd recognized him, in spite of the dim light, in spite of the ten years.

A jinx, he was thinking irritably; this assignment would be a jinx all the way. He'd been assured there had been no hint of trouble, but he'd learned to trust vagaries like instinct and intuition.

A jinx. And stumbling on Conan Flagg in this out-of-the-way burg was only the beginning.

CHAPTER 2

The rain stopped as if in deference to the rising sun, but the wind showed no similar respect. It seemed, if anything, to increase in intensity.

And this dawn didn't come heralded with color. It came imperceptibly, in minute degrees. The white ghosts of the breakers flickered out of the darkness, and slowly the atmosphere assumed a dull, nacreous sheen hardly recognizable as light.

Conan Flagg became aware of the encroaching dawn as he lay stretched across his bed, and he gave the covers an impatient kick. There was no comfort in the pummeled pillows, the twisted, disordered piles of sheets and blankets; the rubble of insomnia.

He swung his legs over the side of the bed with a sigh of disgust and stared numbly at the glowing dial of the clock on the control console.

7:10.

And only beginning to get light. November. Before the winter solstice, it would be pitch dark at this time. The village of Holliday Beach straddled the 45th Parallel and paid for its long summer days with the short and usually rainy days of its winters.

Forty-five degrees north latitude; halfway between the equator and the North Pole. That fact always seemed to have some deep significance, but he'd never decided exactly what it might be.

Forty-five degrees . . . and you're spinning your wheels. He'd been spinning his wheels since one-thirty this morning.

No—his mental wheels began their ceaseless turning yesterday evening when he saw the man in the blue Chevrolet outside the bookshop. But the subsequent events of the night—or rather the early morning—had distracted him from that particular enigma.

Tragedies supposedly came in threes. He wondered how enigmas grouped themselves.

And in this case, one of the enigmas was also a tragedy.

He didn't know yet exactly how to classify the man in the blue Chevrolet. An enigma, definitely, and possibly more. A door opening suddenly into the past; a living question mark.

He turned up the volume on the stereo system; it had been on all night, but the music didn't have charm enough to soothe him into sleep. He felt for his cigarettes on the cluttered bedside table. The flare of the lighter stabbed at his dark-accustomed eyes. Then he took a long drag, resting his elbows on his knees, letting his head fall forward, pulling against the tension of his shoulder muscles.

Rachmaninoff . . . the Second Piano Concerto.

Briefly, he wished for something with less emotional impact. He listened for a few seconds, then pulled himself to his feet and extricated his robe from the tangle of blankets, pulling it on as he walked over to the wall of windows at the west end of the room. He leaned against the glass door, gazing out over the deck to the vague white lines of the breakers.

The roar of those towering cataracts waxed and waned, but never ceased to be less than a roar; a sound that stirred some center of fear and awe in the primate mind buried in the human brain.

It was the first good blow of the season, and Conan reveled in the winter storms as only the desert-born can. Still, he was well aware of the insensate power existing within this vast vortex. The sea was called cruel, but cruelty was a human invention. The sea was only incalculably powerful.

A human being is a frail vessel.

And the juggernaut of the storm had snuffed out a human life in its passing, impersonally and implacably.

Or so it would seem.

But there had been one dissenting opinion. His eyes squeezed shut.

No—*it's not possible! It can't be an accident! Please listen to me—he was murdered!*

He looked down, his eyes slipping out of focus, his consciousness slipping back into memory.

Directly below him to the north of the house was a public beach access. A farseeing Oregon governor had recognized a truth many years ago: the beaches belong to all the people. They were designated public property, and the state maintained these accesses at regular intervals along the coast.

This one was only a small paved area large enough to park three or four cars and provide easy pedestrian passage to the beach.

An empty space now, the pavement wet and oily, streaked with fingers of sand encroaching from the beach. A space as bleak and lonely as a desert expanse for all its small dimensions; a loneliness created by the long-drawn sighs of the wind, the dull, vague light, and the gray mist moving like smoke, gathering the glow of the street lamp in a blue aureole.

This small paved area had provided a stage for the last act of a tragedy only a few hours ago, and he knew he would never again see it as anything else.

Conan had been awake when the curtain went up; he

seldom turned off his lights before 2:00 A.M. The arrival
of the storm front at midnight had distracted him, but only
briefly, from his labored efforts at translating a century-
old book. He'd been so engrossed, he hadn't even heard
the siren until it was quite close.

The siren. 1:35 A.M.

Even in memory that sound sent a chill along his skin,
and last night, when the siren finally separated itself from
the storm sounds, he'd felt the same chill. He'd put his
book aside, thrown back the covers, and paused only long
enough to switch off the reading light before coming to
this window.

There had been more sirens, but all of them sank into
silence by the time he reached the window, and this small
paved area had been crowded with an ambulance and two
police cars, one state, the other local. A Dantean scene in
the black heart of the storm, lit by headlights, spotlights,
flashlights; white shafts glittering with rain. The red emergency lights spun, pulsing reflections wavering and angling down the windows with the wash of rain. Hooded
figures, bent against the onslaughts of wind and rain,
moved in and out of the light shafts.

Conan had observed that scene from the vantage point
of his bedroom, making no move to join the cluster of
curious onlookers already accumulating on the periphery
of the stage—a silent chorus. He waited for the drama to
resolve itself, and it did within the next few minutes.

A pair of headlights came out of the darkness, out of
the sea itself, it would seem. That apparent impossibility
hadn't disturbed him; in this context it seemed reasonable.
And there *was* a reasonable explanation. The tide was going out, and the vehicle was making its way along the
beach.

The Beach Patrol jeep.

The jeep lurched through the sand on its oversize tires,
was caught in the headlights of the cars at the access, and
finally came to a halt beside the ambulance.

Conan was satisfied, even then, to watch the scene from
a distance, but he changed his mind a moment later.

A figure emerged from one of the police cars; the one emblazoned with the shield of the Holliday Beach chief of police. He'd been only mildly annoyed as he watched Harvey Rose make his way around to the passenger side. It was more than the wind that made Chief Rose so unsteady.

Conan changed his mind when Rose opened the car door, and a tall, slender woman stepped out. She was bareheaded, her gray hair slipping from its upswept corona, windblown tendrils streaming unnoticed across her distraught features.

Elinor Jeffries.

This gave the entire scene substance; brought it into jarring, sharp focus. Conan grabbed his robe, pulling it on as he ran out of his bedroom and along the balcony to the staircase.

But he didn't have an opportunity to talk to Nel Jeffries. There was too much confusion, and in the end he'd been too stunned to react before the scene dissolved and Nel disappeared with Chief Rose and the ambulance and the police cars.

He remembered that the front door had jerked out of his hand as he opened it. It was at the north end of the house facing the access, and in the lee of the wind, but some wayward gust pulled it away, and he met a solid wall of icy rain.

He saw Elinor Jeffries near the Beach Patrol jeep, and began working his way through the crowd toward her. Two men were maneuvering a laden stretcher out of the jeep. The occupant of that stretcher was shrouded with a blanket.

But Harvey Rose was bending, turning the blanket back, looking up at Elinor Jeffries, and Conan caught a glimpse of the man on the stretcher before Rose covered the head again.

He recognized him. The victim.

Captain Harold Jeffries, U.S.N., Ret.

A man who had survived thirty years of active duty—most of it at sea—before his retirement.

Conan's next thought had been for Nel. The shock of seeing her husband . . .

But Elinor Jeffries needed no comforting then. She was pleading, but not for comfort.

His memory was focused almost entirely on her face and on her voice. Then, as now, the words were clear, etched indelibly. Her hands locked on Chief Rose's arm, her features taut, intense, Rose making a befuddled effort to calm her.

She wouldn't be calmed. And if her voice was strained with shock, it still carried a solid conviction as chilling as the beating wind and rain.

" . . . it's not possible! It can't be an accident. He was murdered! Please listen to me—he was *murdered*!"

Conan turned away from the window and went back to the bedside table to dispose of his cigarette. The gray morning light, devoid of warmth, made even this room seem bleak and empty.

Murder.

Most foul, as the Bard would have it. It was primarily that word that had deprived him of his sleep last night, not Harold Jeffries' death in itself.

He couldn't regard the death as a personal loss; Jeffries had never been a close friend. Conan hadn't even particularly liked the Captain; he'd always cared a great deal more for Nel than her taciturn husband.

But he couldn't dismiss the memory of that word on Nel's lips.

He lit another cigarette and wandered through the gray shadows back to the window, his eyes drawn inexorably to the beach access.

Shock. Hysteria. Elinor Jeffries had just seen her husband's drowned body when she spoke the "murder."

Yet he knew Nel well enough to call her a friend, and he found hysteria an inconclusive explanation. The Jeffries' marriage wasn't exactly one of deep passion, and Nel wasn't prone to uncontrolled emotional outbursts.

And why would she react in that particular way? Why throw out a word like "murder"?

Conan, son, you're muddlin' yourself. . . .

So Henry Flagg would have dismissed these fruitless speculations.

. . . you're just like your mother, the Lord rest her soul. Always rattlin' up spooks.

But Henry Flagg had been a man with his feet planted firmly on the ground, and hidden somewhere in the recesses of his land-rooted psyche was the conviction that only birds were meant to fly.

And Conan Flagg had been handed, in a period of less than twenty-four hours, two conundrums; two enigmas. It was enough to make him muddle himself.

He took a long drag on his cigarette, letting the smoke veil around his head, his dark eyes narrowing as he gazed down through the less tangible veils of mist beyond the window.

Nel's reaction might be explained as emotional strain. But the man in the blue Chevrolet—that enigma couldn't be explained away so easily.

Major James Mills, Army Intelligence, Retired.

At least, he was retired from G-2.

Conan smiled in retrospect, remembering the jarring shock of recognizing that bland, nondescript, eternally middle-aged face yesterday evening. It had been ten years since he'd last seen James Mills, and half a world away. Berlin.

He found his own reactions vaguely amusing. In spite of the shock, he'd walked past Mills without a word or a hint of recognition. Reflex. He'd taken his cue automatically from the Major; from that disinterested gaze focused across the street.

It hadn't occurred to him until later that what he interpreted as a no-recognition signal might simply have been an attempt on Mills's part to avoid being recognized.

He turned his gaze outward to the headland that loomed to the south; a shadow now, blued with a dense growth of hemlock and jack pine. Jefferson Heights, the natives had patriotically, if unimaginatively, named it. He watched the waves breaking in slow, monumental explosions along the black cliffs at the point of the headland, but he found it impossible to enjoy this vista now, or even to focus his thoughts on it.

Finally, he turned away from the window and walked back to the bedside table, wondering if he'd ever have any answers to the questions Major James Mills called up by his very presence, or to the questions Nel Jeffries called up with the word "murder." It was highly unlikely, and he had other, more mundane problems to occupy his mind.

The rain was beginning again, rattling against the glass and thrumming on the roof. He heard that sound with a little dread. The roof at the bookshop would probably be leaking by now. He should get to the shop early to help Miss Dobie with the buckets and mopping.

And this was Saturday. His housekeeper, Mrs. Early, was due at ten, and he intended to be gone before she arrived. He wasn't equal to a rehash of Captain Jeffries' death as interpreted by the local grapevine.

He switched on the reading light and picked up a book from the table. It was an old, extremely rare, and exquisitely beautiful book entitled *L'Histoire de la Peinture Italienne*. His fingers moved gently, with almost covetous pleasure, across the embossed leather cover. Then he put the book on the bed and took an open notebook from the table, frowning as he read his own scrawling handwriting.

Last night, he'd headed the page: "L'Hist. de la P. It.— Columbia U. Lib. Re: Consultation project: Fabrizi. (Unsigned triptych; nativity)." Under this, in parentheses, was written: "For H. R. Bishop, Montgomery, Alabama."

The rest of the page was blank except for one short entry: "pp. 373–74. Ref. to painter 'Fabrizio'—school of Giotto. Alterpiece (?) Pitti, Florence. Possible alternative spelling of . . ." The entry ended abruptly there.

He'd ceased writing when he heard the mourning wail of the sirens.

Conan dropped the notebook on the table and stood for

a moment with his hands on his hips. Concentrating on mundane problems would be difficult today.

Then he turned, stripping off his robe as he walked to the bathroom, making a mental note to call Nel Jeffries later in the day.

Through the automatic process of showering, shaving, and dressing, he was still preoccupied, his thoughts turning in a repetitive fugue whose major themes were Harold Jeffries and Major James Mills. It wasn't until he stopped to pick up the *Histoire* before leaving the bedroom that he took note of the particular combination of slacks and heavy turtleneck sweater he'd chosen.

He'd dressed himself entirely in black.

And perhaps it was the only appropriate color for the day.

The chime of the doorbell stopped him before he reached the bedroom door. He went to the high, narrow windows on the north wall and saw the town's one-cab taxi fleet retreating up Front Street.

He was only annoyed as the chime sounded again. He turned and crossed the room with long strides, then traversed the balcony and descended the spiral staircase into the living room, his pace quickening as he hurried down the screened passage under the balcony to the front door.

His annoyance was mounting as the chime rang again. He didn't even take time to check the view-hole before he opened the door, and he was entirely unprepared for what he saw.

His unexpected visitor was Elinor Jeffries.

CHAPTER 3

Conan had always maintained that Elinor Jeffries was the most beautiful woman in Holliday Beach.

Hers wasn't the self-conscious beauty of youth, although he doubted she'd ever been less than beautiful. If he'd been asked, he couldn't have guessed her age; with Nel, age seemed irrelevant. And almost inevitably in her presence, such old-fashioned adjectives as "gracious" and "well-bred" came to mind.

She was tall and slender, with fine-boned features, and steel-gray hair worn in a style almost reminiscent of Gibson. She had a smile to light a whole room, and gray eyes that always had a hint of laughter in them. But this morning, there was no life in her eyes, although she was as impeccably groomed, her bearing as graceful as ever.

'Nel, come in. Please.'' He recovered himself finally, and stepped back from the door.

She smiled faintly, turning as he closed the door behind her.

"I'm sorry to burst in on you without warning, Conan. I'd have called, but—''

"I know; my phone's unlisted. And I need no warnings from you, Nel. You know that. May I take your coat?''

"No, thank you. I won't be staying long.''

He hesitated, still a little off balance, then led her down the entry hall. At the kitchen door, he stopped.

"Go on into the living room. I'll put some coffee on.''

"Oh, you needn't go to the trouble for me.'' She stepped down into the living room and paused by the piano, her eyes moving around the room distractedly.

After a moment, he nodded and followed her, stopping to switch on the lights. But the high ceiling and the dark, paneled walls seemed to absorb the light, and the room, which usually seemed so spacious and warm, was bleak and dark. He went to the windows that made up the west wall and started to pull the drapes, then hesitated and glanced at Nel. It occurred to him that she might not enjoy this particular view this morning.

But she smiled at him and walked over to the two Barcelona chairs by the windows.

"Please—go ahead, Conan.''

As he pulled the drapes, she looked out at the surf, her eyes taking on the same clouded, vague light as the sky. Then she sank into one of the chairs, putting her purse beside her on the floor, and began removing her white gloves.

He studied her, not in the least deceived by her outward composure. That was only a product of ingrained self-discipline. She was too quiet; too composed.

"If I can't tempt you with coffee,'' he said, "perhaps I can offer a little brandy.''

"At this early hour?'' She laughed at that, but it was only a frail echo of her usual laughter. "You're leading me astray, but at the moment I'm willing to be led. Yes, I'd enjoy that.''

He went to the bar at the south end of the room, and the brandy was as much for his own nerves as Nel's. He returned with two glasses of Courvoisier and put them on the table between the chairs, then seated himself, all the while watching her. And wondering. But there was

nothing in her expression or attitude to explain this unexpected visit. Under the circumstances, he doubted it
was simply a social call.

She took the glass and raised it to her lips.

"Thank you, Conan."

"Of course. I'm glad I thought of it. The morning
routine of coffee is getting tiresome." He tasted his
brandy, still watching her closely. "How are you, Nel?"

"Oh . . . I'm really quite all right. I'm tired, I guess."

He offered her a cigarette, leaning forward to light it
for her, then lit one for himself.

"Is someone staying with you?"

"Yes. Pearl Christian. She was with me last night, so
she . . . just stayed. Thank goodness for Pearl; I don't
think I could stand anyone else around. She knew Harold, and she can understand how I feel now. Perhaps you
do, too, but not many would."

"And how *do* you feel now?"

She sipped at her brandy, a faint, pensive smile shadowing her mouth.

"Well, to be honest, I'm not really sure yet. You know,
I married Harold rather late in life, in both our lives,
because I was tired of the struggle after . . . Mark died."
She paused. "Harold had many characteristics I didn't
appreciate, and I suppose in some ways I feel a certain
sense of . . . of relief now." She looked up at him, then,
apparently satisfied with his brief smile of understanding,
turned away, her eyes seeming to slip out of focus. "But
even if our marriage wasn't truly a union of love, at least
we had a great deal of respect for each other; I think it
could be called a mutually beneficial arrangement."

Conan laughed a little bitterly. "That's more than can
be said of most marriages. Will you be staying in Holliday Beach?"

"I don't know. I won't make any major decisions now.
Jane and Mark—my children—are coming down this
morning to help with the necessary arrangements. The
funeral will be tomorrow. Then I may go into Portland

and stay with Jane and her husband for a while. I don't know. I might prefer to be alone.''

She paused, and Conan waited, reading the making of a troubled decision in her controlled features; a decision that had nothing to do with Portland or Holliday Beach.

For a while, she seemed unaware of him, taking another swallow of brandy, tasting it as if she were searching for a flavor that wasn't there. Finally, she put the glass on the table with a decisive gesture and turned to face him, something contained and tense in her posture.

''I had a specific purpose in coming here this morning. There's a sign outside the bookshop that says 'Conan Flagg—*Consultant*.' ''

He laughed, a little surprised at the turn of the conversation, and a little uncomfortable with it.

''Nel, you know good and well I added that 'consultant' because I was tired of people asking me to look up information for them—gratis. It's purely accidental that it became a bona fide business. You should know better than to take that sign too seriously.''

''But I *am* taking it seriously.''

He paused, stopped by the cool intensity of her voice.

''All right, Nel.''

''And I . . . I want to consult you. I want to hire you.''

''*Hire* me? Whatever for?''

''I—'' She faltered, but only briefly. ''I know all this will sound like the maunderings of a grief-stricken old woman. I've been told as much, in more or less polite terms, several times in the last few hours. But I'm quite in control of myself, and I'm not sure I could honestly be called grief-stricken. I didn't love my husband, Conan, but we . . . we understood each other.'' She paused and crushed out her half-smoked cigarette, her mouth unnaturally tight. Then she leaned back and carefully folded her hands together.

''Whatever I felt for my husband, he was, in his own way, a good man. Even if he weren't, I don't think it right or just that his murderer should go unpunished.''

* * *

Conan absorbed this in silence, allowing himself little outward indication of surprise. But he felt a chill weight gathering under his ribs.

Murder.

Hysteria might have been responsible for that word last night. But not now. He frowned and tapped his cigarette against the ashtray.

"Nel, I don't understand."

She replied in the same calm, contained tone.

"I think my husband was murdered, but I have no proof. You've made a business, of sorts, of finding the answers to other people's questions, and I have a question. I want to know what happened last night. I want to know who killed my husband and why. I'm quite able to pay for your services."

He waved the last statement aside irritably.

"Your ability to pay for my services is the least of my concerns."

For a short time he was silent, considering Harold Jeffries' death, the man himself. And Nel.

Murder.

The *day* was out of joint, and there seemed to be nothing he could do to set it right.

"Nel, I've known you for a long time—"

"And you think perhaps the shock has been too much? I've flipped my wig?" She laughed, but there was no humor in it.

"No. What I was going to say, is that I've never known you to be unreasonable or illogical. I *don't* think you've . . . flipped your wig. But if you have good reason to think your husband was murdered—and I'm assuming you do—why come to me? If you're right, this is something for the police."

One hand went to her forehead to push a strand of hair back, and her eyes closed briefly.

"Don't you think that was my first thought? *Yes*, I talked to the police. Of course, I didn't expect much from the local police. Chief Rose was too busy trying to sober up last night to pay much attention to me.''

Conan gave a short, caustic laugh. ''As usual.''

''I also talked to the State Police and the County Sheriff's office. All I could get from anyone was that I should talk to the *local* police. It wasn't a state or county matter unless the local office requested assistance. So I was right back where I started—with Harvey Rose.''

''That isn't much of a starting place.''

''No. But I did reach one . . . well, slightly sympathetic ear with the State Police. A man named Travers. He said he was a friend of yours.''

Conan nodded. ''Steve Travers. Yes, I've known him since we were kids. We grew up together near Pendleton.''

''Well, he couldn't help me anymore than the others, although he was courteous enough to check with the patrolmen who were on the scene last night. That didn't seem to change his opinion, but he did tell me it might be 'worth my time,' as he put it, to talk to you.''

He looked at her sharply. ''Why me? Did he say?''

''No. It seemed a little strange, but he asked if I knew you, and I said you were a friend. I suppose he thought you'd be able to calm down the hysterical old woman. I doubt he had anything else in mind.'' She looked at him intently. ''And, Conan, I'm well aware that there's probably nothing else you *can* do for me. I know it's unreasonable for me to come to you with something like this, but if I'm not hysterical, I am desperate. There's no one else I can turn to. I thought perhaps you'd at least listen to me without automatically dismissing everything I say as some sort of delusion.''

He found it difficult to meet her eyes.

''Nel, I'm complimented by your faith, but—''

''I've gone over the whole thing in my mind a thousand times. I just can't believe Harold died as a result of an 'accidental drowning.' It just isn't possible. And I can't simply shrug my shoulders and forget about it. I must know. I must find out what happened last night.''

He raised his glass, then put it down again. The brandy had a flat taste. Then he rose and moved restlessly to the window to stare out at the surf.

He knew what he should do. He should simply say, sorry, but I can't help. It would come to that sooner or later; it might be easier for Nel if he said it now.

If Jeffries *had* been murdered, it seemed unlikely that it had been premeditated. It seemed utterly improbable that anyone would have a motive to kill him. He hadn't been particularly well liked, but neither was he hated. He inspired indifference more than anything else. Why would anyone want to kill him?

But that was the question Nel was asking—not *did* someone kill him, but why. And who. There was no doubt in her mind that he had been murdered.

He turned, finding her calm gaze fixed on him, and in the wan light, her face seemed something drawn in charcoal; all soft grays.

"Nel, Steve Travers may have sent you to me to calm down the hysterical old woman, as you so inaptly put it. But he also knows I hold a private investigator's license, and from time to time I take on problems of this sort. At least, when I have a personal interest in them."

Her eyes widened. "Conan, you—"

"I know. Steve's one of the few people who know about it. I prefer to keep it quiet." He smiled fleetingly. "In this, as in everything else, I'm an amateur. A professional dilettante. And I intend to maintain that status."

"Should I be encouraged that you've told me this?"

He frowned and looked out the window.

"No, not really. I know my limitations. But I'd like to know more about it." He looked around at her. "I'd like to know why you think your husband was murdered."

She seemed to sag, her breath coming out in a long sigh. Then she nodded, lifting her chin slightly.

"To be quite honest, I have nothing you could call concrete evidence, and I haven't the slightest idea what happened last night. I . . . wasn't home when Harold left the house.'' She paused, shaking her head. ''I so seldom went out without him, but Pearl and I had been invited to the Barnhards' for bridge. And on the one night I was gone—'' She stopped, then went on firmly. ''It doesn't matter. Anyway, I don't know what happened last night, and the only evidence I have is my knowledge of my husband. But as far as I'm concerned, it's as concrete as a fingerprint.''

He nodded. ''All right, Nel, go on. I'm listening.''

''Well, that's more than the police would do.''

''They're used to working with more concrete evidence—such as fingerprints.''

''I know, and I can see their reasoning. Harold was seen walking down Front Street in the general direction of the beach access—''

''Who saw him?''

''Alma Crane, our neighbor across the street.'' Her tone was briefly cold. ''Who else? The all-seeing eye of Hollis Heights.''

Conan knew Alma Crane and understood Nel's coldness. He made no comment, waiting silently for her to continue.

''Anyway, a few hours later, he was found washed up on the beach. So the police, quite naturally, I suppose, assumed he went for a walk on the beach and got caught in a high wave.''

''But you have another explanation?''

''No. All I know is *that* explanation is wrong. It sounds reasonable enough, and would be—for anyone but Harold. I knew my husband, Conan. I know it's inconceivable that he would *voluntarily* go out on that beach last night—or any night. And if he didn't go voluntarily, he was taken there forcibly, and he died there. That doesn't add up to 'accidental drowning.' ''

He walked back to his chair and sat down, frowning as he stubbed out his cigarette and lit another.

''What makes you so sure he wouldn't go to the beach voluntarily?''

She hesitated as if she were trying to find the right words.

"You see, Harold had many . . . eccentricities, and one of them was his strange—well, I suppose you'd call it a *fear* of the sea. It *was* strange. He spent most of his life on or near the ocean, and in a way, he loved it; at least he loved his life on the sea. But at the same time, he was deathly afraid of it. I think it started when he lost that ship. That was in the Korean War. He never talked about it much, but I understand there weren't many survivors. At any rate, his attitude toward the ocean was . . . ambivalent, at the least. Fear, is the only word I know for it, and it was getting worse with time."

She sighed and leaned back in her chair, gazing out the window.

"I never did really understand it. I was only grateful he was willing to live here on the coast. That was a concession to me; he knew how I loved it. But when we decided to move down here, there was one thing he was adamant about: he would *not* live on the beachfront. We had a chance to buy the Adams house—you know, that nice place down on the front next to Mrs. Leen's?"

He nodded. "Yes, I know the one."

"It was a real bargain then, but Harold wouldn't have anything to do with it. He paid *twice* as much for the house we have now, and it isn't nearly as nice. And he was always . . . extremely careful with his money. Penurious, to be quite frank." She leaned forward, emphasizing her words. "But the important thing to him was that our house is up on Hollis Heights, a good three hundred feet above the beach level. He didn't seem to mind so much being within sight of the ocean, but he literally couldn't stand being—well, within *reach* of it."

She sighed and leaned back, closing her eyes.

"And Harold did *not* take walks on the beach, day or night. In all the time we lived here, nearly ten years now, he only set foot on the beach three or four times, and that was at my insistence, and always on mild summer

days. He used to get quite upset when I went down to
the beach, and he never wanted me to go alone.''

She looked up, a troubled, reminiscent expression
clouding her gray eyes.

"And those few times he did go with me, he insisted
on waiting until low tide, and all the time he was nervous
as a cat. You'd think he was expecting a tidal wave. The
longest time he ever stayed on the beach with me was
about half an hour. Then he just grabbed my arm and
practically ran for the access. That was also the *last* time
he went to the beach, and that was six years ago. It was
a kind of phobia, I suppose. It was entirely unreasonable,
and even he admitted it. But he couldn't seem to help
himself; even the thought of going to the beach made him
almost ill these last few years. He just couldn't stand to
be that close to the water.''

She paused and looked questioningly at Conan.

"So, can you tell me, in the face of all that, how it
would be possible for Harold to suddenly decide—especially on a very stormy night, with the tide nearly high—
that he wanted to take a little stroll on the beach?''

He was silent, searching for an answer, feeling the
acute sense of discomfort that always accompanied any
confrontation with the inexplicable. He crossed his legs,
settling himself deeper into the chair, frowning as he
took an impatient puff on his cigarette.

"Nel, has Harold been acting strangely? I mean, have
you noticed any change in personality lately?''

She laughed. "You mean symptoms of senile dementia? No, and he was in excellent physical health, considering his age. He had a checkup about a month ago. I
know what you're doing, Conan. I've been doing the
same thing for hours—looking for some simple, logical
explanation for an utterly unreasonable act. I can save
you some time and trouble. Harold was perfectly clear
mentally, and quite stable emotionally, except for his
phobia about the sea, and he solved that problem very
neatly by simply staying away from the beach. Suicide
isn't a possibility. He might complain about the way the

world was going, or about my cooking, but he never complained about himself. He always seemed quite content with his lot in life." She shook her head, her shoulders coming up in an uneasy shrug. "Conan, there is *no* logical explanation for his going to the beach last night."

He leaned forward, resting his elbows on his knees.

"Then perhaps the question is why he left the house, not why he went to the beach. Have you any doubt that he left the house voluntarily?"

She hesitated, then shook her head.

"No. Mrs. Crane saw him leave. He was alone, and apparently under no duress. But I can't guess what prompted him to go out; he said nothing to suggest he had any intention of leaving the house last night. I suppose it's possible he had some sort of secret life; something that would explain his going out without telling me. But knowing him, it's highly unlikely; he wasn't that imaginative. And if he ever had any secret rendezvous, they were few and far between. He has never, under any pretext, gone out alone when I was home, and I very seldom went out without him. He made too much of a fuss about it. Besides, even if I knew why he left the house, it still wouldn't explain how he ended up on the beach."

"It might have some bearing on that."

She pressed her fingers to her eyes tiredly and nodded.

"Yes, I suppose so."

"Nel, did you talk to Mrs. Crane?"

"Of course. When Pearl brought me home and we found Harold gone, I called Mrs. Crane. I knew she'd take due note of it if he left the house. After that, I could hardly get rid of her."

"I suppose she came over to your house."

"Oh, yes. Full of neighborly solicitude."

He laughed briefly. "Alma always likes to be where the action is. What did she tell you?"

Nel took a deep breath. "Not a great deal, although it took quite a while for her to tell it. She said she heard our front door close and looked out her window. That was at eight-thirty. She pinpointed the time by the fact that the Lawrence Welk show had just concluded and she'd turned off her television."

"When did you leave the house?"

"Pearl picked me up at eight. Anyway, Alma said Harold left the porch light on and took time to lock the door, then he walked down Front Street 'at a good clip.' She can see quite a distance from her south windows; she knows he stayed on Front as far as Beach Street. There's a light at the corner there, and he didn't turn off. But it was too dark for her to see him after that."

Conan frowned. Beach Street intersected Front only a block north of his house—and the access.

"Was he alone?"

"Yes."

"You have no idea where he might have been going?"

"No. We don't know anyone down at this end of Front; not well, at least. Except you."

"Well, Harold never paid any calls on me here at home. Is there any reason he wouldn't take the car? I mean, mechanical problems that would preclude his using it?"

She picked up her glass, swirling the brandy idly, smiling with a hint of irony.

"No. The car was *always* in perfect working order. Harold wouldn't tolerate mechanical malfunctions; he ran a tight ship."

"That would suggest his destination was close—within walking distance."

"True, but it doesn't suggest to me what his destination might have been."

"Did Mrs. Crane have anything else to offer?"

"Oh, a great deal, but nothing else that could be classified as factual."

"Nel, what about—" He paused, then, "I don't like to make things worse for you, but was there anything unusual about the body? Any signs of violence?"

She shut her eyes briefly. "I—I don't think so. Nothing obvious, anyway."

"And the official cause of death was drowning?"

"Yes. I've ordered an autopsy done, but I haven't heard anything about it yet."

"Do you know who the examining physician was?"

"Nicky Heideger."

His head came up. "Nicky?"

Dr. Nicole Heideger was probably one of the finest G.P.'s in the country, but because she was too outspoken about local politics, she was *persona non grata* to the administrators of the Taft County Hospital.

"I know it was Nicky, Conan. I talked to her last night at the hospital."

"I was only surprised she'd be called in. Nel, when Harold was found, was anything missing—billfold, money, jewelry?"

She shook her head vehemently. "No. He still had his billfold, and there were forty-five dollars in it. He was wearing a rather expensive watch and a two-carat diamond ring. It wasn't a simple case of robbery."

"All right. What about yesterday? Did anything unusual happen?"

"No. We were both at home all morning, then we came down to the bookshop in the afternoon—you remember."

"Yes. Where did you go after you left the shop?"

"To the post office to pick up the mail."

"Were there any personal letters for Harold?"

"No. The only mail in the box was a letter to me from my daughter Jane."

"And after you left the post office?"

"We went back home."

"Were there any calls or visitors?"

"No, and neither of us left the house. We were together all day until Pearl picked me up for our bridge date at eight o'clock. Everything was perfectly normal; there wasn't the slightest hint that anything was wrong. When I left, Harold was sitting by the fire, peacefully reading a book. He was in his robe, already prepared for bed."

Conan's lips were compressed, and he nearly knocked the ashtray from the table as he put his cigarette out. He despised questions with no answers. Why would a man comfortably reading, already prepared for bed, go to the trouble of dressing and braving a rising storm on foot? Particularly a man like Captain Jeffries, whom the villagers called a recluse; a hermit.

"Did . . . Harold drink much?"

She laughed at that. "He didn't drink at all. That was another of his quirks."

He nodded, staring down at the rich patterns in the Lilihan, his frustration mounting steadily. It was like trying to climb a sheer wall; he kept fumbling for a foothold, and the wall only became increasingly solid, offering not even the slightest crack. He wondered why he kept asking questions.

He shifted his gaze to Nel, still finding her calm a source of amazement.

"What about Harold's financial status?"

"He had a pension from the Navy, of course; that was his sole source of income, and it was quite sufficient for us."

"No investments or anything of the sort?"

"United States savings bonds. Harold was a flag-waver, really; a borderline chauvinist. Nothing else, except some small insurance policies. I kept the accounts, and if he indulged in any financial speculation, it was either before we were married or entirely *sub rosa*. And on a small scale."

"Insurance policies?"

She eyed him obliquely. "I'm the beneficiary of all of them—and his sole heir. He has a brother still living, but Ben did quite well for himself in real estate in California. Harold didn't think he needed anything from him." She pulled in a deep breath, her weariness coming through. "It's ironic. If you're looking for someone with a reasonable motive to kill him, I'm the only one."

Conan rose and went to the window again, finding

immobility intolerable. And he was running out of questions.

"Nel, haven't you any thoughts, any speculations, however irrational? For instance, when you reached the conclusion he'd been murdered, did anyone—or anything—come to mind?"

Her head moved back and forth slowly.

"No one and nothing. And I have no speculations, irrational or otherwise. All I know is that Harold didn't go out to the beach of his own volition."

"Did he leave any messages? A note, perhaps, or—"

"No. I looked for one both before and after he . . . he was found." She frowned and leaned down to open her purse. "There was something, though; but I'm not sure it means anything."

He tensed, the frustration translating itself into reined excitement. Hope. A fragment of a hint, something, *any*thing that would give him a small foothold. . . .

He walked over to her and took the sheet of paper she proffered, studying it almost hungrily. It was from a notepad and bore the navy insignia and Jeffries' name and rank. A telephone number was written across the lower part of the page.

"This is Harold's handwriting?"

"Yes."

"Where did you find it?"

"It's from a notepad by the telephone. It's a local number by the prefix, but it doesn't belong to any of our friends. I checked our address book."

He stared at the number, his frustration returning with a rush that made his shoulders sag. He saw his own disappointment reflected in Nel's eyes.

"What is it, Conan?"

He returned the sheet to her. "That's the bookshop number."

"It's what?"

"The bookshop."

"Oh." Her hand moved spastically, crumpling the paper, and for a moment she seemed on the verge of weep-ing. Then she pressed the paper flat and put it in her purse, managing a short, brittle laugh.

"Well. So much for my one concrete piece of evidence. I wonder why he wanted the bookshop number."

Conan frowned, walking slowly back to the window.

"I don't know, but I doubt anyone at the bookshop had anything to do with his death."

Again she laughed. "Well, I can't see you or Miss Dobie doing him in, and that leaves Meg. She's out on the basis of the feline aversion to water."

He called up a smile at this, more for the effort behind it than the humor. She was at the frayed end of hope.

"Nel, you found nothing else?"

"You mean in the form of written messages? No. Pearl and I searched quite thoroughly. We even sorted through the ashes in the fireplace." She paused, watching him, and her voice had a dull, final tone. "I've given you nothing to work with."

He turned, drawn by her weary, weighted resignation. There was no hint of recrimination in her eyes, but she seemed immensely tired. And age was a part of her now; he could well believe she was a grandmother. Before, it would have been irrelevant to call her old; now it was only unkind.

"Nel, I'm an amateur. I'm not equipped to deal with this. If there's an answer, it's probably buried in Harold's past. Or his death might be a psychotic and random act, entirely unmotivated. In either case, getting at the truth would challenge the facilities of a fully equipped police force." He turned away. "I could tell you I'd investigate it, but it wouldn't mean anything. It would be a hollow promise."

She rose and walked over to the window beside him.

"Conan, do you believe me?"

"Believe you?"

"Do you believe there *is* something wrong here? That Harold didn't die accidentally?"

He took a deep breath and finally nodded.

"At least, I believe something's wrong, and it's quite possible he didn't die accidentally."

"Thank you."

He frowned irritably. "For what? The only thing I can do is talk to Steve Travers, but his hands are tied officially, unless Rose requests state assistance, and that's highly unlikely."

"I know, but—"

"Nel, I can't help you. I'm . . . sorry."

And he couldn't meet her gaze. He could only stare out at the rolling surf, still thinking over every piece of information he had, still trying to find a foothold.

"Conan—"

Her hand on his arm brought his head around; she was smiling gently.

"You've already helped me, and I'm the one who should be offering apologies. Forgive me for burdening you with this, but consider yourself *un*burdened. Please. I wanted someone to hear me out, and you did. And I said I had no one to turn to but you, so if you're powerless, then I've done all I can." She smiled again, her hand tightening on his arm. "I just don't want you falling into the typical male reaction of feeling inadequate when you can't accomplish the impossible."

He laughed at that. "It isn't a question of ego bruising. I want to know the answer myself."

"Perhaps you will—we both will—somehow." She glanced at her watch and sighed. "Jane and Mark are probably at the house by now, and they'll worry about me. I'd better get home." She went back to her chair for her purse, pausing to pull her gloves on.

"I'll drive you home, Nel."

"No, you needn't. I could call the cab; but I think I'll walk. It isn't far, and I'd enjoy it."

He regarded her dubiously a moment, then nodded. He could understand her need for solitude, even if it meant a walk in a pouring rain.

"All right. And if there's anything I can do . . . I mean, anything—"

"You've already done more for me than you know. Don't worry about me. And again, thanks."

He accompanied her to the front door, feeling vaguely uncomfortable. Thanks for having ears, perhaps. That was all. He watched her walking up the street, her back straight with that graceful Victorian carriage; then finally, he turned away and closed the door.

She could unburden him of any obligation to her, but she couldn't unburden him of the cloying, nagging frustration fostered by the unanswerable questions she'd raised.

CHAPTER 4

As he drove past the post office, he saw that Miss Dobie had already arrived; her red Porsche, Beatrice Dobie's private declaration of independence from the confines of middle age, was parked south of the bookshop.

He parked the Microbus and walked through a haze of rain, squinting up at the sign over the door.

Consultant . . .

Hubris. Or as Henry Flagg would have expressed it—damnfoolishness.

When he opened the glass-paneled door, he was greeted by an assortment of sounds: The jangling of the bells hung on the door; Miss Dobie's shouted, "Good morning!" from the second floor; and inevitably, the melodic pinging of water dropping into buckets.

Then came a demanding, husky-toned meowing. Meg was waiting for him on the cash register counter across the room from the entrance. His tense features relaxed into a smile as he swept the cat into his arms.

"Meg, I hear you, but I don't believe a word of it."

She closed her sapphire eyes as he stroked her back, her complaints lapsing into a rumbling purr. She was a blue-point Siamese, of not particularly good form; a little too square in the face, and her back feet were pigeon-toed. But she had fine, large eyes of the deepest blue.

Meg was the bookshop's—or it was hers; Conan wasn't sure which. But she had decided long ago that the shop was her home and her domain, and he was too inordinately fond of this feline doyen ever to contest her sway.

He gave her a final vigorous rubbing.

"All right, Duchess, that's it. I have things to do."

But Meg protested, locking her claws in his jacket as he tried to put her down. After a moment, he desisted and reached for a piece of scrap paper from the counter, wadded it into a ball, and rolled it along the floor. Meg leaped for it avidly, making a skidding turn as she landed.

He watched her, laughing at her tiger feints and lunges. Paper was Meg's hang-up. She'd received hundreds of toys from her admirers, all designed to delight the feline heart, but even the fanciest bored her. Her favorite plaything would always be any loose bit of paper.

At the jingling of the bells on the door, he looked up to see Ellie Todd, one of the local high school girls, coming in.

"Good morning, Ellie. May I help you with something?"

"Oh, hi, Mr. Flagg! Uh . . . yes, just a second."

He watched, fascinated, as she rummaged through a large, gaily colored receptacle which he assumed she called a purse. Finally, she brought forth a wrinkled mimeographed sheet, loosing a long sigh of relief.

"Oh, *here* it is—thank goodness! Mr. Flagg, I've got a book report to do, and I have to have it in by Monday, and they don't have *any* of these books in the school library. I hope you've got at least one of them, or I'm just *sunk*!"

He took the paper, frowning at the date on it.

"Procrastinating again, Ellie? This assignment's three weeks old."

She grinned sheepishly. "Yeah. I guess I sort of forgot about it."

"Obviously. Of course, I *should* just let you suffer the consequences." Then he smiled at her. "Don't look so worried; you know I'm a soft touch. And don't give me that fluttering eyelash bit. It may devastate the football team, but I'm immune."

She laughed at that. "Why, Mr. Flagg!"

"Now." He studied the list. "I think I saw this one upstairs yesterday. Dana's *Two Years Before the Mast*."

"Really? Oh, that'd be groovy! I saw the movie on the late show last month."

Conan sighed. "Well, I hope you won't be disappointed with the book. Come on, let's see if we can find it."

As he led the way to the stairs at the north end of the building, he noted that Miss Dobie had already put out buckets and cans and mopped the floor, but he saw a pile of water-soaked books in one corner. He'd never been able to understand how it was possible to have leaks on the first floor of a two-story building, but that was only one of the shop's many quirks.

The bookshop was badly lit, dingy, full of odd rooms, unexpected corners, and low beams. Still, his clientele insisted, it was a place of unique and comfortably anachronistic charm.

And Conan agreed. He'd been quite content to leave the building in its charming state when he bought it, except for some direly needed structural work.

He led Ellie up the creaking staircase into the quiet, attic-like gloom, hearing a distant swishing and thumping—Miss Dobie mopping up in the Reference room at the far end of the second floor.

The fiction was arranged in more or less alphabetical order according to author. Conan found the D's and glanced down the titles, then gave a satisfied, "Ah!" and pulled out the book in question.

"*Voilà!*" he said, handing it to Ellie with a flourish. "You're saved."

"Oh, wow, Mr. Flagg! That's just groovy!"

He winced, and while she thumbed through the book,

he automatically noted a Rex Stout which had been put on the wrong shelf. He reached for it, then stopped abruptly.

Somewhere in the back of his mind, a dim alarm was ringing. Not for the Nero Wolfe, but for the book just next to it. He pulled out the other book, frowning, wondering why he'd noticed it at all.

It was only a common, red-jacketed Modern Library edition of *Crime and Punishment*.

Yet when his eye chanced upon it, he felt a shiver of apprehension, and irrationally the sound of sirens came to mind.

"Mr. Flagg?" Ellie was watching him inquisitively.

He smiled at her and started to put the Dostoevsky back on the shelf, then hesitated, and instead tucked it under his arm.

"I was just trying to remember something, Ellie. Come on, I'll check out your book for you."

Downstairs, Conan returned to the counter. The process of "checking out" the rental books was simple enough. He stamped the date on the library date card that was kept in an envelope in the back cover of the book. The cards were only a convenient means of marking the date on which a book was taken out; they were always left inside the books, and only referred to when a book was returned in order to calculate the nominal daily rental fee.

He stamped the date on the card, returned it to its envelope, then handed the book to Ellie.

"Here you are, and good luck."

"Oh, thanks, Mr. Flagg—ever so much."

When she was gone, with an unnerving jangling of the door bells, he picked up the *Crime and Punishment* again, studying it curiously. Then he shrugged; he'd have to ask Miss Dobie about it.

He checked to see if the cash was in the register—knowing it would be—then, with the Dostoevsky in hand, went into his office.

Conan had made certain concessions to modernity in his office—or rather, to his privacy. The room was soundproofed, and the "mirror" on the door was a one-way glass. The door, marked with a small sign reading PRIVATE, was behind the counter and a little to one side, so that from his desk, he had only to turn his head to the left to see both the cash register and the front entrance.

And he'd made concessions to his pleasure. The small room was carpeted with a ruby-hued Kerman, the wood-paneled walls adorned with a few of his favorite paintings. It was furnished with an old Hepplewhite desk, two comfortable chairs for visitors, and a Louis Quinze commode housing a stereo and a small bar and supporting the coffeepot, which was always full when the shop was open. The one window opened to the west, giving him a view over the rooftops of the village to the sea.

There was also an antique safe. He never kept money in it, however; it served as a storage place for a few especially rare volumes.

He put the *Crime and Punishment* on the desk and hung his jacket in the small closet behind the door, then poured a cup of coffee and sat down at the desk to check the mail. It was laid out in two neat stacks—"personal" and "business."

He glanced through the personal mail, noting return addresses, and ripped open a letter bearing the Circle-10 insignia of the Ten-Mile Ranch Corporation. This would be from his cousin, Avery Flagg. As he read, he heard Miss Dobie approaching, and looked up as she sauntered in.

"Well," she said, pausing to prop a wet mop against the doorjamb, "the rains have come."

Conan laughed. "The monsoon season. Thanks for taking care of the bucket brigade."

"Sure." She poured herself a cup of coffee then settled in the chair across the desk. "That roof is really getting bad. We'll have to hold a *rain* sale pretty soon."

He glanced up at her briefly as she loosed a long, weary sigh. Beatrice Dobie was somewhere in her fifties, trim-figured, but with a square, broad-featured face that made her seem heavier than she was. Her hair was a deep auburn, and she went to some trouble to keep it that way.

Miss Dobie had her quirks; she could be exasperatingly long-winded and occasionally stubbornly perverse in her convictions, but he was well aware of her special gifts; particularly the gift of a card file mind. She was an indispensable part of the shop.

He finished the letter from Avery and tossed it on the desk.

"That roof isn't just *getting* bad, Miss Dobie, it's gone." He sighed. "You'd better get your notebook. There are quite a few things to take care of today."

She went out to the counter and returned with a stenographic notebook and a pen.

"Well . . . this looks like a good day to get things done," she commented, resuming her seat. "There won't be many people out in this rain."

"Oh, there'll be some locals," he said, opening another letter and glancing through it. "The post office parade should be starting soon."

"At least they'll have plenty to talk about today. Did you hear about Captain Jeffries?"

He didn't look up. "Yes."

"You know . . . it's hard to believe. And to think the Captain and Nel were in the shop just yesterday." Miss Dobie shook her head ponderously. "You'd think a man who spent his life on ships would know better than to go out on the beach on a night like that. Seems strange." She sighed. "But I guess the sea takes its own."

Miss Dobie had a penchant for such weighty observations. Conan's jaw tightened and he continued his examination of the mail without comment. Finally, he put aside the business stack.

"There's nothing imminent here," he said. "Just bookkeeping." He turned to the personal stack again and handed Avery Flagg's letter to her. "You can send a reply to this. Tell Avery—again—he has my proxies and my good faith, and I will *not* attend his damned board meeting.

Why the hell does he think I made him chairman of the board?''

She scribbled a few quick shorthand notes, making no response, knowing none was expected, and knowing the letter she wrote would be couched in more polite terms.

"About the roof," he said, as he glanced through another letter, "you'd better call old Hitchcock. See if he's sober enough to give us an estimate." He separated three letters and handed them to her. "These are inquiries on consultation projects. Tell them I'm tied up at the moment. They sound about as interesting as stale macaroni."

She took the letters with a faint smile.

"What about the Fabrizi project? Did you find anything in that French book?"

"Oh—that reminds me." He straightened and reached for a battered three-by-five-inch card file.

This was the File, always spelled with a capital letter in his mind; the heart of his consultation business. It contained the names of the top authorities in almost every field of human endeavor. It had been years in the making, and he considered it one of his most precious possessions. Miss Dobie had standing instructions: in case of fire, save the Morris Graves and the File first.

He looked under "Art," flipping through the cards hurriedly.

"Yes, there was a possible lead in the *Histoire*," he said. "But I was thinking about that man in Florence. I dealt with him on that pseudo da Vinci business a few years ago." He paused, pulling out a card. "Ah. This is the one. Luigi Benevento."

"I remember him." She studied Conan thoughtfully. "Shall I write to him, or are you going to see him yourself?"

He looked up at her sharply. "What makes you ask that?"

"Oh . . . you just had that nostalgic look on your face." She leaned back, giving him one of her slow, maddeningly knowing smiles.

"Nostalgic?"

"Well . . . it's been months since you've been away from the shop, and every time you start getting itchy feet and thinking about faraway places, you get that nostalgic look."

He smiled, then took out a cigarette and lit it, for a moment indulging himself in a warm, sienna- and ochre-toned vision of Florence. Business would be slow this time of year; Miss Dobie could take care of the shop easily enough. There was nothing to keep him here now except . . .

His smile faded and he dropped the card on the desk.

"It's a beautiful idea, Miss Dobie, but I'll . . . have to think about it."

She raised an eyebrow at that, then shrugged.

"Shall I write to Benevento?"

"I'll do a rough draft for you. I have some specific questions and—" He frowned at the shrill ring of the phone, and when he made no move to answer it, Miss Dobie leaned forward to pick up the receiver.

"Holliday Beach Bookshop."

He stared at the Benevento card, listening to her mon-osyllabic responses, hoping the call wasn't for him, but knowing it probably was.

Finally, she covered the mouthpiece with one hand.

"It's Avery Flagg."

He reached for the receiver, his frown deepening.

"Where's he calling from?"

"The Pendleton office. Shall I leave?"

"What—oh, no. Hello."

It wasn't Avery who responded, but a crisp, feminine voice.

"Mr. Flagg? Just a moment, please. I have Mr. Flagg on the—"

"Oh, for God's sake, Carrie, this isn't Wall Street. Get Avery to the phone."

He heard a muffled giggle. "Yes, sir."

The next voice was Avery's, and it had an edge of anxiety in it.

"Conan, I'm glad I caught you."

"Caught me? Where the hell did you think I'd be?"

"Well, with you, I never know."

He leaned back and took a quick puff on his cigarette.

"Yes, I know. I'm such a gadabout. But I'm glad you called. It'll save me some postage and Miss Dobie some wasted time. I just got your letter."

"Letter?" A brief pause. "Oh, yes. That one."

"That one. The answer is no. Don't expect me at the meeting."

Avery sighed, but didn't press the matter, which surprised Conan.

"Well, we were going to discuss the Vanstead ranch; they've dropped the price another ten thousand, but that wasn't what I wanted to talk to you about."

"I'm relieved."

"Conan, I just had a call from Hendricks at the Portland office. He has a friend in the state tax office in Salem; records division. Anyway, he picked this up and tipped Hendricks about it, and—"

"Is this third or fourth hand?"

"Who knows. But the word is, someone's digging into corporate records and asking a hell of a lot of questions about *you*; financial status, where you fit in with the company, that sort of thing."

Conan laughed, finding Avery's tone of mixed chagrin and suspicion ironic.

"Who's supposedly asking the questions?"

"I don't know. Government boys. And I don't mean *state*."

"Federal, then? Well, that's a relief. I thought it might be the Mob, or whatever it's called these days."

Avery Flagg wasn't amused.

"Conan, this is serious."

"No doubt. And no doubt you're thinking of the IRS."

"It crossed my mind. Look, if there's anything—"

"Avery, we have an excellent and overpaid staff of accountants to deal with problems of that sort. If you're worried about the IRS, consult them. I'm the last one to ask when it comes to the intricacies of taxes."

"I just thought . . . well, if there was something I should know about."

Conan knocked the ash from his cigarette into the ashtray with an impatient snap.

"I'm sorry, I can't help you. My life's an open book. At least, my financial life. I haven't time to waste trying to hide anything from the all-seeing eye of the IRS."

Avery sighed. "All right. You're sure there's nothing you've . . . uh, forgotten, maybe?"

"Quite sure. And now, if you'll excuse me, I have some important business to attend to." He caught Miss Dobie's eye, exchanging a wry smile with her.

"Sure. Well, thanks anyway."

"You're quite welcome. Good-bye, Avery."

He cradled the receiver, pausing to take a slow drag on his cigarette. That possible inquiry into the business affairs of Conan Flagg vibrated in his mind like a dissonant chord.

Then he leaned back and turned his attention to Miss Dobie, who was waiting patiently. And silently. For all her tendency to verbosity, she could be admirably tight-lipped about matters she knew to be private. She wouldn't question him about the call.

And he wouldn't allow himself to be concerned over a piece of gossip.

"Now, Miss Dobie, where were we?"

"Luigi Benevento."

"Oh, yes. I'll take care of that later."

"Okay. Say, what about the Dell order?"

"Oh. I forgot about that. Joe Zimmerman was here—as usual." He opened the top drawer of his desk and pulled out a duplicate order form, and as he handed it to her, he fixed her with a suspicious look. "You certainly timed that hair appointment well."

She tried to look innocent, but only succeeded in looking sheepish.

"Well . . . one thing you can say about Joe Zimmerman, he's as regular as clockwork."

He nodded glumly. "Sure. You can set your calendar watch by him. Every second Friday of the month, and neither rain, nor snow, etcetera, will stay him on his rounds. Unfortunately, I forgot what day it was." He paused, then added, "Obviously, *you* didn't."

She glanced over the order form. "Oh, he's not such a bad guy, really."

"No. Just the world's biggest bore. The All-American Failure."

"Well, he's harmless enough."

Conan hesitated. "Yes, I suppose so. But I always wonder about a man whose capacities fall so far short of his ambitions."

"Well, we only have to put up with him once a month." She laid the order form aside. "Oh, by the way, there was a telephone repairman here this morning before you arrived."

"Telephone repairman?" He focused intently on her.

"I guess there was some trouble up the line. He said he was just checking."

Conan considered this piece of news, and perhaps it was only intuition that set his teeth on edge; or nerves. Or the fact that the local telephone company seldom checked its equipment except on urgent demand.

"Who was it—Frank Beasely?"

"No, it was a new man. He says he's only been with the local office a couple of weeks. I think he said his name is Evans. Nice young man, and that's a pleasant change."

He smiled at that, then reached for the telephone and unscrewed the mouthpiece. Miss Dobie watched him curiously, but he gave her no opportunity to question him.

"Did he check the extensions?"

"Oh, yes. He was very thorough."

He nodded as he replaced the mouthpiece and cradled the receiver. No doubt the "telephone man" would, indeed, be very thorough.

The phone was bugged.

He felt the heat in his cheeks; a reaction to anger. The whole day was assuming the irrational aspect of a dream, and not a pleasant one. The bug made absolutely no sense. Who would want to. . . ?

Major James Mills.

Conan almost laughed. Who else? And perhaps Avery's third- or fourth-hand information was more than gossip. And the Major's appearance outside the shop yesterday— perhaps that was more than a chance encounter.

But why?

The bells on the front door jangled, and he came to his feet, waving Miss Dobie back to her chair.

"I'll take care of it. You finish your coffee."

CHAPTER 5

He greeted Miss Hargreaves and Miss Corey, two of the local teachers, with his customer's smile.

"How are you ladies this morning?"

"Well, we're just fine, Mr. Flagg," Miss Corey replied. "But, my goodness, isn't this a terrible day? And wasn't that awful news about Captain Jeffries?"

"Yes, a terrible thing," he responded tersely. "May I help you with something?"

Miss Hargreaves piped, "Oh, no. We're just on our way home from the post office, and we thought we'd stop in and look around upstairs for a while."

"Fine. If you need any help, let me know."

The Bobbsey Twins, he called them privately, and he smiled faintly as he watched them walk away toward the stairs, in perfect step, as usual. Then he went over to the door and opened it, and leaned against the jamb, his preoccupied frown returning.

The sun was shining dimly through a break in the clouds and bringing out the local citizenry for what he termed the "post office parade." With no house-to-house delivery, the daily pilgrimage to the post office was an important ritual of village life.

He saw Mrs. Edwina Leen coming up the sidewalk from the north, her long, threadbare coat fluttering around her legs, her white hair constrained with a babushka-like scarf.

He smiled to himself; Mrs. Leen's name was a tempting source for jokes. She was no more than five feet tall, and weighed at least 190 pounds. She was one of the many Social Securitied widows living in Holliday Beach.

Mrs. Leen was a relative newcomer; she'd taken up residence in a beachfront cottage half a block north of Conan's house a little over a year ago, but from the beginning, she'd fallen in with the pervading rituals and rhythms of the village, and she passed this way every day, rain or shine.

He waved and shouted a good morning to her, but she only squinted vaguely at him through thick, gold-rimmed glasses. He raised his voice; she was quite deaf and probably hadn't heard him.

"Good morning, Mrs. Leen," he shouted. "Nice to have the sun out for a little while."

Her pink face crinkled in a friendly smile.

"Mornin', Mr. Flagg. I'm sure glad the sun decided to come out."

She didn't pause, her rolling, stiff-legged gait carrying her past him and on toward the post office. She'd probably be back to check out a book on her way home; Mrs. Leen seldom missed a day at the shop, and had already nearly exhausted his supply of mystery books.

"Hey! Mr. Flagg—"

Conan turned, then smiled as he recognized Olaf Svensen trudging along the sidewalk.

"Well, Sven, how are you?"

The old fisherman came as close to smiling as he ever did.

"Purty good, purty good," he rumbled. "I be better when this blow be over. Can't be takin' my *Yosephine* out in this."

"No, it'd make for rather rough going."

The brief break in the storm was passing, and a sprinkling of rain began. The fisherman eyed the cloudy sky balefully.

"Ha! Look at that. Startin' in all over ag'in. On'y fisherman catch anyt'ing in this weather's them damned Rooskies. Them wit' their big boats; yust like the *Queen Mary*. They be out catchin' fish like crazy—*our* fish. And me—I can't even get my *Yosephine* out of the Bay!"

Conan studied Svensen intently.

"The Rooskies? That Russian fishing fleet is back?"

"Ya, they be back. Me and Hap been up nort' by Tillamook Head couple days ago. Sighted 'em up there, movin' sout'. They always stayin' yust outside the t'ree-mile limit. But the damned fish—*they* don't know nothin' about t'ree-mile limits!"

"I suppose as long as they stay in international waters, no one can touch them."

"Oh, they be doin' a lot of talkin' in Washington, but that's all is goin' to come of it, yust *talk*." He shrugged and paused, preoccupied; then his features relaxed slightly. "Hey, Mr. Flagg, you hear about ol' Cap'n Yeffries?"

Conan nodded. He suspected he'd be bearing about it all day.

"Yes, I heard."

"Strange business, that. I wouldn't be surprise hearin' some of them damn-fool toorists 'round here gettin' drowned. But ol' Cap'n Yeffries—I just don' know."

The rain resumed in earnest now, the wind rising in intensity. Svensen turned up his collar, pulling his head down, turtle-like, and cast another vengeful look heavenward before he started off down the sidewalk again.

"Damned Rooskies!" he muttered. "I be seein' you, Mr. Flagg."

"Take care, Sven."

He retreated into the shop as Svensen went on his way, but he didn't go back into the office. He closed the door and thrust his hands into his pockets, staring at the miniscule, sliding lenses of raindrops on the glass.

The business about the trawlers was interesting, particularly in light of Major Mills's unexplained, and perhaps inexplicable, arrival on the scene. But, of course, the Russian fishing fleets had worked the coast in this area before.

And it wasn't the "Rooskies" that made his black eyes opaque and cold, but the activities of a certain pleasant and very thorough "telephone man." Mr. Evans, whoever he might be, hadn't bugged his phones on a personal whim; he was acting under orders. Orders from James Mills.

The Major.

A door opening into the past.

The last time he'd seen Major James Mills was at an airport in Berlin.

Conan's departure from Berlin had been involuntary, as was his transfer to desk duty in Washington. He'd left Berlin on a stretcher.

The scar was still with him, like the memories. Both were permanent parts of his being. The scar traced a thin line from his right clavicle, angling down to the eighth rib on his left side, ending there in an inch-long cicatrix of heavier scar tissue.

Major Mills hadn't been with him the night he acquired that scar; he'd been alone. But the Major had done some after-hours checking and sent another agent, Charlie Duncan, to the site of that ill-fated rendezvous. Just in case. Conan owed his life to Duncan.

Later, the Major had taken time to see Conan off at the airport, which was typical of him. It was also typical that, from that day, there had been no communication of any kind between them. Mills didn't indulge in casual exchanges of letters or Christmas cards.

That had been ten years ago.

And four years ago, Major Mills had retired from G-2. Conan knew this from Charlie Duncan, and he was a dependable source of information. Mills's retirement could be accepted as fact. At least, his retirement from G-2.

But he hadn't retired from the business.

The rain increased in tempo until the glass was only a

blur of distorted images, and it seemed appropriate some-how, that wracked view.

That hadn't been a no-recognition cue yesterday; Mills had hoped to avoid *being* recognized. Yet if he intended to spend any time in Holliday Beach, he would be well aware of the risk that Conan might recognize him in the future; and if Mills was working under a cover identity, that could be highly dangerous.

The safest course of action for the Major would be to set up a private meeting on his own terms and warn him of his presence in the village.

But Mills hadn't taken that course; instead, he was monitoring Conan's phones, and someone from the federal government was digging into state tax and corporate re-cords and asking questions about his financial status.

Briefly, Conan considered making some inquiries at the telephone company about their new "repairman," Mr. Evans. But that would be futile. Undoubtedly, Mills had the official leverage to enlist their full cooperation and insure their silence. And the bugging was only a symptom.

Apparently, Major Mills regarded Conan Flagg as an object of suspicion for some unknown reason, and found it necessary to investigate him. He wondered grimly if he were also under surveillance.

But why?

In Berlin, Mills had gone so far as to give him a few reserved, and rare, words of praise, as well as a recom-mendation for a promotion when he was forced to leave his command.

And he was wondering who the Major was working for now.

At least Avery would be relieved to know it wasn't the IRS who was so interested in the Ten-Mile Ranch Cor-poration's majority stockholder.

But why was anyone interested, and, for that matter, why was Mills here at all? Conan didn't flatter himself that he was the reason for the Major's appearance in Hol-liday Beach; he was probably only an annoying compli-cation.

Holliday Beach was only a small coastal community, dependent on lumber, fishing, and tourists. It was tourism that was the mainstay of life in the village. And Social Security. The coast attracted many retired people.

But what attracted Mills?

There were no military installations, no research facilities, not even any factories, other than a few lumber and pulp mills, anywhere near the village.

Of course, there were rumors that some of the new resort complexes near the town were backed with syndicate money, and the local government had its share of graft and corruption. But the area was relatively undeveloped, and he doubted there was enough money to be made here to attract criminal activity on a large scale.

And the Major's specialty had been counterespionage.

More questions without answers.

Finally, he turned away and walked back into the office.

Miss Dobie was on her feet, scrutinizing a book held in one hand, but he was hardly aware of her.

"Where ever did you find *this*?"

He slumped into his chair, resting his chin on his folded hands.

"What?"

"This book. *Crime and Punishment.*"

His eyes came into focus on the book abruptly, and on Miss Dobie's perplexed expression. And again, he heard that dim alarm ringing in the back of him mind.

"Upstairs. Why?"

"*Where* upstairs?"

"In the Fiction, under the D's; exactly where it belonged."

She blinked at him, the corners of her mouth pulling down with chagrin.

"Oh, dear, this is *terrible*."

"Terrible? That I found it where it belonged?"

"No, that's not what I meant." She opened the book to the back cover, then sighed. "Well, it *must* be one of ours. This looks like my handwriting on the price mark."

He came to his feet slowly, the alarm ringing louder.

"Did you think it might not be one of ours?"

She put the book down and shrugged uneasily.

"Oh . . . it's just that I was so sure we didn't have a copy of *Crime and Punishment* in stock. I checked just last week. We picked up a copy in that estate sale last August, but I sold that to Mrs. Church a month ago. At least, I *thought* it was the only one we had. Of course, I have it on order, but we haven't had anything from Modern Library since May tenth. That new shipment's late, too." She frowned irritably. "I suppose I'd better write and—"

"Miss Dobie, what about *this* book?" He leaned forward and picked up the Dostoevsky.

"Oh—that. Well, apparently we *did* have a copy. I just can't understand how in the world I could've missed it, not to speak of forgetting all about it. I guess it's just old age creeping up on me."

He felt the tension sagging from him and a vague sense of disappointment.

"Well, we're all capable of error, and I certainly wouldn't characterize this error as 'terrible.' "

"Oh, I wasn't," she replied flatly. "I mean, not just missing the book. I was only thinking it was terrible because now it's too late." She gazed absently at the Dostoevsky. "He was always so methodical about his reading. He'd pick an author or nationality, and go right down the line—alphabetically, yet."

The tension returned with a whispering chill. He stared at her, feeling the uneasy stirrings of memories; small, insignificant memories. And Miss Dobie rambled on in her flat, laconic tone.

"He was working on Russian authors, and he asked me about *Crime and Punishment* last week, and I looked all over this place for it. I was just *sure* we didn't have a copy, but I checked anyway. I suppose it was right under my nose all the time. And now it's too late."

"Too late for *what*? Miss Dobie, who wanted this book?"

She looked at him blankly. "Oh, I meant Captain Jeffries. Didn't I say so?"

Conan felt his way back into his chair, aware of the dull thuds of his pulse, and the memories were falling into place now; small fragments of trivia forming an image whose dimensions he couldn't assimilate yet. The jingling of the door bells shivered through him, a sensation close to pain.

He turned his distracted gaze on the entrance. Mrs. Edwina Leen, pink-cheeked, smiling vaguely. He was in no state to deal with her communication problem now.

"Miss Dobie, would you mind?"

She glanced out into the shop, then frowned anxiously.

"I'll take care of her. You don't look too well, Mr. Flagg."

Conan waited, motionless, until Miss Dobie left the office and shut the door on the high-volume conversation that ensued. Then he closed his eyes, savoring the quiet of the blessedly soundproofed room.

Finally, he picked up the Dostoevsky.

But it was only a mnemonic device. He was still concentrating on memories; on yesterday afternoon.

Harold and Elinor Jeffries.

When they brought their books to the counter, he'd waited on them. Miss Dobie had already departed for her hair appointment, adroitly avoiding Joe Zimmerman. The salesman had been at the office door, making his impatience known; the order hadn't been completed yet. And Conan had taken a perverse pleasure in spending more time than was necessary with Nel and her husband.

Four books.

One for Nel, the other three for the Captain.

Conan couldn't name the book Nel had rented, but he knew Jeffries' methodical reading habits and found them faintly amusing. Otherwise, he wouldn't have noticed his selections.

Jeffries had worked his way up to Pasternak and Sho-

Iakov. The Dostoevsky was out of sequence, but now he understood why.

But it had been a peripheral awareness at the time. He was preoccupied with his conversation with the Captain and Nel, with two more customers waiting to be helped, the Dell salesman's impatience, and his own impatience at Miss Dobie's very convenient hair appointment.

The Dostoevsky had been the last book, and it was clear in the inner eye of memory now, as he put it on top of the other books and handed the stack to Harold Jeffries.

We're all capable of error . . .

But Beatrice Dobie was virtually infallible when it came to books. She hadn't made an error. None of this would make sense if she had.

Please listen to me! He was murdered. . . .

He opened the book to the back cover and took out the date card. He noted the blackened border at the bottom, but his attention was focused on the last date.

November 12. Yesterday.

Yesterday, Jeffries took this book from the shop. Last night, he died. This morning, the book was waiting on the shelf—exactly where it belonged.

He took a deep breath, his eyes narrowed, intent, but focused on nothing.

Then he reached for the phone.

CHAPTER 6

"Nel, are you alone?"

There was a brief hesitation. "Why, yes. For the moment, at least. I'm in my room, resting. Is something wrong?"

He leaned back, looking down at the Dostoevsky.

"No. I just wanted to ask a couple of questions about the . . . matter we discussed this morning."

Again, a hesitation, and a hint of anxiety in her tone.

"Well, I'll answer any questions I can, Conan, but I told you, you needn't worry about—"

"I'm stubborn, if nothing else. First, you said you left Harold 'sitting by the fire, peacefully reading a book,' if I remember correctly."

"Yes."

"Can you tell me what book he was reading?"

"What book? Well, I . . . I'm not sure."

"Please, try to remember. It's important."

"The book?" She gave a short laugh that was only a mask for uncertainty. "Well, let me think. It was one of the books he picked up at the shop yesterday. He was on a Russian kick, you know. Let's see . . . something about

54

the Don? No, that wasn't the one. Oh—and Conan, I must get those books back to you before I leave. I asked Pearl to gather them up, but she said she could only find three. I was sure we had four, but perhaps not. Anyway, if there's one missing, we'll find it sooner or—"

"Nel, don't worry about the books, please. The shop won't go out of business without them." He didn't add that she'd never find the fourth book. "Now, what about the book Harold was reading last night?"

"Oh. Let me think a minute—" Another pause, then, "Yes, now I remember. He said he was so happy to find it; something about asking for it earlier and you didn't have it. Let's see . . . Dostoevsky. Yes, that was it. *Crime and Punishment*. I'm sure that was it."

His breath came out in a long sigh.

"Thank you. Now, I'd like to ask something else. You and Harold were upstairs for at least a half hour yesterday, weren't you?"

"Yes. Perhaps a little longer."

"Did you see anyone you knew?"

She sighed. "Oh, dear. Well, there were quite a few people. Not all at once; coming and going. And there were a number of strangers, of course." She paused, and Conan waited patiently. "But I do remember some of the local people. Mrs. Hollis was there. I remember wondering how she ever manages those stairs."

"I know; I always wonder. My liability premiums go up every time she sets foot in the shop. Anyone else?"

"Yes, there was Mrs. Leen. I talked to her for a while— or tried to. It's a little difficult sometimes with her hearing problem." She laughed briefly. "She was in the D's looking for Dashiell Hammet. And then later, I saw the Manley girls. Trish said she got that scholarship to Reed College. And the new Methodist minister's wife was there. I can't remember her name."

"Oh, yes. Mrs. Hopkins, isn't it?"

"I think so. And that's all, really. I can't remember anyone else, except that young man—I don't know who he is, but I've seen him around the shop before. He was downstairs by the counter when we left.''

Conan frowned, then nodded to himself.

"Yes. He's just a salesman. Are you sure you can't think of anyone else?''

"No, I'm sorry. There was no one else I recognized, at least. Conan, what's this all about?''

"I'm not sure yet, but I've decided to look into the matter we discussed a little further.''

"You're going to inves—''

"I'm going to do what I can, but don't get your hopes up. I told you I'm an amateur.''

"Oh—'' The sound was close to a sob, and he expected the pause, the time necessary for her to regain her control. "I don't know what to say. But you mustn't feel under any obligation. I mean—''

"I don't, Nel, and probably nothing will come of it, but I'll give it a try.''

"But what happened? I mean, what made you change your mind?''

He looked down at the Dostoevsky, but made no effort to explain his decision.

"It doesn't matter. Now, if you're to be my client, I'll have to exact a promise of you.''

"Of course. Anything you ask.''

He laughed. "That's faith. I must ask you to tell no one about this, or that I'm involved in any way. And please, don't discuss your suspicions about Harold's death. Not with anyone.''

There was a shading of doubt in her voice, but she acquiesced without argument.

"All right, if you wish.''

"Another thing, have you made a decision about going into Portland after the funeral?''

"Oh . . . more or less. I told Jane I'd probably stay with her for a week or so.''

"Good. I insist that you do. As far as I know, there's no cause for alarm, but I know almost nothing. I'd feel better if you were . . . well, away from the scene.''

If this hint of personal danger disturbed her, she gave no indication of it.

"All right, Conan. You can reach me at Jane's. You can't tell me any more?"

"No, not now. I'll talk to you when—or if—I have something concrete to offer."

"Please, let me know."

"I'll let you know; don't worry. Now, get some rest."

"I will, but . . ." Her voice was suddenly tight. "I guess I hadn't thought it out this far. If—if I'm right about Harold, I may be putting you in danger. Oh, Conan, please be careful."

He laughed briefly. "Don't worry about me, Nel."

The die was cast.

He wasted perhaps ten seconds considering his decision, but his mind was already moving past it, sorting possibilities and potentials and alternatives. Even the physical weariness, a product of a long, sleepless night, was gone. Later, perhaps, he'd have second thoughts, but there wasn't time now.

The book. *Crime and Punishment.*

There were ironies enough in the choice of title. And it was a tenuous foothold. But that didn't matter; it was all he had.

He put the book in front of him on the desk. It was new, showing little sign of use. First, he shook it, letting the pages hang loose, but nothing fell out from between them. Nothing was hidden along the spine that a careful probe with a letter opener would dislodge. He flipped through the pages, searching for notations, any variation in paper stock or type style, noting the sequence of page numbers. He examined the inside of both covers, finding no obvious evidence of regluing, and the paper was consistent with the rest of the stock.

Finally, he concentrated on the inside back cover, studying the price mark in the upper corner. He knew it to be a forgery—assumed it—but he wouldn't have recognized it as such otherwise, nor had Miss Dobie, and it was supposedly her handwriting. It was the work of a professional.

He frowned at that, then pulled out the date card, checking the envelope first. Both were the same kind used in the bookshop, but they could be procured at any library supply outlet.

He looked up, distracted by a movement at the counter. But it was only Mrs. Leen. He started to resume his examination of the book, then paused, studying the old woman curiously through the one-way glass.

She'd returned from upstairs without a book, which surprised him. Miss Dobie was attempting to carry on a shouted conversation with her, but Mrs. Leen seemed quite distracted. She dropped her purse, then got her scarf tangled as she tied it under her chin. Finally, she said what was apparently a quick good-bye to Miss Dobie, and rushed out the front door.

He wondered vaguely what brought on this precipitous exit; it was odd. In spite of her communication problem, Edwina Leen was always even-tempered and friendly.

He shrugged and concentrated on Dostoevsky. No doubt Miss Dobie would enlighten him on the cause of her apparent pique sooner or later.

He studied the date card, noting first that all the dates had been made with a different stamp from the last one. He'd stamped the last one himself. The others were simply protective coloration, done with a similar stamp. Very similar. And again, he found himself wondering at the careful preparation implicit in this attention to detail.

He gave his full attention now to the blackened, irregular bottom edge. It had been burned, and it must have happened after Jeffries rented the book yesterday; otherwise, Conan would have noticed it when he was checking it out for him.

Both sides of the card were marked with a few soot-smudged fingerprints. The scorched area extended no more than an inch into the card, curving around one corner; only a quarter inch at the most had actually been destroyed.

He frowned at the card, handling it carefully by the edges. Both he and Miss Dobie had added their fingerprints to the book itself, but he could refrain from adding more, or smudging any in existence on the card.

An attempt had been made to repair the burned border. Cellophane tape had been applied, folded over as if to seal the ragged edge. And this seemed quite incomprehensible. The scorching itself made no sense. He put the card back in the envelope and paused to light a cigarette.

It made sense. At least, he could make a reasonable conjecture.

Harold Jeffries sat by his fireplace reading this book last night. Peacefully, as Nel put it. Conan knew something else about the Captain's reading habits other than his methodical approach. Jeffries wouldn't consider dog-earing a book, and he habitually used the date cards as a convenient place marker. Conan had found the cards between the pages often enough when the books were returned.

It wasn't unreasonable to assume Jeffries had taken the card out of the envelope, or that he'd let it slip out of his hand into the fire. And that attempt at repair was characteristic of him; a stuffily conscientious man.

That might answer the question of the burned edge, but little else.

But he expected little else at this point, as he expected little of his cursory examination of the book. A real examination would mean tearing it apart, page by page, subjecting it to chemical and microscopic study, and that was something for experts. For legally authorized experts.

He rose and took the book to the safe, and when he closed the heavy, cast-iron door, it had a curiously final ring.

Then he walked slowly back to his chair, veiling himself in tenuous clouds with slow puffs on his cigarette.

He couldn't even speculate yet how the Dostoevsky made its way from Jeffries' hands at eight last night to its proper place on the shelf upstairs this morning. The only important fact now was that it *had* been returned. It had been waiting this morning.

Perhaps this explained Major James Mills's arrival in Holliday Beach. The return of that book all but shouted *drop*.

An information exchange, and a classic ploy. Conan couldn't guess why a drop here, why Holliday Beach, but at least he could understand the Major's suspicious attitude now.

If the bookshop was being used as a drop, then it was natural enough to investigate the owner of the shop—particularly when he'd had experience in the field of espionage. Agents, or ex-agents, had been known to switch to the other side of the fence often enough.

It was entirely reasonable, the Major's suspicion, but highly inconvenient. That could only be called an understatement. It might be crippling.

Mills should know about Jeffries; about the Dostoevsky.

But until he was sure of Conan's innocence, it was unlikely that he'd initiate direct contact, and he'd regard anything Conan might offer with a jaundiced eye. The only hope of real cooperation was to bring the mountain to Mohammed; to induce Mills to come to him on his own terms.

And there was an element of perversity in the decision not to approach Mills directly. He'd worked in the Major's command for two years under conditions to try the worth and loyalty of any man. If Mills still couldn't trust him, he'd have to pay the price.

Conan pulled the phone closer and took a Salem directory from his desk. He was well aware that his every word would be duly recorded; his call to Nel was already on record. He could have removed the monitor, but he had no intention of doing so. That was his only link with Mills.

He wouldn't attempt a direct appeal to the Major yet; but perhaps if he gave no hint that he was aware of the bugs, but enough hints about the book and Jeffries to pique the Major's curiosity . . .

That wasn't his primary problem now.

Someone, other than Harold Jeffries, was interested in

Crime and Punishment, and it had been returned to the shop for a reason. It had been waiting.

The primary problem now was to get the book back on the shelf and hope it wasn't too late; that the person for whom the book was waiting hadn't already come for it and found it missing.

CHAPTER 7

The first call went to the J. K. Gill Bookstore in Salem. Conan's wholesale outlets were in Portland, but Salem had an advantage over Portland that was crucial at the moment: it was an hour's traveling time closer to Holliday Beach.

He asked for the manager, explained his needs, then leaned back and waited for the expected outburst.

"Good God, Conan, we don't even *deliver* here in Salem. And a couple of cheap ML editions—you're nuts!"

Conan only laughed. "Well, that shouldn't come as a surprise to you, Ed. But I'm not unreasonable, whatever my mental state. Those books are worth fifty dollars apiece to me—*if* you get them to me within an hour."

"Fifty bucks apiece? For a couple of dollar ninety-five books? You *have* flipped out."

"Possibly. But I mean it."

There was a long sigh. "Okay. I can't turn down that kind of profit, even if it means taking advantage of a deranged man. Two Modern Library editions of *Crime and Punishment* coming up. But with this rain, it'll take a *full* hour."

"Right. Oh—I'd appreciate it if you handled this as discreetly as possible. Don't discuss it with anyone."

Another resigned sigh. "Nobody'd believe me, anyway. Where do you want them—the bookshop?"

"Yes. And thanks, Ed."

"Sure. Uh . . . take it easy, huh?"

Conan cradled the phone and looked at his watch, then reached for the File. He flipped through the cards and finally pulled one out and studied the name typed across the top: "Charles Duncan, the Duncan Investigation Service, Inc., San Francisco." Another graduate of Major Mills's very special institute of espionage in Berlin.

A faint smile relaxed the tight lines of his face; he was thinking, with a little malice, of what this call would do for the Major's blood pressure.

Eventually, he worked his way through a receptionist and a secretary to Duncan, and his ebullient voice boomed from the receiver.

"I'll be damned—Conan Flagg! So you're still alive and kicking."

"Mostly kicking. How are you, Charlie?"

"Can't complain. Where're you calling from, anyway?"

"Holliday Beach; the bookshop."

"Still at the sedentary life, huh? How's the book business?"

"Lousy, but it keeps me occupied."

Duncan snorted. "So what more can you ask—a profit? Anyway, what can I do for you?"

"Well, I have a little problem up here, and I need some—ah, professional help."

"That's what I'm selling. What's the problem? Somebody steal one of your books?"

"No, as a matter of fact, someone left me a book, but I doubt it was intentional. Anyway, I need a couple of operatives up here as soon as possible."

"Somebody left you a book, and you want that investigated? Must've been a damned strange book."

"Yes. Well, there's more to it than that. A man was drowned here last night, and there are some rather peculiar circumstances connected with the death. The official verdict was accidental drowning, but I'm not convinced it *was* accidental."

Duncan gave a low whistle. "Murder?"

"Probably."

"Well. Maybe the book business isn't as dull as I figured."

Conan laughed. "Oh, it has its moments."

"You said you want two men?"

"Yes, that would give me a start, anyway."

"Okay, but I'm a little shorthanded right now. Let me check and see who's available. Hold on."

As Conan waited, he turned his chair and stared idly out at the counter, listening to the rain pounding monotonously on the window behind him until finally Duncan returned to the phone.

"Any luck, Charlie?"

"Well, not much. I only have one good man available; name's Carl Berg. He's been with me for quite a while." Duncan hesitated. "You can't tell me anymore about this business?"

He pulled in a deep breath. "There really isn't much to tell at this point, but there's one aspect of it that makes me wonder. Anyway, I want to find out more about it."

"Aren't you wandering a little far afield from the book business? Sounds like you're trying to move into *my* territory."

Duncan wasn't among the few people who were aware that Conan was also a card-carrying member of the private eye fraternity, nor did Conan intend to make him one.

"I wouldn't think of infringing on your territory," he replied with an easy laugh. "That's why I'm calling you— for expert advice."

"Sure. You can lay off the snow job, Chief." Duncan paused. "Damn. I don't have anybody else available with the experience to handle something like this."

"One's better than nothing."

"If you've got a murder on your hands, one man could get himself in a hell of a lot of trouble. Look—" He hesitated, then, "Look, maybe I could take a week or so off. You know, it might be kind of nice to spend a little time at the beach."

"Charlie, that would be great, but I haven't much you can get your teeth into."

"Well, even if it's a wild-goose chase, I might get in a little fishing."

"There's that to recommend it."

"Okay. I'll have to shift some schedules, but I'll be there." He paused briefly. "Say . . . I was just thinking, seeing as how this might turn out to be a fishing trip, how about me bringing the wife and kids along? They're crazy about the beach."

Conan didn't answer for a moment, a vision of sandy little feet trampling the Lilihans passing through his mind.

"Uh . . . well, Charlie, I only have one guestroom—" Duncan's big laugh rolled out.

"I figured that'd bring you up short. Don't worry, I wouldn't do that to you; not the kids, anyway. And I wouldn't trust you with my wife. It'll just be me and Carl. How soon do you want us up there?"

Conan breathed a quick sigh of relief.

"How about tomorrow?"

"Short notice, but I guess we can make it."

"Any idea when you might be arriving?"

"Oh, depends on what flight we get to Portland. Early afternoon, probably. How do I find you?"

"Take Highway 18 out of Portland; it joins 101 just north of Holliday Beach at Skinner Junction. Call me from there and I'll give you further directions. You'd better have both the shop and my home phone numbers. And don't lose the home number; it's unlisted." He gave Duncan the numbers and waited for him to write them down. "What about a car? I can have one of the corporation cars meet you at the airport."

"No, I prefer rentals. Makes it a little harder for anybody to get back to my clients."

"All right. I'll probably be at the shop when you arrive."

"Okay. I'll get my fishing gear together and see you tomorrow."

"You'd better bring more than fishing gear—just in case. Take care, Charlie. And thanks."

"Sure, Chief. But don't thank me till you get the bill."

Conan didn't hang up, but pressed the cradle button and began dialing. Again, Salem was the destination of this call, but not a bookstore; the call went to the headquarters of the Oregon State Police.

"Steve Travers, please," he said, as the usual cool receptionist's voice answered; then when the connection was made, "Steve—Conan Flagg."

There was a faintly sardonic laugh at the other end of the line.

"Oh, hello, Conan. I figured I might be hearing from you today. Did that Jeffries woman get hold of you?"

"That 'Jeffries woman' happens to be a *lady*; one of the last of a vanishing breed."

Travers sobered. "Oh. Then she *is* a friend of yours."

"Yes, and she did get hold of me."

"Well, I hope you got her calmed down. She was kind of hysterical. I'm sorry if I was out of line, but I wasn't just buck-passing. I figured if there *was* something screwy going on, you'd be the one for her to see. There wasn't a damn thing I could do for her. I checked with the patrolmen at the scene, and there was no sign of foul play. God, Conan, she was going on about *murder*."

"Well, I did manage to get her calmed down."

"I'm glad. I really felt sorry for her, but I couldn't help her. Anyway, what's on your mind?"

"Elinor Jeffries."

"I thought you took care of her."

"I did. I'm taking her case."

There was a slight pause, then a burst of laughter.

"You're *what*? Conan, that's going a long way just to calm her down."

He smiled faintly. "You just don't know Nel Jeffries, Steve. I couldn't say no."

"Sure. You're a real marshmallow. Okay, so what do you know that I don't? How come you're taking her so-called case?"

"Oh, I don't know," he replied casually. "Maybe Nel just has an honest face."

"And a pretty one? I didn't check *Mrs.* Jeffries' vital statistics last night."

"No, nothing like that."

"Well, come on, Conan—what's going on?"

He smiled at the sharp edge of curiosity in Travers' voice, and purposely ignored the question.

"Say, Steve, I understand you've been talking about me behind my back lately."

After a brief silence, Travers asked suspiciously, "What are you talking about?"

"I hope you had a chance to meet Major Hills in person. He's quite a guy."

"Now, listen, I don't know any Major Mills, and I—"

"I said *Hills*, Steve. You must be confused."

"Hills, shmills. I've got nothing to say about—"

"All right, I'm putting you on the spot, and I apologize. I must be getting paranoid in my old age."

"Sure. But I accept the apology; you owed it. You've got a long nose, friend. Now, what about your—your client, Elinor Jeffries? I want to know what's going on."

Conan pulled in a deep breath, thinking bitterly that Steve wasn't alone in that.

"Actually, nothing at the moment. Maybe it's just the old hackles rising."

"In other words, you're not saying."

"Not now."

Travers sighed. "Okay. Let me guess your next question."

"Be my guest."

"You want information; anything I can dig up on Harold Jeffries. Right?"

Conan laughed appreciatively. "Right. Can you do it?"

"Sure, but it'll cost you."

"What? My immortal soul?"

"No, there's no market for souls anymore. But one of these days—and soon—we're going to get together, and you're going to tell me exactly why you're taking on the Jeffries case."

"All right, Steve, but meanwhile—"

"I know. Meanwhile, I'll see what I can dig up for you on Jeffries."

"Thanks. Oh—and you don't need to discuss this with any of the local boys in blue."

Travers gave a short laugh. "No faith in your local stalwarts?"

"You know Harvey Rose. He's inept, at the very least."

"Yes. Well, you've got a point there. Anyway, your little excursions into never-never land are your own damn business."

"I appreciate that—and the information."

"Sure. It's the least I could do, after sending the . . . *lady* to you. Now, stay out of trouble—okay?"

"Okay, Steve. Take care."

Conan filled his coffee cup, then went to the window; he found the small room oppressively confining. But there was nothing more to do until the books arrived from Salem. Except more muddling.

He grimaced at the scalding temperature of the coffee and put the cup down on the sill, watching a patch of fog form on the cold glass.

Asking Steve about Mills had been a shot in the dark, but one with a good chance of hitting the target. Mills would naturally go through police channels in his investigation, and it was all but inevitable that he'd encounter Steve Travers. Finding a division chief of detectives among Conan's friends must have been a boon to the Major.

Steve must know who Mills was working for, but obviously he wasn't free to discuss it. Not with Conan.

He frowned irritably and looked at his watch, then took his jacket from the closet and went out into the shop, locking the door behind him. Miss Dobie's eyebrows came up at that; he seldom locked the office door.

"Miss Dobie, I'm going out. I'm expecting a delivery from Gill's in Salem, but I'll be back before it arrives." He zipped up the jacket and crossed to the front entrance.

"Oh . . . uh, all right. Mr. Flagg, did you get a letter drafted for Benevento? I'll type it up for you."

He opened the door, glancing back at her distractedly.

"Benevento? Oh. No, Fabrizi will have to wait." Then at her perplexed expression, "Something's come up."

CHAPTER 8

He had no specific purpose in mind when he left the shop, except to escape its confines for a short while. He walked south, head down against the wind-driven rain, past the random assortment of shops and the post office to the first corner, then west toward the ocean. He scarcely looked up as he walked the two blocks down the sloping street. The way was quite familiar to him; it took him to the beach access only a few steps from his house.

If he had any destination in mind, it wasn't home. The access, perhaps. Again, a mnemonic device. But as he approached the house, he slowed his pace and pulled the hood of his jacket up—not against the rain, but to shadow his face against possible recognition. And he found himself smiling; a tight, ironic smile that had no humor in it.

A telephone company truck was parked outside his house. His home phones were also being "checked." Mr. Evans was no doubt accepted as unquestioningly by his housekeeper as he had been by Miss Dobie.

But at least that invasion of his privacy, even though it

brought a flush of anger to his cheeks, wasn't so inexplicable now, and for the moment he put it out of his mind.

He stopped across the street from the access, bracing himself against the intermittent assaults of wind. The rain was letting up, but it still found its way under the hood and ran in chilling rivulets down his chin and neck.

He was standing at the juncture where Harold Jeffries would have walked out onto the beach last night, according to the official version of his death.

He turned and looked north along Front Street, which paralleled the shore behind a row of beachfront houses. Front began here, making an L with Day Street, and continued several blocks straight north, then wound its way up onto Hollis Heights, finally dead-ending a few doors north of the Jeffries' house high on the wooded headland.

He turned his gaze westward, out to the roaring breakers, but he wasn't seeing them. He was thinking of Harold Jeffries' uncharacteristic nocturnal walk, and wondering what his intended destination might have been.

Jeffries had walked straight down Front Street from his house, but if Nel judged her husband well, the beach access wasn't his destination. Yet, according to Alma Crane, he'd stayed on Front past the corner of Beach Street, and that was only a block to the north.

But there were still a number of possibilities. He could have stopped at one of the houses on the way, or even if he stayed on Front until he reached this point . . .

Conan turned abruptly, staring up at the tiered slabs of silver-shingled walls and the banks of rain-washed windows of his own house, and his pulse quickened.

If Jeffries had come this far, he could have turned right to the beach—an impossibility, according to Nel—or left up Day Street to the highway. Or he could have continued straight ahead to Conan's front door.

He stood perfectly still for the space of a minute, unaware of the chill rain wetting his face. The idea had definite possibilities.

But guessing at the Captain's *intended* destination was an exercise in futility now. All his guesswork and conjecturing were an exercise in futility. Muddling. Still, he knew it would be equally futile to attempt to turn his mind from that muddling.

He took a last look at the telephone company truck, his eyes assuming the cold sheen of obsidian, then he thrust his hands into his pockets and set off northward along Front Street, the wind gusting fitfully at his back.

His feet led him on, a kind of automatic homing instinct guiding his steps. He was too preoccupied to be aware of his surroundings or destination. He turned east at the next corner, toward the highway, still lost in concentration, wrapped in the rain-born solitude of the empty street.

When he reached the highway, he quickened his pace. The air had a cutting chill now as he turned south by the grocery store, walking straight into the wind. He was only a few steps from the bookshop entrance, when he finally looked up, toward the highway.

Perhaps his eye was drawn by the flash of blue. He didn't break step, or turn his head, but he watched the blue Chevrolet closely as it passed.

Major James Mills was at the wheel.

Conan's jaw was aching with tension as he opened the door of the shop. Sooner or later, he'd find it necessary to talk to the Major, and he could only hope he wouldn't have to force the meeting. That could be potentially dangerous for Mills if he was working under a cover identity.

"Ah! Misster Flack—"

Conan closed the door, bringing his thoughts into focus with an effort. Then he found himself relaxing, his smile coming easily.

Miss Dobie was at the counter checking out some books for Mr. Dominic.

Anton Dominic was one of his favorite local characters, and a welcome diversion at the moment. He was a retired carpenter, an immigrant from Greece, and Conan had become quite fond of him in his two-year residency in Holliday Beach.

"Well, good morning, Mr. Dominic."

The old man's face was creased with a broad grin, his sky-blue eyes glowing behind his thick glasses; but his wispy gray hair and moustache were even more unkempt than usual, and he wore a cumbersome wool scarf around his neck. His thin, pointed nose was red, and there was a pale cast to his skin.

"Mr. Flack, how are you being today?"

"Very well, but what about you?" He crossed to the counter, pushing back the hood of his jacket. "I haven't seen you for a couple of weeks."

"Oh, I been a liddle—as you say—under the weather. But I be fine now."

Miss Dobie frowned solicitously. "You really should have let us know."

He looked down at the floor shyly, burying half his face in the scarf.

"No, no, Miss Dobie, you should not be worry about me. I only haf liddle cold iss all."

Conan smiled privately as he glanced at the books Dominic was checking out: a book on recent developments in nuclear particle accelerators, and a thin, scholarly treatise published by MIT on Mu mesons.

"I'm sorry you've been ill, Mr. Dominic, and you *should* have let us know. Oh—by the way, I saved my last copy of the *Scientific American* for you."

Dominic's lively eyes glinted with anticipation.

"Ah, that iss be very nice, Mr. Flack."

"It's in my office," he said, taking out his keys. "I'll go find it for—" He stopped, looking past Dominic as the front door opened.

Major James Mills.

Mills nodded impersonally as Miss Dobie smiled and wished him a good morning.

"Can I help you with something?" she asked.

"No, just browsing, thanks."

His eyes shifted curiously around the shop, then he moved to one of the paperback racks lined up to the north of the entrance and began looking over the books. He didn't so much as glance in Conan's direction.

Conan refocused his attention on Dominic, who was still smiling diffidently, sparing Mills only a brief, disinterested glance.

"Wait just a minute, Mr. Dominic," Conan said as he unlocked the office door. "I'll find that magazine for you."

He stripped off his dripping jacket, then went to the desk and began searching through the drawers hurriedly, his brows drawn together in an intent, angry line.

Why was Mills here? Why was he taking the risk of open recognition?

Testing, perhaps. Testing Conan's reactions.

That was the only reasonable explanation, and it wasn't too reasonable. But it was too early for the monitored phone calls to have brought him around; his attitude suggested no willingness to talk. Of course, those calls might have aroused his curiosity enough to induce him to scout out the situation in person, if not to discuss it.

Conan found the magazine, closing the drawer with an unintentionally hard push that sent a pile of papers fluttering off the top of the desk. He returned to the counter, noting that the Major was still at the paperback rack, apparently fascinated with the books.

He called up a smile and handed the magazine to Anton Dominic.

"Here you are. Sorry it took so long to find it."

The old man took the magazine with an expression of delighted, almost hungry anticipation.

"Ah, t'ank you, Mr. Flack. T'ank you very much. I bring it back soon."

"No hurry. I have plenty to keep me occupied."

Dominic took a knit cap from his pocket and pulled it down over his wispy hair almost to the top of his glasses. He smiled at Miss Dobie as he put the magazine in the sack with his other books.

"And t'ank you, Miss Dobie, for finding the pam—what you call? Pamlet?"

"Pamphlet," she said, smiling warmly. "You're certainly welcome. Now, you take care of yourself."

He picked up his sack and started for the door.

"Do not be worry, please. Good-bye. I be back, day or so."

As the door closed behind Dominic, Conan looked over at Mills, waiting—hoping—for a cue. But the Major only glanced at him briefly, and there was nothing in his expression to suggest he'd ever seen him before in his life.

And that was the cue: no-recognition. Conan's mouth tightened, but he looked away, his features reflecting the same casual indifference.

"You know," Miss Dobie said, "for a retired carpenter, that man has the most extraordinary tastes in reading matter."

She was watching Anton Dominic through the windows fronting the shop as he trudged down the highway. He lived nearly a mile to the south, and he didn't own a car, but he walked to the shop several times a week. The exercise was good for him, he always insisted; good for his old man's heart.

Conan nodded absently. "Well, Miss Dobie, as you always say, you can't judge a book by its cover."

"Mm. Well, this book may be in a plain wrapper, but the contents are amazing. He's such a nice old man, and here he's been down with a cold for two weeks, and I didn't even call. He probably could've used some fresh reading material."

There was another book of extraordinary contents in a plain wrapper here, but Miss Dobie seemed entirely unaware of him. Conan knew he wouldn't have been, either, if he didn't know him; nor would he have taken note of his departure now, if he weren't so acutely conscious of his presence. That virtual invisibility was a talent of the Major's.

Casually, the "browsing tourist" sauntered to the door, and with only a faint jingling of the bells slipped out into the rain. Conan watched him cross the highway and get into the blue Chevrolet, then drive out of sight toward the south.

" . . . walking around in this downpour, Mr. Flagg."

He frowned with annoyance. "What, Miss Dobie?"

"I said, you're *soaked*."

"Yes, I noticed that."

He turned away abruptly and went into the office. She followed him as far as the door.

"You'd better go home and get into some dry clothes. You'll catch your death."

"Miss Dobie, I'm fully capable," he said curtly, "of recognizing and dealing with any risk to my health."

"Oh . . . yes. I'm sorry."

His shoulders sagged at her subdued tone. He crossed to the percolator to pour some coffee, mustering a smile for her.

"Don't mind me. I'm just a little wound up today."

And as if to prove that statement, he nearly spilled his coffee as Meg skidded around the corner into the office, a crumpled wad of paper between her teeth.

After a moment, he laughed, put his cup down carefully, then leaned down and swept the cat unceremoniously into his arms.

"Aha, tyger tyger burning bright—what've you got your teeth into now?"

As Meg fought for her prize, he pried it out of her mouth, then put her down on a chair and smoothed out the paper.

"I thought so," he said reprovingly. Meg turned back her ears, her tail jerking back and forth petulantly, as he handed the paper to Miss Dobie.

"Oh, the Dell order," she said matter-of-factly.

"Joe Zimmerman would choke if he knew how his orders are handled around here." He smiled at that thought, then reached down to scratch Meg behind her ears. "You wreak havoc with the filing system, old lady. You know, Miss Dobie, somewhere in this building, this cat has a cache of valuable and irreplaceable papers. If the IRS ever decides to audit us, all we can do is refer them to Meg."

She laughed at that. "Sounds like a good idea. Come on, Meg, I'll get you something else to play with." She picked up the cat and started out to the counter.

"Miss Dobie, have there been any calls for me?"

She paused at the door. "No. And no one from Gill's yet."

He nodded, glancing at his watch. It was still too early for the delivery. And he wondered grimly if it weren't too late for it to make any difference.

The books were delivered exactly fifty-eight minutes after he placed the order. Conan gave the clerk a check in a sealed envelope and ushered him hastily from the office, then closed the door before Miss Dobie could get out more than a bewildered sigh.

Ten minutes later, she sighed again as he emerged from the office and headed for the stairway without so much as a glance at her.

He found only one customer upstairs: an adolescent boy sprawled in a chair in the Non-fiction section, completely absorbed in a book which, Conan noted absently, was from the "Erotica" shelf.

He checked all the upstairs rooms, then returned to the Fiction section. The two copies of *Crime and Punishment* from Gill's were tucked under his arm, hidden in the package in which they'd been delivered.

He went to the D's and took one of the copies from the sack, then hesitated, studying it critically.

Both copies were now outwardly identical to the one in the safe. He'd pasted envelopes in the back covers for the date cards, used old cards taken from other rental books, stamped yesterday's date on them, and imitated Miss Dobie's handwriting on the price mark to the best of his ability.

He hoped they would pass muster; and he hoped it wasn't already too late. He glanced at his watch and pulled in a quick breath. Nearly noon.

He put one copy on the shelf, exactly where he'd found the original, then he frowned as he considered where to put the extra copy for safekeeping. Finally, he took it back to the Reference room and put it in the Anthropology section.

As he walked back to the stairway and passed through the Fiction room, he glanced over at the substitute copy waiting on its shelf.

The trap was set.

He could only hope the intended victim would take the bait.

If he, or she, didn't there was little chance of getting another lead on Jeffries' killer. Conan felt a momentary chill that was more than cold and dampness.

He'd now passed a point of no return.

CHAPTER 9

"Forester and water, please, Mary."

Conan sank wearily into a chair as the waitress took his order.

"Okay, Mr. Flagg. How are you this evening?"

"Damp, but otherwise fine."

She grinned. "Another few years in this country, and you'll develop webbed feet. Just be patient." She turned and headed for the bar.

He leaned back and lit a cigarette, feeling the dull ache of tension in his neck and shoulders. He'd chosen a table away from the bar near the glass doors that opened onto the swimming pool. The pool was lighted from beneath and cast wavering, blue-green reflections into the shadowed room.

When Mary brought his drink, he signed the tab, then turned his chair toward the pool again. The Surf House Lounge was thinly populated this evening, and he found himself relaxing with the solitude and the bourbon.

Still, he wasn't capable of relaxing enough to stop the ceaseless process of muddling; reexamining and dissecting the events of the day, worrying every slight hint or anomaly like a dog with a bone. It had been a long day, but as far as the Jeffries matter was concerned, not very productive.

He'd had an opportunity to waylay Alma Crane, the Jeffries' busybody neighbor, on her way to the post office, creating an excuse for accompanying her by mailing a stack of unaddressed, unstamped, and empty envelopes taken hurriedly from his desk.

Mrs. Crane was enjoying the limelight as the last person to see Captain Jeffries alive, and she told her story with only the slightest prompting. But it added little to his fund of knowledge, except that she was sure Jeffries was carrying something when he left his house. She couldn't identify it, however, except that it was small and red.

The Dostoevsky. But this only confirmed what he'd already assumed: that Jeffries had taken the book with him when he embarked on his solitary and fatal sojourn.

There was nothing else to show for the day's efforts. Major Mills had put in no more appearances, and no one had checked out the *Crime and Punishment*. When he closed the shop, it was still on the shelf—waiting.

"Conan, you look like the bottom just dropped out of the stock market."

He looked up to see Nicky Heideger standing across the table from him. He laughed and rose to pull out her chair.

"I never believed in stock, Nicky, except the four-legged kind." Then as he resumed his seat, he met the quiet look of amusement in her eyes with a warm smile. "It's good to see you. I appreciate your taking time to talk to me."

"My pleasure. It's a relief to talk to someone who isn't sick, or doesn't at least think he is. I'm sorry I'm late. The Hicks kid broke his wrist."

She took a package of Camels from her purse and leaned forward as he lit one for her. Then she settled back in her chair, her head tilted to one side, and studied him curiously.

Dr. Nicole Heideger was an attractive woman who might have been beautiful, but there was little time in her life to waste on cosmetic embellishment or fashion. Her dress was simple and practical, her straight, dark hair cut in a boyish style. Her brown eyes were quick and alert, crinkling at the corners now as she smiled.

"As a matter of fact," she said, "you've been much too healthy lately. I haven't seen you for weeks."

The waitress came to the table and Conan ordered another bourbon for himself and scotch for Nicky.

"Well, I'm sorry about my good health," he said when Mary left. "But if it'll make you happy, I'll try to work up a case of typhoid or diphtheria."

"Thanks a lot, friend. All I need is an epidemic. Try something simple, like a good case of lumbago or gout."

He gave her a crooked smile. "No, if I'm going to suffer, I want something that'll get me a little sympathy. All I'd get with lumbago or gout is snickers."

"Sympathy, you want." She laughed, tilting her head back. "Try a broken leg, then. At least it isn't contagious." She paused to inhale on her cigarette, squinting at him through the smoke. "Anyway, now that I'm here, what were you so anxious to talk to me about?"

He took time to glance around to make sure no one was within earshot, the glint of laughter in his eyes fading to black opacity.

"Nicky, this is going to seem strange, I know, but I need some information."

"I gathered that from what you said on the phone. What about?"

"Harold Jeffries."

Mary returned with their drinks, and Nicky waited until she had departed. Then she raised her glass and nodded to Conan, her eyes slightly narrowed.

"Thanks for the drink. Now, what do you want to know about Jeffries?"

"Anything you might know."

"You mean the man himself, or his death?"

"His death."

She took a swallow of her scotch, eyeing him skeptically.

"Conan, I realize you have a problem controlling your curiosity—note, I'm being polite and not using the word 'nosiness'—but why are you so interested in Jeffries' death?"

"Well, that's where the strange part comes." He paused, tapping his cigarette against the ashtray, then looked up at her. "Nel Jeffries thinks her husband was murdered."

If Dr. Heideger was surprised, she didn't show it.

"And you're playing detective?"

He shrugged. "You might put it that way. I suppose I was the last resort; no one else would listen to her."

Nicky gave a short laugh. "You always were a sucker for a damsel in distress."

"Perhaps, but Nel doesn't quite fit the damsel image. Maybe your diagnosis was correct; plain nosiness."

"Maybe. Do *you* think he was murdered?"

"I think it's very probable."

She was silent for a while, considering this; then she leaned forward, resting her elbows on the table.

"Okay. I've been around enough to know it's possible. Of course, if it's *probable*, then it isn't very smart of you to get involved."

"I know, Nicky, but some very peculiar things have been going on. Something's happening, and—"

"And you can't stand it until you find out *what*?"

He laughed, his shoulders rising in a quick shrug.

"I guess that's about it."

"All right. I'm not asking any more questions. Ignorance is sometimes less than bliss, but it's a hell of a lot safer." She took another swallow of her drink and leaned back. "Unfortunately, there isn't much I can tell you. The only reason I was called in on this, was because Dr. Callen was out of town, and old Spenser was drunk." She smiled sardonically. "It must've galled Harvey Rose to have to call *me*. Anyway, I only examined the body and signed the death certificate. They brought him to the hospital a little before 2:00 A.M. I can't say exactly how long he'd been dead, but at least three to six hours. As far as I could determine, he died by drowning.''

''Nel ordered an autopsy done. Have you any idea when the results would be available?''

''Available to whom?'' She eyed him suspiciously, then shrugged. ''The autopsy was probably done today. Dr. Callen is back and he usually handles the pathology.''

''Nicky, I want to know the results of that autopsy.''

She studied him a moment, a frown drawing a strong line between her brows. Finally, she sighed.

''You want to look at the report *personally*?''

''Not necessarily. I just want to know—''

''The results.'' She sighed again, her mouth tight. ''Okay. I can probably get a look at it. I'm not making any promises, but I'll see what I can do.''

''Thanks, Nicky.''

''Sure.'' Then she grinned at him. ''I'm sorry I didn't find any bullet holes. Would that have helped?''

''I don't know. Was there anything . . . anything at all unusual about the body? Perhaps some small mark or injury, particularly around the head?''

She thought a moment, then nodded.

''Well, yes, there was something. But it was only a bruise and some very minor lacerations on the right side of the jaw.'' She pointed to a spot on her own jaw, just to the right of her chin. ''About here.''

Conan looked at her intently.

''You said the *right* side? Are you sure?''

''Yes, it was the right side, but it wasn't necessarily inflicted by a human hand. There *are* a few rocks out in that surf, you know.''

''Not until you get down around the base of Jefferson Heights. Jeffries was drowned on an incoming tide. I doubt he ever got far from the beach, even after he died. Were there any other bruises?''

''No. Nothing recent, anyway.''

''Is there anything that makes you think that bruise *couldn't* have been inflicted by a human hand?''

She hesitated briefly. ''No. It *could* have been.''

He leaned back, lost in concentration, his fingers drumming on the table. After a while, Nicky laughed softly.

"Well, I'm glad I gave you something to think about."

"Oh, I have plenty to think about, but I don't know how far it'll get me."

She sipped at her drink thoughtfully.

"Conan—"

He looked up at her distractedly. "What?"

"Look, I don't know what you've gotten yourself into, but in my business, I see a lot of the end results of violence. If there *is* a possibility you're dealing with murder, my doctorly advice to you is to be careful."

He smiled faintly. "Nicky, I *have* had a little experience . . . well, along similar lines. Anyway, I don't intend to—" He stopped, looking past her to the entrance of the lounge. "Well. Here comes the honorable Chief Rose."

Her eyes went hard and cold. "Making his nightly rounds, I suppose—of the bars."

"No doubt."

Nicky turned and watched Rose as he sauntered up to the bar and greeted the bartender familiarly; then she tipped up her glass and finished her scotch.

"I wonder," she said caustically, "if he swaggers like that without that fancy uniform and that .38 on his hip."

Conan laughed. "I doubt he can stand up without them."

Rose glanced around the room and nodded as he recognized them. Conan managed a small, tight smile of acknowledgment, wondering at his own uneasiness, and what it was about Rose that inspired it.

Harvey Rose was a big, rawboned, short-necked man with a ruddy complexion and thin, sandy hair. But for all his size, he moved awkwardly, and there was a softness about him; a softness that was soul deep. The source of any apprehension he inspired had to be in his eyes. A pale, watery blue, fringed with blond lashes, his eyes seemed always in motion. Like a cat's.

Nicky put out her cigarette and picked up her purse.

"Conan, thanks for the drink, but if you'll excuse me, I think I'll take off. It's been a long day."

"I'm with you, Nicky." He rose and came around the table to help her with her coat. "The atmosphere is getting unpleasant in here. I'll walk you to your car."

.

The rain had stopped, but the highway was still wet and slick. Conan was driving the black XK-E, which he considered his nonbusiness car; the Microbus was for hauling books and other such mundane pursuits. But the Jaguar was one of the real pleasures of his life, not because he was concerned with such vague abstractions as compression ratios and horsepower, but because it was a thing of beauty and a constant joy to the eye.

It was only a mile from the Surf House on Holliday Bay to the center of town, but tonight it seemed unusually long. He was mentally and physically drained, anticipating a warm fire, a quiet supper alone, and some Sibelius, perhaps, on the stereo. *En Saga* or *Oceanides* . . .

He flipped on his turn signal as he neared Day Street and glanced into the rearview mirror. A pair of headlights glared back at him. Mumbling a few choice comments on tailgaters, he swung off the highway, looking back as he completed the turn.

The other car roared on, but as it passed under the street lamp, he recognized the insignia on the door.

It was Police Chief Harvey Rose's car.

CHAPTER 10

When Conan and Miss Dobie arrived at the bookshop, it was nearly noon, and a few tourists were already waiting impatiently at the door. There would be few locals today; it was Sunday, and the post office was closed. As soon as he had the front door unlocked, he went upstairs, ostensibly to turn on the lights.

The *Crime and Punishment* was still in place, and apparently untouched.

On returning downstairs, he unlocked the office then opened the safe. The original copy was also still in its place.

He started the percolator and fed Meg, who had followed him every step of the way, noisily reminding him that she wasn't accustomed to late breakfasts. As he finished this task, he heard Miss Dobie in conversation with one of the customers, then footsteps and voices fading as she went upstairs to search out the requested book.

He went to the window, gazing out at the satin grays of the sea, calm now that the worst of the storm was past.

The cause of their late opening was Captain Harold Jeffries' funeral, and he was thinking of Nel, suffering the graveside ceremony in silence, calm and entirely composed.

Nel was on her way to Portland now. It was something of a relief to have her away from Holliday Beach; at least until he knew more about her husband's death.

The jingling of the bells brought his head around abruptly. He frowned, then went out to the counter as a black-uniformed state patrolman walked into the shop.

"May I help you?" Conan asked, noting the large manila envelope in his hand.

"Yes, I'm looking for Conan Flagg."

"I'm the only one around who answers that description. What can I do for you?"

"I guess it's a matter of what I can do for you, Mr. Flagg," he replied, smiling politely as he held out the envelope for him. "Steve Travers asked me to drop this off for you."

"Ah." This would be the report on Jeffries. "Thank you. I hadn't expected such fast service, or a personal delivery."

"I had to go down to Westport today, so it was no trouble."

"I appreciate it, and thank Steve for me."

"Yes, sir, I will." He touched his fingers to the bill of his cap. "If you'll excuse me, I'll be on my way."

"Of course. Thanks again."

Miss Dobie approached the counter, eyeing the patrolman curiously as he left the shop.

"Well. Looks like they finally caught up with you, Mr. Flagg."

"They always get their man. Excuse me."

He turned and went into the office, closing the door behind him, then sat down at the desk and tore open the manila envelope.

Ten minutes later, he stuffed the papers back into the envelope with a sigh of disappointment. His quick perusal turned up nothing new or unexpected. Jeffries had been a cadet at Annapolis and spent his life in the Navy, working up through the ranks with steady, but unremarkable consistency. His record showed no irregularities, and his reputation was unimpeachable.

The only item of interest was the fact that he had once been attached to the Navy Code Section in Washington.

Conan glanced out at the counter, then put the envelope in his desk drawer and locked it.

Another source of information had already proved even less fruitful. He'd called Nicky Heideger before he left home for the funeral on the off chance that she might have had a look at the autopsy report.

He was in luck, but only to the extent that Nicky had to make an early call at the hospital, and she'd taken the opportunity to look through the files. The report was notably uninformative, except in a negative sense. She assured him that Dr. Callen had done an adequate job on the autopsy, but the cause of death was simple and uncomplicated. Drowning.

That didn't preclude murder, but it added nothing to his scant fund of knowledge concerning Jeffries' death.

The item about his connection with the Navy Code Section was interesting, but aside from that, he had nothing to go on but a book that shouldn't have been on the shelf, a widow's knowledge of her husband's eccentricities, and a bruise on the right side of the victim's jaw.

But perhaps he'd catch something in the little mousetrap he'd set upstairs. And Charlie Duncan would be arriving this afternoon; maybe he'd have some ideas.

Conan rose and poured a cup of coffee, then went out to the counter. Miss Dobie looked up at him questioningly.

"Anything special to do today?"

Sure, he thought—just find a murderer.

"No, Miss Dobie. You probably have some orders to take care of. I'll watch the counter for a while."

She nodded and started for her office.

"There's always plenty to catch up with on my desk. I'd better check that Doubleday order; it's late."

"Fine. I'll call you if I need any help."

He sat down on the stool behind the counter, and a

few minutes later heard the distant clatter of Miss Dobie's typewriter. There were quite a few tourists in the shop; more than usual for November. He smiled and greeted a young couple as they came in, automatically pegging them as newlyweds on their honeymoon.

But his mind wasn't on the customers.

He'd sent Miss Dobie away because he wanted to be at the counter in case anyone checked out that copy of *Crime and Punishment*.

Waiting—for anything—wasn't Conan's idea of a good time.

For well over an hour, he sat behind the counter, occasionally tending the needs of customers and constantly restraining his rising impatience, before the monotony was broken by so much as a familiar face.

He was stubbing out his tenth cigarette since the beginning of his vigil, and as he looked up at the jingling of the door bells, his eyes widened.

Joe Zimmerman, the Dell salesman.

For a moment, Conan didn't credit his own vision. Joe Zimmerman had never, in all the time he'd been on this route—over a year, now—set foot in the shop except on his regular second Friday of the month.

But here he was, the All-American Failure, big and square, but showing a tendency to a thickening around the middle; his hair cut short in a crew cut fashionable in his varsity football days.

"My God, it must be Friday," Conan commented.

Zimmerman's broad face was a study in confusion for a moment; then he grinned, that cocky, self-sure grin Conan always found so irritating.

"Nope, you only get one Friday a week, and you had that already. You know, *some* people get a vacation now and then."

"I wouldn't expect you to spend any part of your vacation in a bookshop, Joe."

Zimmerman shrugged, sauntering over to the counter and leaning on it with one elbow, bringing his face uncomfortably close, a habit Conan found particularly annoying.

"Oh, I just figured I'd see what goes on here when my back's turned."

"I'm afraid you'll find what goes on here rather boring," Conan replied, leaning back against the wall.

"I doubt that, ol' buddy. Say—I've got a complaint to make to the management."

"I'm the management."

"Well, the sign on the door says you're supposed to open at ten every day except Mondays, right?"

"That's what the sign says."

"I was here at ten-thirty, and the place was closed up tighter'n a drum." He paused, then added archly, 'You keeping banker's hours?"

Conan started to reply, but was distracted as Meg trotted around by his stool, using his lap as a launching pad to leap up onto the counter. At that, Joe straightened and backed up a step, and Conan restrained a smile. Meg had an unerring instinct for people who didn't like cats and inevitably chose to lavish her attention on them.

"Well, Joe," he said, ignoring his reaction to Meg's proximity, "some people can afford banker's hours."

Joe glanced uncomfortably at Meg. "Yeah . . . must be nice."

"It is. Anyway, I don't like schedules."

"That's a hell of a way to run a business." Then he smiled quickly. "But it's *your* business. I'm happy as long as you pay your bills. Keeps the boss off *my* neck."

"I promise you, I'll do my best to keep your account paid up." He reached out and stroked Meg's silky back. "How long will you be staying in our fair city?"

"Oh, I don't know. I'm only taking a week off now. If this weather doesn't clear up, I may just go on back to Portland."

"From all reports, you'll be in luck." He lit a cigarette without offering one to Joe. "It should be clear by tomorrow."

"Yeah? Well, those damned meteologers can't be

wrong *all* the time." He glanced at Meg, then thrust his big hands into his pockets, and finally, seeming to find nothing more to say, and getting no encouragement from Conan, he shrugged. "Well, I guess I'll browse around upstairs while I'm here."

"Good. Buy a book. It'll make it easier for me when it comes time to pay up your account."

Zimmerman gave a short, caustic laugh.

"Listen, buddy, if you can afford banker's hours, you don't need *my* business." He started for the stairs, his hands still in his pockets. "See you later, Cone."

Conan winced. He did not like his name reduced to "Cone"—at least, not by Zimmerman. Then he smiled to himself as Meg leaped from the counter and set off after Joe.

He rose as a woman came to the counter with some books. Taking care of her purchases, with the usual time out for polite palaver, occupied only a few minutes. He'd just settled himself on the stool again after her departure, when Zimmerman returned from upstairs.

Conan took a drag on his cigarette, studying the salesman through a haze of smoke. He was empty-handed, which was to be expected. When he came on his monthly rounds, Zimmerman usually looked at the books upstairs while he waited for Conan or Miss Dobie to complete their order, and occasionally he even bought a used book. But those occasions were rare; Joe might be a seller of books, but he wasn't a reader, and never had been.

Conan said quietly, "That was short. Nothing upstairs you haven't already read?"

Joe was on his way to the door, and he seemed peculiarly nervous and ill-at-ease.

"What? Oh. Well—" A quick shrug. "Maybe I'm just not in the mood for reading." His hand went to the door.

Conan took a perverse pleasure in delaying him; he was so obviously anxious to leave.

"That's too bad. A nice rainy day like this—perfect for curling up with a good book."

"Sure." He called up a crooked smile. "Listen, ol'

buddy, if I'm going to do any curling up, it sure as hell won't be with a book. I'm on vacation, remember?" He started to open the door. "Anyway, I've . . . got something to take care of right now. I'll see you around."

Conan laughed. "What's her name?"

Zimmerman eyed him sharply, then gave him a sly grin.

"Whose name?"

"Your new girlfriend."

"Who says she's *new*?" He opened the door. "But don't wait for me to tell you what you been missing out on around here. See you later, Cone."

"Sure, Joe. Have fun."

He wondered vaguely who Joe's local girlfriend might be, but it was a matter of indifference to him, except that it explained his unexpected appearance in Holliday Beach.

After Zimmerman's departure, the quiet descended, and the minutes seemed to space themselves at longer and longer intervals.

As the afternoon wore on, he gave himself up to aimless muddling, welcoming every customer's question or need as a diversion. And every time a book was brought to the counter, he looked for that small, red-jacketed book.

It seemed there was an unusually high ratio of red covers on the books he handled, but none of them was the Dostoevsky.

During the hour following Zimmerman's departure, all the customers were strangers, with one exception. The old fisherman, Olaf Svensen, came in, pausing for a few terse words before he went upstairs, rumbling about some engine trouble in the *Josephine* confining him to shore in spite of the clearing weather.

In response to Conan's question about the Russian trawlers, Sven's bristling face screwed up in a glowering frown.

"*Sure*, they still there! You yust look out you window.

I bet you see 'em from you own house, now. They be out there, all right—yust outside the t'ree-mile limit. And they *be* there till the damn fish runs out!"

He hadn't pursued the subject, seeming to find it too disgusting. He'd only lumbered off toward the stairs, mumbling to himself.

At two-ten, Conan looked at his watch again and lit one more cigarette, scorching a finger when he was distracted by the door bells.

Again a familiar face, and a particularly welcome diversion. Anton Dominic.

The old gentleman was grinning happily as he walked up to the counter and laid a flat paper sack on it.

"How are you being today, Mr. Flack?"

It would have been difficult, had he wished to, not to respond to that ingenuous smile.

"I'm fine, Mr. Dominic. I hope you're well."

"Ah, yes, I be completely better now."

Conan looked down at the sack. "Good. What's this?"

"Oh. I haf return your *Scientivic American*."

"Anything of interest in it? I didn't get around to looking through this copy." He didn't get around to looking through most of the copies of the magazine; the subscription was more for Mr. Dominic than himself.

"Oh, yes." The old man nodded enthusiastically. "I be stay awake until midnight reading last night. Iss very good article on research being done on Pi meson."

Conan took the magazine from the sack and flipped through the pages.

"I'll have to read that, although I'm sure it'll be way over my head. I've been trying for years to get the various nuclear particles straight, but I didn't get much past Bohr's neat little diagrams."

"Ah, well, you should not be surprise to be confuse. A few years ago, iss thirty-four different atomic particles identify, and still they be find more. Iss some that maybe be what they are call 'anti-matter.' The alpha boryon negative particle, that iss such a one."

Conan smiled, enjoying the light of enthusiasm in the old man's eyes.

"Now, there's a fascinating subject—anti-matter. It suggests some sort of reversed world; a mirror universe." He shrugged, giving a short laugh. "At least, to a few science fiction writers."

Dominic laughed at that. "Ah, yes, and perhaps iss not be all fiction; perhaps such a—a mirror universe could be exist. But I am not so sure." He shook his head thoughtfully, and his eyes seemed to be focused somewhere far beyond Conan's ken. "No . . . I am not so sure. I am think perhaps this 'anti-matter' be relating to *speed* of particles. I mean, even what are call 'normal' particles. Maybe . . . maybe iss somet'ing happens if particle move *beyond* speed of light. Maybe Einsteinian limits can be—"

Suddenly Dominic stopped, and he seemed momentarily confused, as if he'd just remembered something.

"I . . . I am sorry, Mr. Flack. I am sometimes be— how do you say? Carry away? I should not be boring people with my foolish old man's thinkings."

Conan frowned, feeling a biting regret for that painful lack of assurance, and he wondered at its source. It seemed to come so often with age, and perhaps that was the source for Anton Dominic.

"Mr. Dominic, whatever made you think you were boring me? And what you have to say is far from foolish."

He gave Conan a small, shy smile, apparently fascinated by the scuffed toes of his shoes.

"T'ank you. You are always be very kind." He thrust his hands into the pockets of his heavy, oversize coat; a hand-me-down garment that always made him look like some lost urchin bundled up for a long, cold winter. He gave a wheezing sigh and looked up at Conan. "Anyway, I go upstairs, now, and see what I find new to be reading."

Conan studied him a moment, then nodded.

"All right. Oh, by the way, I have a new shipment

coming in next week. There may be some books you'll be interested in.''

Some of the light came back into his eyes.

''Ah, t'ank you. I—I am always be grateful you haf think of me when you are order books.''

''It's my pleasure.''

And that was a simple truth. He watched the old man trudge off toward the stairway, a frail, bent, and somehow sad figure, and he was feeling mixed emotions of sympathy and curiosity. An extraordinary book, indeed, and a fine mind wasted on carpentry. But no doubt he'd been an extraordinary carpenter, too.

The jingle of the door bells interrupted his reverie, and as he turned he felt a tightness along his shoulder muscles.

Major James Mills.

It occurred to him that it was odd Mills should come in at this particular time, when Dominic was in the shop. Dominic had been here yesterday when the Major appeared.

Then he shrugged mentally, as an elderly couple approached the counter with three books to purchase.

Twice didn't make a trend.

He was distracted while he took care of his customers, but when they were gone he noted that Mills was again perusing the paperbacks. The Major glanced at him briefly, but his disciplined face gave no hint of recognition.

Impatiently, Conan crushed out a half-smoked cigarette. So Mills still wasn't ready to talk to him. But he must have checked those monitored calls by now.

He brought his annoyance under control, but only with an effort. He couldn't wait indefinitely for the mountain to come around.

For a while, he only watched Mills out of the corner of his eyes; then he reached for a piece of paper and wrote his home phone number on it, adding a brief message: ''I must talk to you—urgent. Possible drop. CJF.''

He waited a full minute before he made another move, watching the customers. The Major had undoubtedly chosen his position carefully; he had a clear view of the entrance, as well as most of the downstairs section, including the stairway. But this meant he was also exposed to observation. Conan folded the paper and slipped it under the sleeve of his sweater; it would be necessary to exercise a little discretion.

Finally, he walked over to the paperback rack and began busily straightening the books, nodding casually to Mills as he worked.

"Nice day today."

Mills smiled briefly; the kind of impersonal smile that passes between strangers.

"Yes," he replied distantly, picking out a book and thumbing through it. "Looks like the storm's about over."

"I hope so. May I help you with anything in particular?

"Oh . . . I was just looking for something light."

Conan noted the title of the book he seemed to find so engrossing, then pulled another book from the rack and handed it to him.

"I see you're an Agatha Christie fan. Have you read this one? It's one of her best."

Mills hesitated, then reached for the book, and the firm control faltered for a split second as he saw the slip of paper barely protruding from the pages, his features displaying a flicker of surprise.

"Yes, I enjoy some of Christie's books," he said slowly, "especially the Poirots."

"Then you'll like this one. She gets Poirot involved in a bit of international intrigue; espionage, and all that. Quite well done."

At the word "espionage," Mills's grayish eyes narrowed slightly, then he smiled and nodded.

"Sounds good. Maybe I'll give it a try."

Conan turned, hearing footsteps behind him; Mr. Dominic returning from upstairs. He went to the counter to check his books out, and waved as the old man went out the door, his good spirits apparently restored.

Within less than three minutes—Conan timed it out of curiosity—Mills came to the counter and paid for the Agatha Christie without comment. But as he was leaving the shop, he paused briefly, looking directly at Conan.

"Thanks for the recommendation."

He didn't wait for a response; he turned abruptly and closed the door between them.

CHAPTER 11

For a while, Mills's parting remark gave him a little hope to ease the tension of his vigil, but as the slow minutes ticked by, he became increasingly restive. At 2:45, Miss Dobie went next door to the Chowder House for lunch and brought a sandwich back for him, but most of it went untouched, and she retired to her office on finding him entirely unresponsive to her attempt at conversation.

By four o'clock, he was feeling like a caged lion too confined even to pace. He took advantage of a lull in business to go upstairs and check the *Crime and Punishment*.

It was still on the shelf—still waiting.

And the phone was ominously quiet during the long afternoon.

He went into the office to refill his coffee cup, wondering why he hadn't heard from Charlie Duncan. The jingle of the bells brought him back to the counter, where he resumed his seat with a sigh of disappointment.

It was only Edwina Leen, her round, pink face crinkling with a vacuous smile.

He took a deep breath, mustered a smile, and shouted, "Good afternoon, Mrs. Leen. How are you today?"

"How's that, Mr. Flagg?"

"I said—*how are you today*?"

"Oh, I'm just fine. How 'bout you? You was late openin' this mornin'."

"Miss Dobie and I went to Captain Jeffries' funeral."

"What'd you say?"

He leaned closer. *"We had to go to Captain Jeffries' funeral!"*

"Oh, yes, I heard 'bout the Cap'n. Too bad. When'd you say the funeral's goin' to be?" She tilted her head, bringing her right ear—presumably her better one—around toward him.

"It's already *been*," he shouted. "That's why we were late."

"Oh. Then I guess I missed it." She shrugged, pursing her thin lips. "But then, I never knowed the Cap'n too well, anyhow. He a friend of yours?"

"Well, not a close friend. He came into the shop quite a bit."

"How's that?"

"He wasn't a *close* friend; just a *customer*." Then before she could reply, he shouted, *"May I help you with something?"*

"Oh, no, nothin' partic'lar. I'll just go on upstairs and see if I can find somethin' to read."

"Fine, Mrs. Leen." He sighed. "Good luck."

He wasn't sure she actually understood his last words, but to his relief, she only smiled in her usual vague manner and headed for the stairs. He slumped down on the stool, staring after her. He'd forgotten to ask Miss Dobie why she'd seemed so upset yesterday morning.

Then he tensed at the ringing of the phone and reached for the counter extension. This *had* to be Charlie Duncan.

"Holliday Beach Bookshop."

"Conan?"

"Yes, Charlie. Hang on a minute." He covered the receiver with one hand. "Miss Dobie!"

A few seconds later when she came around the corner from her office, he handed her the receiver.

"Watch the counter for me. I have an important call."

She blinked and nodded. "All right."

Inside the office, he closed the door, took up a position behind the desk where he could see the counter and entrance, and picked up the phone.

"Thank you, Miss Dobie." Then when she hung up the counter extension, "Charlie, where are you?"

"Just outside town; Skinner Junction. I'm in a phone booth."

"Is Berg with you?"

"Yeah, and we're at your disposal."

He hesitated. "I'm not sure exactly how to dispose you until we've had a chance to talk, but for the time being we'll keep Berg out of sight. I don't want him seen around the shop *or* me. Find him a place to stay, then you—" He stopped cold, feeling the solid shock of adrenalin hitting his nervous system.

Through the one-way glass, he'd seen a flash of red.

Outside the counter, Miss Dobie was opening a red-jacketed book to the back cover and removing the date card.

"Conan, are you still—?"

"Hold on a minute, Charlie."

He dropped the phone and moved to the door, watching intently as Miss Dobie methodically stamped the date on the card, returned the card to its envelope, and closed the book. It was a Modern Library edition. He couldn't see the title, but it could be the Dostoevsky. Then Miss Dobie handed the book across the counter.

And there, smiling beatifically, was Mrs. Edwina Leen.

Not Mrs. Leen. That muddled, bumbling old woman . . .

She must have picked it up by mistake—if it *was* the *Crime and Punishment*.

He fought the blind impulse to rush out and snatch the book from her. The original copy *couldn't* have been meant for her. It was a mistake; it had to be.

He pulled in a long breath, forcing himself to relax.

Anything was possible. And yet his mind balked at accepting this possibility. It *had* to be a mistake.

Or perhaps it wasn't the Dostoevsky.

Miss Dobie was chatting amiably with Mrs. Leen, an exchange he watched with almost uncontrollable impatience. Finally, he moved back to the desk and picked up the phone, his eyes still focused on Mrs. Leen's smiling face.

"Charlie—"

"Yeah. What the hell's going on?"

"I can't explain now. What's the phone number in that booth?"

Duncan gave him the number, then started to protest.

"Listen, Conan, will you just—?"

"Stay put. I'll call you back in a few minutes."

He didn't wait to hear Duncan's reply. Mrs. Leen was leaving the shop. He hung up the phone, then crossed to the office door and threw it open.

"Miss Dobie, what was the title of the book she just checked out?"

Beatrice Dobie turned, so startled she dropped the cigarette she'd been about to light. She laughed as she leaned down to retrieve it.

"You mean Mrs. Leen? Well, I'm afraid she's in for a big disappointment."

"The *title*, Miss Dobie."

"Oh. Well, it was *Crime and Punishment*. She thought it was a mystery."

"She *what*?"

"She thought it was a mystery story."

"Good God, didn't you tell her it wasn't?"

"Well, yes, but it didn't seem to make any difference."

"Are you sure she understood you?"

She shrugged, looking up at him anxiously.

"I think so, but with her you never know. Why? What's wrong?"

Conan brought himself under control and mustered a brief smile. His reaction would make no sense to her.

"I'm sorry, Miss Dobie. Nothing's wrong." He paused,

then pulled the office door shut and locked it. "I'll be back in a few minutes."

"Say, about that book, Mr. Flagg—"

But he was already at the front door. He closed it behind him and turned, scanning the highway and sidewalk. A moment later, he was running toward the north corner.

He stopped when he reached the corner, staying close to the building as he looked down the side street. Mrs. Leen's stout figure and rolling, stiff-legged gait were unmistakable; she was about a block away, moving at a surprisingly fast pace.

He waited, studying every car and window, every shadow along the street; but if there were any observers along the way, they were well hidden. Then, as Mrs. Leen turned left onto Front Street, he started after her.

He took the first block and a half at a full run, then reduced his pace to a casual stroll, and finally just far enough past the wall of the corner house to have a view down Front Street.

Mrs. Leen was perhaps a hundred yards down the street, and he saw a bit of red protruding from her handbag.

She still had the Dostoevsky.

He watched her until she stepped up onto the porch of her tiny, age-worn cottage, then he drew back a pace. As she paused to unlock her front door, she took a long look up and down the street, then stepped inside, and he heard the distant slam of the door.

Conan stared at the shabby little cottage, swearing inwardly at the awkward timing of Duncan's arrival. He had no choice but to leave Mrs. Leen unwatched until he could get Duncan or Berg down here.

And the sooner the better.

He turned and set off for the shop at a dead run.

CHAPTER 12

C onan knelt by the hearth and touched the match to the kindling, then waited patiently until the flames took hold. For several minutes, he stared into the burgeoning fire, absently listening to the rhythmic strains of *The Moldau*. Finally, satisfied that the fire was well established, he wandered to the window wall on the west side of the room.

He heard the small sounds from upstairs: Charlie Duncan moving around, unpacking, checking his equipment. When he heard Charlie speaking in subdued tones, he turned and looked up toward the balcony and the door of the guest room. Then he smiled faintly. Duncan was checking out his contact via two-way radio with Carl Berg.

Conan looked out at the blood-red sky, watching the sun curdling into a heavy bank of clouds. It was a profound relief to have Duncan on the scene. A big, sandy-haired, freckle-faced Scot who reminded him of Henry Flagg in his pragmatic, matter-of-fact attitude. Charlie didn't believe in rattling up spooks, either; he considered it a waste of time.

Conan had left Miss Dobie to close up the shop; left her staring blankly at him and sighing. Then he'd broken every speed limit making his way out to Skinner Junction to meet Duncan and Berg.

Carl Berg was now ensconced in a house across the street and two doors south of Mrs. Leen's, and in the process was risking a charge of breaking and entering.

It was a risk taken out of desperation. Berg needed a vantage point; he couldn't watch Mrs. Leen from his car. The house was a weekend cottage belonging to the Alton family, and Conan knew them through the bookshop. At least, he knew that Thomas Alton was a professor at the University of Oregon, and it was highly unlikely he'd be using the house before the next weekend.

That was the only real risk—an unexpected visit from the Altons or some of their friends. Berg had the tools, and a little practice, as he put it, to walk into the house as easily as if he had a key, and Conan had instructed him to do so, using the front door. There was little risk that the neighbors would question a stranger walking into the house; it was quite common for people to rent or loan their weekend cottages.

Conan had given Duncan a tour of Holliday Beach—the geographical points of interest in the Jeffries case—and told him everything he knew about it. That had been a pitifully short account. There hadn't been time yet to go past the facts, and the only decision reached was that Berg would maintain surveillance on Mrs. Leen, keeping their rental car with him, and Charlie would move into Conan's guest room. The old army buddy. That would satisfy the local grapevine.

He turned at the sound of footsteps to see Duncan coming down the spiral staircase.

"Find everything you need, Charlie?"

"And more. That so-called guest room of yours is more like a suite." He came over to the window and looked out at the red sky. "Poor old Carl. I think he got the raw end of this deal."

"Don't be too sure. This is just the beginning."

Duncan grimaced. "Yeah, I was afraid of that. Oh, I

checked with Carl. He's all settled in. The utilities are all hooked up, by the way, including the phone."

"Yes, I thought they would be. People don't bother to cut off the utilities in these vacation houses when they're gone; the local hook-up fees are too exorbitant. What about Mrs. Leen?"

"She's safely at home; no action."

"Good. How about a drink? Supper, such as it is, is in process."

"That's encouraging. I'm starved."

"Well, don't get your hopes up. I've no delusions about my culinary skills."

"Right now, I'm not particular, and I'll have that drink. That's the best idea you've come up with so far, Chief."

Conan smiled faintly as he crossed to the bar on the south wall; he'd forgotten that "Chief."

"What'll you have, Charlie? Still scotch and soda?"

"Right." Duncan sank wearily into one of the Barcelona chairs by the window. "Man, I'm bushed."

"Well, this might pick up you a little," Conan commented as he mixed the drinks, "or at least make my cooking more palatable."

He returned with the two glasses, putting them on the marble-topped table between the chairs. Then he seated himself, watching Duncan with a little amusement as he tasted the scotch critically, then smiled and settled back with a contented sigh.

"Mm. Beautiful booze and classy accommodations. This is my kind of job." His eyes swept the darkening vista of surf and sky. "Look at that view."

Conan was already looking. A hint of a smile curved his lips.

"It isn't bad."

"Sure. You know what a view like this would cost in California?"

"Charlie, in California, you'd never *find* a view like this unless the smog lifted."

"That's just a myth, Chief. It's just plain fog."

"Of course. Just don't ask me to breathe it."

Duncan laughed, but his amusement faded after a moment. He took another swallow of his scotch and leaned forward, resting his elbows on his knees.

"Okay, I'm enjoying the view *and* the fresh air, but I came up here to do a job of work, so maybe we better get back to business."

Conan nodded, focusing his thoughts on the "business" of Jeffries' death with some reluctance. Then he frowned irritably and started to rise.

"Damn. I meant to get that book from the safe before I left the shop." He hesitated, and finally sank back into his chair. "I'll get it after supper. It'll only take a few minutes."

"It won't help much for me to look at it anyway. If there was anything to find, you'd have caught it."

"Not necessarily. There's nothing obvious, however."

Duncan frowned into his drink.

"Crime and Punishment—good Lord."

"Apparently, someone along the line has a sense of humor. A little macabre, perhaps."

"Sick, is more like it. Okay, so what's your theory about this business? You must have one by now."

Conan laughed. "Of course. Theories are easy."

His hand moved almost reflexively to his pocket for his cigarettes. He offered one to Duncan and lit one for himself before he went on.

"All right, Charlie. A theory. First, I'm hypothesizing an information system based in Holiday Beach with the bookshop as the point of exchange, and the information carried in books. Harold Jeffries checked out a book intended for an agent in the system, and the agent—or courier—saw him take it. That night; Jeffries found something in that book that made him wonder. And remember, he was once attached to the Navy Code Section. Anyway, he left his house with the book intending to ask me about it, but he was being watched. The agents involved obviously didn't want to lose the book, or whatever it contained."

"So, he was intercepted along the way, clipped on the jaw—"

"The right side of the jaw."

"Yeah, so maybe you're looking for a southpaw. Then he was held under until he drowned. Right?"

"Right." He studied Charlie over the rim of his glass, watching him as he pursed his lips, his hazel eyes narrowed thoughtfully, then finally nodded.

"Okay. We'll just ignore the little problem of what he found in that book for now, but tell me this—why was it put back in your shop, if that's what they were after?"

"The killer was only a hired man. The agents would avoid that sort of personal risk if possible, and they'd also avoid direct contact with the flunky. That's why it was put back, so it could be picked up later by the person it was actually intended for. The only hitch was that Miss Dobie has a digital memory for books."

"That wasn't the only hitch, if your theory holds water. I mean, having a guy like Jeffries pick up the damn book; somebody with the experience to recognize a code, or whatever."

Conan nodded, studying the red reflections in his bourbon.

"I know. But this system has probably been in operation for some time. Mrs. Leen's been living here for well over a year, so we can assume a number of exchanges during that time—*if* she isn't just another innocent bystander. The more exchanges, the more chances of failure. The real hitch on this one was in choice of title. Jeffries was looking for *Crime and Punishment*."

"But they couldn't know that."

"No. And they chose a standard title in a common edition that would normally attract no attention. Neither Miss Dobie nor I would've looked twice at it, if it hadn't been for Jeffries. I'm sure we handled a number of other books in the exchanges without being aware of it."

Duncan nodded, pulling on his cigarette, squinting at Conan through a haze of smoke.

"There's another possibility you haven't mentioned. It could be Jeffries was *part* of the system, and maybe there was some sort of disagreement among the comrades."

"Yes, it's a possibility, but I just can't buy it."

"Why not?"

"I don't know. Jeffries. I can't see him playing the role of enemy agent."

"Maybe that's because he was good at it."

Conan rose and walked to the window, the smoke from his cigarette taking a reddish cast from the sky. After a moment, he laughed and shrugged uneasily.

"Maybe. And I'll admit I'm having a hard time figuring out why it was necessary to murder him, if he were only an innocent bystander. You know the cardinal rule in this business—don't make waves. You'd think they could get that book from him somehow without taking the risk of killing him. I keep wondering if he didn't know too much; if he was killed in order to silence him—not just to get the book."

"Well, maybe he *was* an innocent bystander, but there was enough in the book itself to make him dangerous."

"Possibly, but I doubt that. They wouldn't pass anything easily recognizable or readable by that means; the information would be coded. Jeffries may have had some experience with codes, but he wasn't a genius. Nel left him at eight. At eight-thirty, he left his house. Would any self-respecting espionage agency use a code that could be broken in half an hour, even by an expert? And I doubt Jeffries qualified as an expert. It's been a long time since his Navy Code Section days."

"But he'd sure as hell know a code when he saw one, even if he couldn't break it."

"That's what I'm assuming." He gave an impatient sigh. "But how would the killer know how much Jeffries knew? Possession of the book wouldn't indicate knowledge in itself. I doubt the agents were aware of his experience with codes; it would take time to get that information. They had absolutely no reason to assume he knew a code—or anything—was hidden in the book. Not unless he *told* someone."

Charlie was silent for a while, his brow furrowed with parallel creases. Then he shrugged.

"Okay. For the time being, we'll just say Jeffries was an innocent bystander. So, you figure he was on his way to talk to *you* about whatever it was he found?"

"Yes. He found the book in my shop; he walked within a block of my house on his own; and there was that phone number Nel found. If he asked Information for my number, the bookshop number is the only one he'd be given, so he couldn't call me at that time of night. If he wanted to talk to me, he'd have to come to my house."

"But would he trust you?"

Conan looked over at Duncan, considering the question. Finally, he nodded.

"I think so. Harold and Elinor Jeffries have been regular customers since I bought the shop. I haven't stayed glued to the shop all these years, but I saw them often enough to know them fairly well, and for them to know me. Of course, I was closer to Nel, but I think the Captain would trust me."

"Nel." Duncan gave a soft laugh. "Damn, she must really be something to get you mixed up in this thing. Or was it just a conditioned reflex from your G-2 days?"

"Maybe a little of both. And curiosity."

"You know, there's an old saying about curiosity. Something about killing the cat."

Conan smiled obliquely. "Yes. But there's another old saw about cats, Charlie—cats have nine lives."

"Okay. Touché." He held on to a wry smile, but only for a few seconds; it faded into a disgruntled frown as he tipped up his glass. "God, this thing's weird. If it wasn't for the Major, I'd say you were out of your head."

"Is the Major all that assures you of my sanity?"

"Well . . . that book showing up after Jeffries died is a little suspicious."

"A little."

"The Major." He smiled to himself, taking time to puff on his cigarette and send out a slow stream of smoke. "That son of a gun. He never did trust anybody."

"Apparently." Conan folded his arms, focusing on the red-hued, tumbling breakers, recognizing the tightness within him as resentment, but still finding it hard to control. "Charlie, have you any idea who he's working for now?"

"No. I should've known he wouldn't be content to sit back and collect his retirement pay, though. And I'd say you've got something special going on in this burg if he's in on it. He isn't exactly a second-class legman."

"True. But I'll be damned if I can figure out what attraction Holliday Beach has for Mills."

Duncan shrugged. "An information exchange, maybe."

Conan turned, thrusting his hands in his pockets.

"But why an exchange *here*? It just doesn't make sense."

"We don't know enough about this yet to say whether it makes sense or not."

"You have a point there."

"For that matter, we can't even be sure of Mrs. Leen. You said maybe she picked up the book by mistake."

"Another point." He went back to his chair and sagged into it, scowling at a sunset that would have commanded his admiration under other circumstances. "And we can't be sure the *real* agent didn't come in yesterday morning, find the book missing, and take off for parts unknown."

Duncan laughed. "Will the real spy please stand up?"

"If he's still around, he probably will, one way or another. They seem rather anxious to get hold of that book." He glanced at his watch. "Damn. Someone should be watching the bookshop now."

"Just keep calm, Chief. I'll go up to the shop later, but let me get this thing straight in my head. Okay?"

Conan sighed. "Okay."

"Now." Duncan folded his big hands, studying them absently. "There *is* one possibility for getting a line on the Major and who he's working for. I know a guy in D.C.—Stewart Roth. Remember him?"

"No. Should I?"

"Maybe not. No, I guess he joined the Berlin group after you left with your punctured lung. Anyway, he went into the CIA and did all right for himself. If I put it just right, I might find out if the Major's with the CIA."

"That might at least eliminate a possibility. And we have two other potential sources of information. The Major's partner; that bogus telephone man. But I haven't even had a look at him."

Duncan gave a short laugh. "I doubt he'll oblige you, anyway, if Mills won't talk to you. So, what's source number two?"

"Steve Travers. Oh—you'd better make a note of his name; it might come in handy. He's with the State Police."

Charlie took a notepad and pen from his breast pocket and wrote down the information as Conan gave it to him, one eyebrow arching up at Travers' official title.

"He'd be a good contact in *my* business."

"Yes, well, he's an old friend from my youth."

"Another cowboy, huh? So, how does he rate as an in on the Major?"

"I'm sure Mills talked to him in the process of investigating me. But Steve isn't free to discuss it. At least, he wasn't yesterday."

"I doubt he'll be any looser today. But maybe the Major will take you up on that little invite you slipped him this afternoon."

"Maybe." He picked up his glass, then put it aside irritably and came to his feet, again drawn to the windows. "While you're making notes, you'd better have Miss Dobie's home phone. And Nicky's."

Duncan hesitated, his pen poised. "Nicky?"

"That's Dr. Nicole Heideger."

"Oh. The examining physician. You sound like you're expecting trouble."

He laughed at that. "No, but if it shows up, you'll know who to call." He gave Duncan the numbers, then took his key ring from his pocket, removed one key and handed it to him. "That's for the VW, in case you need transportation when I'm not around. I don't have extra keys for the shop or the house, but I doubt you'll have any trouble with those doors.''

Duncan pocketed the key, eyeing him suspiciously.

''I'm on my own, is that it? And what'll you be up to in the meantime?'' He sighed and put the notebook away. ''I have a feeling I'll regret signing on for a job with you. You'll probably wade right into this thing, and take my 'expert advice' if and when you damned well please.''

''Charlie, you worry too much.''

''Sure. Maybe I just have a good memory.''

''Then you'll remember I never believed in sticking my neck out unnecessarily.''

''I remember you believed in sticking your nose where it didn't belong a hell of a lot.''

Conan laughed, turning to look out the window, and his laughter faded, his eyes focused intently on the horizon.

Only a livid red streak marked the meeting of sea and sky now, and along that line was a string of tiny lights.

''Charlie—''

''Yeah? What is it?''

He waited until Duncan rose and joined him at the window.

''Those lights on the horizon—see them?''

''Sure.''

''Another interesting item. That's a fleet of Russian trawlers.''

Duncan's eyebrows shot up. ''Russian?''

''Yes. But they've worked this coast before, and of course, they're always careful to stay outside the three-mile limit.'' He turned away and glanced at his watch. 6:20. The shop had been closed for over an hour.

''Charlie, I think I'll go up to the shop and get that book now. Maybe I'll . . . check around a little.''

''Around what? Look, Chief, if you're so worried about the shop, I'll go on up there and—''

''No, not yet.'' He crossed to the telephone on the bar. ''I'd just like to have that book safely in hand. And besides, my father always told me, never put a man to work on an empty stomach.''

"Well, maybe your old man had a point there.'' He sniffed the air, looking toward the kitchen. "Something smells good, anyway. What's on the menu?''

Conan was looking for the Altons' number in the local phone directory; he gave Duncan a sidelong glance.

"Sheepherder's stew.''

Charlie sighed and walked over to join him at the bar.

"Well, I said I wasn't particular.''

"An eastern Oregon delicacy,'' he commented as he began dialing. "I'm going to check with Berg. Do you want to talk to him?''

"No, not unless he's had some action.''

Carl Berg answered in a guarded tone, "Hello?''

"Conan Flagg, Mr. Berg. Anything to report so far?''

"No. Nothing special, anyway. There are lights in Mrs. Leen's house, and I saw her moving around inside earlier. The shades are drawn now. But apparently she's alone, and no one's been in or out of the house.''

"Any cars around?''

Berg hesitated. "Well, it's hard to say, since I don't know what cars would normally be around the neighborhood. The Police Chief drove by about fifteen minutes ago. He was moving pretty slow; probably just making his rounds.''

Conan laughed inwardly at that. Harvey Rose wouldn't be making official rounds at this time of day; he considered himself off duty at 5:00 P.M.

"Did the Chief stop anywhere?''

"No, just moved right along and turned at the next corner. But there was another car I wondered about; this was a few minutes later. I noticed it because it took two turns around the block, going slow both times.''

Conan's hand tightened on the receiver.

"What kind of car was it?''

"A blue Chevy, new model.''

"Did you get the license number?''

"Yes. Oregon, FAM811. I couldn't see much of the driver, but it was a man. Alone."

Alone. Of course. Conan pulled in a long breath.

"Very good, Mr. Berg. Anything else?"

"No, not so far."

"All right, thank you. Charlie or I will bring you some food and coffee later. We can come up the alley without being seen."

Berg laughed. "That's good news—I mean, the food. But give me a call before you come."

"I will. Good-bye."

When he hung up, Duncan gave him a questioning look. "Well?"

Conan leaned against the bar, his features set in a preoccupied frown.

"Damn, if Berg's just on a wild-goose chase—"

"Well, it won't be the first one he's been on. Now, what was that about a car license?"

"A blue Chevrolet took a couple of slow turns around the block a few minutes ago."

"Carl get a license number?"

"Oregon, FAM811. That's Mills's car. Maybe my message got some sort of reaction from him. Or maybe he's just cruising."

Duncan took out his notebook and wrote down the license number, a disgruntled sigh escaping him.

"Why the hell would he be cruising around here?"

"Waiting for me to do something incriminating, no doubt." He went to the table for his cigarettes and put them in his pocket. "Charlie, what are the chances of getting a bug on Mrs. Leen's phone?"

"Well, I don't know. It might be done if you could get her out of the house long enough, but it'd be risky."

"It may not be worth the risk. I doubt she carries on any important business over her own phone. Give it some thought, though. And you might try calling that friend of yours in Washington while I'm gone; your CIA contact."

"Okay, I'll give it a try, but it'll take awhile to get

through to him this late—and assuming he's not on assignment in Inner Mongolia.''

"See what you can do, and you might remove the Major's bugs for that call. But be careful, and put them back when you're through.''

"Right. I'd like to take a look at them, anyway. Might pick up some pointers.''

Conan glanced at his watch and started for the entry hall.

"I'll be back in about fifteen minutes. And, Charlie, if the Major should happen to call or drop in before I get back, tell him for God's sake, whether he thinks I'm an enemy agent or not, I must talk to him.''

Duncan laughed. "I'll give him the message.''

CHAPTER 13

The wind had switched to the east, and the temperature was dropping. Conan rounded the corner at the post office, his head down against the biting wind that made a mournful keening in the harp strings of the power lines. The beat of his footsteps echoing against the deserted shops was a lonely sound.

He reached into his pocket for his keys as he neared the bookshop, then slowed his pace. A car was parked at the north end of the block; a blue Chevrolet.

There were no other cars in sight, but he couldn't be sure one wasn't parked around the corner beyond the grocery store. He quickened his pace, intending to take a look at the Chevrolet, thinking it would be a good idea to check around the corner while he was at it.

But as he passed the entrance of the bookshop, he came to an abrupt halt, a sensation like a primordial raising of hackles crawling along the back of his neck.

The door was slightly ajar.

For a moment, he stared at the door, forgetting to breathe.

Of course, it was possible that Miss Dobie hadn't locked

116

it firmly when she closed the shop; the lock was some-times cranky.

Possible, but knowing Miss Dobie, not probable.

He looked up at the windows.

No lights.

And they always left one light upstairs and one down-stairs at night.

The book.

If someone found that book . . .

His hand shot out for the door under the impetus of the solar plexus shock of anger and anxiety. But before he even touched the knob, he stopped short.

Slow down. A headlong rush into the building wasn't the smartest—or safest—course of action.

He let his hand rest on the knob and slowly pushed the door back until he had a scant two-foot clearance, then he paused again, waiting, every sense alert.

Then he slipped inside the shop and stood pressed against the wall, listening and letting his eyes adjust to the faint light that filtered in from the street lamps. But his straining eyes caught no hint of movement, and the only sound was the whine of the wind.

Light. He needed some light. But he wouldn't risk turn-ing on the shop lights yet. There was a flashlight in the drawer under the cash register, but it hadn't been used for months, and it was doubtful that the batteries were still operable. But at the moment, he could think of no other alternative.

He moved cautiously across the room, felt his way around behind the counter, opened the drawer, and searched blindly inside it with his fingers. And in spite of his intense concentration, he wondered where Meg might be.

Finally, his fingers closed on the flashlight, then he felt along the wall to the office door. It was also slightly ajar, and there was no doubt in his mind that he'd locked this door before leaving the shop.

His mouth was compressed into a grim line as he pushed

the door open, waiting, poised. And again, no sound; only black silence.

He shifted the flashlight to his left hand and gripped the doorknob firmly. He half expected someone to be waiting behind the door, and he was tensed, ready to act.

But no movement—not even a sound—greeted him as he slipped into the office. He started to close the door behind him, realizing he'd be silhouetted against the dim light in the shop, but left it open a few inches, remembering the soundproofing.

Then in the darkness he paused, listening—*feeling*—for any living presence. There was still no sound or movement, and yet his pulse quickened, and he knew, or sensed somehow, that the room wasn't empty. At least, he knew it had been occupied within the last few minutes. Some faint odor, perhaps. He couldn't be sure.

Finally, he pressed the switch on the flashlight.

It flickered, almost fading out, then steadied to a pale yellow glow. The light was dim, but it was enough.

Enough to show him that the office was in chaos; drawers opened, papers strewn around, broken glass littering the carpet, a chair overturned. The safe was wide open, a gaping black hole, its contents of rare books thrown in careless heaps on the floor.

And sprawled in front of the safe among the scattered books, a silent shadowy hulk.

He knew what it was, but he was incapable of movement; he could only stare, incapable even of comprehension.

At length, with every breath catching in his constricted throat, he forced himself to move, one slow step at a time, toward that still form.

Major James Mills.

And he was dead.

CHAPTER 14

Conan's first reaction was purely visceral; a deep and solid nausea. He sank helplessly to his knees, staring transfixed, directing the pale light of the flashlight onto those familiar features, now quiet, still as stone.

Dear God—why didn't he call me?

The flashlight slipped out of his grip, and his hands went to his face, covering his eyes.

And the question kept repeating itself in his mind.

Why didn't he have that much faith? Why—over and over again—*why?*"

He pressed his palms against his burning eyes, crouching by that still, empty hulk—that wreck of a man; that silent remainder of a life—aching in every nerve, choking on the wordless cry rising in his throat.

Why?

The first coherent thought that came to him was that Major Mills would have regarded this blind, uncontrolled surrender to emotion with the most scathing contempt.

There would be time for grief.

But now it was a luxury; one he couldn't afford.

He turned his awareness outward, focusing all his faculties on the work at hand. At first, he was perfectly still, listening, wondering if, in his unthinking reaction, he might have missed some sound or movement from outside the office.

Then he set to work.

He picked up the flashlight and leaned over Mills's body, automatically checking for a pulse, finding none as he expected. The body was still warm to the touch.

He began searching through Mills's pockets, maintaining a cold, objective mental containment. He found nothing unusual; some loose change, cigarettes and lighter, a billfold.

There was nothing in the billfold to indicate the identity of the Major's employers. If he'd been carrying official identification, it had been removed. The gun from his belt holster was also missing.

And something else was missing.

Keys.

There were no keys at all on the body; not even car keys, and Mills was too careful a man to leave the keys in his car. But the car was still outside.

Conan frowned as he continued his examination in the waning light of the flashlight. There were numerous cuts and bruises around the face and head, and a massive contusion behind the right ear; the knuckles of the right hand were bruised and smeared with blood. And there was a small hole in the right temple, surrounded by a grayish halo. Powder burns.

He studied that small wound, and it seemed bitterly ironic, almost inconceivable, that such an outwardly insignificant injury had been the cause of death.

But the bullet had been well placed; Mills had probably been unconscious when the shot was fired. Conan looked down at the bloodied knuckles. At least, the Major had put up a fight before he was knocked out.

He turned the head and carefully examined the left side. The bullet hadn't emerged. He drew back, trembling, aware that the wetness on his hands was blood.

Ballistics.

He concentrated on that dispassionate word; it was the only frame of reference he could tolerate for that bullet.

A ballistics check on the bullet . . . Travers . . . he'd have to call Steve . . .

He froze, one thought driving everything else from his mind.

The book.

He turned away from the body, the fading and flickering of the flashlight lending urgency to his movements. He examined every book, searched every square foot of the room, looking behind and under every piece of furniture.

But it was futile. He knew that even before he began.

The Dostoevsky was gone.

Finally, he sagged against the cold metal wall of the safe, choking back the rage as he thought of Mrs. Leen. Berg should have been watching the shop, not her. She'd sprung his trap, and yet he still couldn't be sure he'd caught the intended victim.

The only piece of concrete evidence he had was that book, and he'd let it slip through his fingers.

No—here was another piece of evidence. He looked down at Major Mills and closed his eyes. What a price to pay. . . .

Abruptly, every muscle in his body snapped tight, the physical reaction coming almost before he realized what had triggered it.

A sound.

He heard a faint creaking sound from somewhere outside the office.

It could be Meg, or the wind, or simply the groanings of old timbers. And it could be the Major's killer. He hadn't been dead long.

Conan switched off the flashlight and moved quietly to the door. Again, the creaking. It seemed to come from upstairs.

He almost smiled. It was an old building, and it would be all but impossible to move around in it silently.

Then he slipped out of the office and started making his

way toward the stairway. And he found the problem of moving quietly on the old floors a double-edged sword.

He reached the bottom of the stairwell without incident, but the passage took a full five minutes, testing the floor and listening intently before every step. And he heard no further repetition of the creaking sound.

He stared up into the almost tangible darkness of the stairwell, his breath coming fast. He was all too familiar with the groanings of those stair treads under the lightest foot.

At length, he pulled in a lungful of air, letting it out slowly, feeling the dampness of his palms as he tightened his hold on the flashlight and gripped the banister with his left hand, leaning hard on it to lighten his weight on the stairs.

Then he started up into the darkness, slowly and carefully, easing his weight onto each step, flinching at every creak, prickling with an overwhelming sense of vulnerability.

There were thirteen steps, he knew, and as he counted them off, he was thinking that thirteen might, indeed, be an unlucky number for him. He could feel the leaden beat of his heart in his clenched hands as he counted off the last steps.

Finally, at the top step, he paused; then still hearing nothing, he began to relax. In all probability, Mills's killer was long gone by now, and his groping through the dark was in pursuit of nothing but the sighing of old timbers. He shifted the flashlight to his left hand, and with his right felt along the wall for the light switch.

But before his fingers touched the switch, the silence exploded. A banshee howl, and a tumbling of books.

Meg . . .

Then a rush of footfalls slamming against the floor. He switched on the flashlight, but its fading light revealed only a looming shadowy figure plunging toward him.

And now Meg was under his feet; howling deep in her throat, clawing desperately at his legs. He stumbled, twisting around to catch the banister, and his senses were wracked with a coruscating flash and a shattering concussion of sound. The solid impact of the wrenching blow against his shoulder threw him forward, off balance.

The flashlight flew out of his grasp, and he reached out blindly for support, his hands closing on thin air. The stairwell opened beneath him, and he was tumbling downward, reflexively curling into a fetal position—his mind so buffeted with sensation, he couldn't separate pain from sound.

He was only aware that he'd reached the bottom of the stairs as his body, slamming against the shelves, loosed an avalanche of books upon him. He gasped for air in the sudden quiet, powerless to move.

The last thing he remembered was Meg's terrified crying fading into the distance.

CHAPTER 15

Nicky Heideger stepped out into the quiet hospital corridor, closing the door behind her. She glanced at her watch, then looked up at Charlie Duncan, and he echoed the gesture, almost unconsciously. 11:30. He was vaguely surprised it wasn't later.

"How is he, Doc? What's the diagnosis?"

She gave a quick, disgusted sigh, then laughed.

"He's vocal—and asking for you. I decided I'd better let him talk to you now; otherwise, he'll give me trouble all night." She glanced back at the door, frowning slightly. "As for the diagnosis, the main problem was the bullet wound. But it went in at a shallow angle across the shoulder blade; lodged against the spine of the scapula. He'll have no permanent damage, but he won't be using his right arm for a while. At least, he'd better not. There were quite a few bruises and abrasions, and a couple of bad lumps on his head. I had some X rays taken; I'll know about possible head injuries tomorrow when I see them." She paused and looked up at Duncan. "What in God's name happened? He looks like somebody gave him a hell of a beating."

Duncan frowned darkly. "I wish I knew, but maybe I can find out."

"All right. You can go on in, but don't stay too long. I'll be back to check on him in a few minutes. And he's still feeling the anesthetic to some degree. He may not be too clear."

He nodded and started for the door. "Okay, Doc. And thanks."

"Charlie, thank God you're here. What happened? Nicky said—"

"You know, for a second there, I thought you were glad to see me for friendly reasons; but I should've known better. All you want is some answers."

Conan laughed, wincing a little. "Well, perhaps my motives are mixed."

"Yeah. I know all about your motives."

Duncan came around to the left side of the bed, studying him, a worried frown furrowing his brow.

His right arm was bound across his ribs, the shoulder heavily bandaged; the left arm was strapped to a board to keep him from dislodging the needle taped at the crook of his elbow. He was unnaturally pale, his forehead marked with a livid, swollen bruise, but he was apparently fully conscious. And impatient to the point of distraction. Still, he seemed to find it hard to keep his eyes in focus.

Duncan noted the line of the old scar across his chest and smiled faintly. This made twice he'd been ready to give Conan Flagg up for dead.

"Conan, how're you feeling?"

He pulled in a long, cautious breath.

"Not bad, considering. I can't say I'm happy about my surroundings."

Duncan pulled a chair up by the bed and straddled it, resting his folded arms across the back.

"Well, it's not bad as hospitals go."

"Which isn't saying much." He sighed and frowned up at the plasma bottle. "Damn, I wish Nicky'd get me off this thing. I feel like I'm in a straitjacket. Charlie, what time is it?''

"Eleven-thirty."

He closed his eyes as if he were reacting to an unexpected flash of light; his breathing quickened and Duncan could see the pulse beat in his throat. It was too fast. And it was too soon for him to try to talk.

"Conan, maybe I better come back later. You don't—"

"*No*. I'm all right."

Duncan waited, watching him, not particularly surprised to see his breathing even out, his pulse rate slow. But he was wondering at something he read in the black Indian eyes; a pain that wasn't physical. And questions. He seemed on the verge of exploding with them. Still, his tone was quiet and controlled when he voiced the first one.

"Charlie, where did you find me?"

"Find you?" That question was something of a surprise. "In the bookshop. Where did you think—?"

"No, I mean where in the shop?"

Duncan's eyes narrowed. "In the office. The place had been ransacked. You were lying in the middle of the floor—"

"There was . . . no one else?"

"No one else? What do you mean?" He saw him turn even paler, and for a moment wondered if he would remain conscious. "Conan, what the hell's wrong? Look, you'd better tell me what happened—if you feel up to it."

He nodded slowly, seeming to gather his strength.

"All right, I'll give you a quick rundown, then I want to know what's been going on while I was out of commission."

"Well, it'll probably *have* to be quick. The Doc said she'd only give me a few minutes with you, and she had fire in her eyes."

Conan laughed weakly. "Then we'd better make it fast. I'm not up to taking on Nicky right now."

* * *

When Conan had finished his brief account, Duncan was silent for a while, his features tight, devoid of expression, his shock hidden somewhere behind his narrowed eyes.

Conan was equally silent, waiting for him to absorb the fact of Major James Mills's death. Charlie had worked with the Major longer than he had, and come to know and respect him as much or more.

And he waited for him to absorb the fact that the Major's body had been removed; and the fact that the Dostoevsky was gone.

Conan closed his eyes. It was so difficult to think; the anesthetic and the constant pain. Strange that his head seemed to ache more than his shoulder.

"Damn it, why didn't you call me when you found the Major?" Duncan was recovering himself. "What the hell did you hire me for if—"

"I know, Charlie, I should've called you, but I was . . . preoccupied. I wasn't thinking too clearly, I suppose."

"It doesn't matter." He fumbled for his cigarettes, then seemed to change his mind and put them back in his pocket. "Damn. The Major. It just doesn't seem . . . right, somehow."

Conan turned away. "Why didn't he have a little faith in me? If I could have talked to him—he didn't have to die, damn it."

"Hey, Chief—" Duncan's voice was level; a quiet reminder. "Take it easy."

He nodded silently, intensely aware of the pain and a palling lethargy. Grief was still a luxury; there wasn't time for it yet. There was too much he didn't know; he had to keep his head clear. He had to think.

"All right," he said finally. "Now, what's been going on while I was out of circulation?"

"A hell of a lot. You missed all the fun."

"Yes. Take it from the top, Charlie. Everything."

Duncan pulled in a deep breath and ran his hand through his already disheveled hair.

"Well, after you left the house, I got on the phone and tried to track Roth down—with no luck. Then I realized you'd been gone nearly half an hour, so I called the shop. When I got no answer, I hightailed it up there to see what the hell was going on. The front door was unlocked, and I found you on the floor in the office, bleeding all over the place."

"Of course. That would very neatly cover any traces of blood left by the Major's body." He frowned thoughtfully. "I can't understand why *I* was left alive."

"Don't look a gift horse in the teeth." He shrugged, then added, "Maybe whoever shot you thought you *were* dead. You damn sure had me fooled at first."

Conan raised an eyebrow and nodded.

"That's quite possible. We aren't dealing with a pro here; a pro would never get himself bottled up like that. He was probably badly shaken by the time he got around to disposing of me."

"At least you got the *luck* of the Irish from your old man. Anyway, I thought about calling the cops, but I figured you needed a doctor more, so I phoned Nicky Heideger. Then I figured it might be a good idea to call Miss Dobie. Sometimes it's handy to have a native around when you're dealing with local cops." He paused, smiling to himself. That's quite a doctor you have there, by the way. She sure gave that Rose the word."

Conan stared at him, attempting to raise his head, but quickly giving it up. The aching in his head threw his eyes out of focus.

"Rose? Harvey Rose?"

"Yeah. About the time the Doc and Miss Dobie arrived, Chief Rose drives up, and—"

"Did anyone call him?"

"No. I was waiting for Miss Dobie before I called in the troops, and this wasn't ten minutes after I found you. He just walked right on in. Damn, I almost took a potshot at him until I saw the badge. Anyway, he was making with the big Sergeant Friday bit. Wanted to know what happened, and if you'd said anything. We took you out to the Doc's car, and Rose kept on asking questions. Nicky finally got fed up and told him to get the hell out of there.''

Conan smiled faintly. ''Did he leave?''

''Yeah. Said for Nicky to let him know when you were up to talking.''

''I'll have her tell him I'm in a coma.'' He paused, his eyes narrowing. ''I wonder what got to Rose. That sort of attention to duty is nothing short of a miracle.''

''I don't know. He said he was just cruising around and saw the lights in the shop and the Doc's car.''

''It doesn't matter. What about Miss Dobie?''

''She locked up the shop and came to the hospital with me. As soon as the Doc had a good look at you, she said we might as well leave, since she had a little stitching to do. I took Miss Dobie back to the shop so she could pick up her car, then she went on home. I'd better give her a call; let her know you're still with us. Poor old gal was really shaken up.'' He paused, then laughed to himself.

''What's so funny?''

''Well, she kept complaining about how the burglar— or whoever—dumped all those rare books out of the safe, then you bled all over them; said they'd be practically worthless. Thousands of dollars' worth of autographed first editions down the drain.''

Conan laughed. ''That's my Miss Dobie.''

''Well, you know how people get in a situation like that. She was really worried about you.''

''I know. Anyway, what next?''

''I went on into the shop and called Carl. This was about eight-thirty. I didn't have a chance to call before with so many people around.''

''What did he have to say?''

Duncan took his notebook from his breast pocket.

''Nothing happened at his end until seven-thirty. Then Mrs. Leen left her house, on foot, and walked up to the corner by the grocery store—you know, just north of the bookshop.''

Conan focused intently on him, unaware of the pounding ache in his head engendered by the quickening of his heartbeat.

"Did Berg follow her?"

"Sure. But he couldn't get too close; too much open space. She stopped at the corner and took out a flashlight and looked around the foundation of the store. Then Carl says he's sure she took something out from between the chinks, but she had her back to him, and he couldn't see what it was."

Conan almost laughed aloud; the sudden relief was overwhelming. For a moment, he was lightheaded with it.

Berg *hadn't* been wasting his time watching Edwina Leen. That nocturnal stroll stilled any doubts about her involvement with the book.

"Beautiful. At least, I caught the right mouse with my trap."

"Some mouse," Duncan commented sourly. "Anyway, she didn't move for a couple of minutes. Carl figured she was checking whatever she picked up. Then she turned around like she was heading home, but after a few steps she stopped and turned around again, and took off north up the highway."

"That's strange. She had what she wanted."

"The book? Yeah, I guess so."

"Where was she—?" Then he nodded. "North. The filling station. There's a phone booth there."

"Right. She made a call, talked for three or four minutes, then went straight home. She hasn't set foot out of the place since."

Conan was silent for a while, thinking over the report.

"Who the hell was she calling, Charlie? It wasn't the hired man. She wouldn't go out to a phone booth every time she had to contact him; she'd have a more efficient means of communication set up." He paused, then gave a quick sigh. "When you went up to the shop, did you see a car parked in front of the grocery store?"

"No. Why?"

"The Major's car was there when I arrived. But, of

course, it would be gone by the time you got there. That's probably how the body was removed. His killer had already taken his car keys when I found the body. Anyway, go on.''

Duncan took a deep breath, frowning down at the floor.

''Well, I'll have to admit I goofed here, Chief. I decided to take a look around the shop, and it finally came through to me that the place had been searched—*after* I went to the hospital with you.''

''Afterwards? But she had the book. Why would—'' Then he closed his eyes with a tight smile of satisfaction.

Something had gone wrong for Mrs. Edwina Leen. He had no way of knowing what it was, but somehow—even though she had the book—she still wasn't satisfied.

''What do you mean about goofing, Charlie? That's the best news I've had all night. We're still in business; she didn't find what she was looking for. And now we can be sure she's involved.'' He hesitated. ''You know, I'll give you odds that deafness routine is an act. It *has* to be.''

''Deafness? I've never met the lady, you know.''

''From all outward appearances, deaf as a post.'' He shook his head in amazement. ''She's a pro, Charlie. But something must have been missing from that book. The shop was searched after she picked it up. That might even explain the phone call. She was calling in someone to make the search. The third man.''

''What do you mean—the third man?''

''I . . . just a figure of speech. The important thing is she didn't find what she wanted in that book.''

Duncan nodded glumly. ''Yeah, I figured it that way, too, but the trouble is, I didn't realize the place had been searched until after I called Carl. Then I checked for bugs. The GI bugs the Major had installed have been replaced. I know, because I took a close look at the ones on your home phones. These are brand X. *That's* what I mean about goofing. She has every word of my call to Carl.''

"Oh." Conan considered this piece of news. "Well, all she could find out was that she was being watched, and perhaps your names."

"First names only. Conan, I'm sorry. The place was in such a hell of a mess already, it took me awhile to catch on."

"It's all right. It might even prove useful; the fact that my phones were already bugged should confuse her, for one thing, and the extra pressure might serve to force her hand. Did you find anything else?"

"Yes. I began to smarten up a little, so I went over to your house and checked. Same story."

"Did you remove the bugs?"

. "No, not yet."

"You'd better get rid of them. Damn, I hate to lose the Major's bugs. That was my only means of reaching his employers. What else?"

"Nothing. I relieved Carl for a while. I checked with the hospital a couple of times, and finally the Doc said you were beginning to come around, so I came on down here. I figured you might have a few questions."

"A few." He closed his eyes; the constant pain was beginning to tell on him. It was becoming increasingly difficult to keep his eyes—or his thoughts—in focus. "It's been a busy night all around."

Duncan came to his feet. "Chief, you look like hell. I'd better take off and let you—"

"No. Wait, Charlie." He took a deep breath. "Let me think a minute. There's something I want you to—" He stopped at a knock on the door. "Yes?"

Dr. Heideger came in, followed by a starchy nurse.

"Sorry, gentlemen, but I'll have to interrupt this."

Conan frowned. "Nicky, I still—"

"Tell me about it later."

She came around to his left side, and Charlie moved to the other side of the bed, while she removed the intravenous needle and unstrapped his arm.

"You can take this with you," she said to the nurse, indicating the transfusion equipment. "And prepare a diamorphine injection for me. I'll administer it." She reached into the pocket of her skirt, pulled out a prescription pad, and made a few cryptic notations, then handed the sheet to the nurse.

The nurse glanced at the form as she took it.

"Anything else, Doctor?"

"No, not now. Thank you, Jean."

Conan flexed his arm, watching silently as the nurse wheeled the plasma rack out of the room and closed the door behind her. Then he looked up at Nicky, who was studying him with a slight frown. She took his hand in hers for a moment, but it wasn't a gesture of affection, he knew; only one of her many unobtrusive diagnostic measures.

"How do you feel, Conan?"

"Fine."

"Sure." She looked cross the bed at Duncan, but before she could say anything more he raised a hand to quiet her.

"Okay, Doc, I know I shouldn't have stayed so long."

"Wait, Charlie," Conan injected.

"It's not you I'm worried about, Mr. Duncan. Harvey Rose just arrived, and unfortunately the nurse at the desk told him you'd been in to see Conan, so he's champing at the bit out there."

Conan's jaw went tight. "He's taking his job damned seriously all of a sudden."

"I'll be happy to get rid of him for you."

He looked up at Nicky, and seeing her sly smile, knew she'd *enjoy* getting rid of Rose, and his first impulse was to let her have her way. An encounter with Rose seemed to be asking too much of his waning physical resources. Then he hesitated.

"No," he said finally, "I'll talk to him. But I'd appreciate it if both of you stayed here. Particularly you, Charlie. I still have something to talk to you about before you leave."

Nicky raised an eyebrow, then acquiesced with a sigh.

"All right, I'll call Rose in. But I'm giving notice

now, Conan. I'm clearing everybody out of here in fifteen minutes, and giving you something to shut you up for a while.''

CHAPTER 16

Harvey Rose followed Nicky into the room, darting quick, suspicious glances at both Duncan and the doctor. He went to the end of the bed and leaned against the railing, while Nicky silently took up a position at Conan's left.

Rose's pale, restless eyes shifted incessantly. His face seemed even redder than usual, and his cheek was blotched with a swollen bruise.

Conan watched him through half-closed eyes, wondering how sober he was; more so than usual for this time of night, no doubt. He deliberately neglected to introduce him to Charlie.

Rose cleared his throat nervously.

"Well, uh, Mr. Flagg, I'm glad to see you're . . . uh, feeling better."

Conan smiled with more than a hint of irony at that expression of concern. Strange—he'd never noticed before, but Rose wore his .38 on his left side.

"I appreciate your taking time to come by, Mr. Rose. I know this is after your normal working hours."

The policeman seemed unaware of the faint overtones

of sarcasm in that statement. He only smiled and shrugged.

"Well, in this business you have to expect a little over-time. Criminals don't work eight-to-five shifts, you know."

No, Conan thought bitterly, but the honorable Chief Rose did. At least, he usually did.

He made no response, giving Rose what he hoped was a sufficiently appreciative smile, watching him as he reached into his breast pocket for a notebook and pen.

"Well, Mr. Flagg, if you . . . uh, feel up to it, maybe you could tell me what happened tonight."

He started to reply, then hesitated, staring at Rose as he made a quick notation at the top of the page, his arm twisted with the overhanded writing position typical of the left-handed. And the knuckles of his left hand were skinned and bruised.

Rose looked up at him sharply. "Mr. Flagg?"

Only Charlie Duncan was aware of the slight change in Conan's attitude; he recognized a faint light hidden behind the opaque black eyes.

Finally, Conan said, "Well, I'm afraid you've put yourself out for no purpose."

"How's that?"

"Mr. Rose, I *can't* tell you what happened."

Duncan threw him a quick, speculative glance, but neither he nor Nicky showed any overt reaction to this statement.

"What d'you mean, you can't tell me?"

"I can't tell you because I haven't the slightest idea what happened myself. It's a complete blank."

Rose eyed him suspiciously. "But you must remember *something.*"

He shook his head. "I wish I could. I don't like the idea of getting shot at. I've been trying to remember, but except for this shoulder—and a hell of a headache—it might as well have happened to someone else."

"But before you got shot—can't you remember anything about that?'' Rose's tone was sharp and insistent.

"No. I remember I was going to the shop to pick up a couple of books I'd saved for Charlie.'' He glanced briefly at Duncan.''

"Then you *do* remember going to the shop?''

"No . . . not really.'' He frowned as if concentrating on calling up the memory. "I remember leaving the house, but that's all. I don't even remember arriving at the shop.''

"Are you sure, Flagg? Come on—just try to think back. You must remember more than that.''

"No, I'm sorry.''

"But that was before you got shot. You must remember what happened before that!''

"I told you,'' Conan said wearily, "it's a complete blank.''

Rose's face was flushed, his eyes narrowed to slits.

"What d'you mean, a *blank*? Listen, Flagg, if you—''

"Mr. Rose—'' It was Nicky, her tone sharp and cool. "Conan suffered a severe blow to the head. Surely, you're aware that partial amnesia, particularly affecting the time span near the injury, is quite common in such cases.''

Rose turned on her, and there was an almost tangible clash as their eyes met—and held. Finally, it was Rose who backed down. He looked away, then concentrated on the problem of returning his notebook and pen to his pocket.

"Well, sure I realize head injuries can cause . . . uh, problems like that.''

Conan was silent, watching this encounter with a certain relish, as Nicky went on coldly.

"My concern is for my patient, Mr. Rose, and I consented to let you see him tonight only because you insisted. But I will not tolerate your badgering him. I think it must be obvious, even to you, that he can't answer your questions, so I'll ask you to leave now.''

Rose shot her a venomous look, then glanced uneasily at Conan, then back to Nicky.

"You . . . uh, figure the memory will come back?"

She hesitated, then caught Conan's almost imperceptible negative head shake.

"That's hard to say," she replied thoughtfully. "I suppose the amnesia could disappear, but it's been my experience with a cranial injury of this type that the trauma apparently blocks the memory functions in the frontal lobes, so there's actually no imprint made on the memory-storing cells. Even events preceding the trauma are permanently obliterated. I've seen some cases where the result was *total* amnesia."

Rose regarded her with a peculiarly blank expression through this dissertation, then finally turned to Conan.

"Well. I—I'm sorry to bother you, Mr. Flagg, but you understand, it doesn't make my job any easier."

Conan mustered a polite smile. "Of course. I suppose you'll want everything left as it is in the shop until you've had a chance to check it—fingerprints, and all that."

"What? Oh. Yes, of course. I'll . . . send somebody down first thing in the morning."

"What time? I'll have Miss Dobie open the shop for you."

"Well, I—about nine, I guess."

"Good. I'll tell her."

Nicky glanced at her watch, then fixed Rose with a cold, unblinking gaze.

"Now, Mr. Rose, if that's all—"

He glanced suspiciously at her, then cleared his throat.

"Yes, that's . . . all. I'll be in touch with you, Mr. Flagg," he concluded lamely, then turned and hurried from the room.

Conan closed his eyes, shivering involuntarily.

Footsteps. Charlie going to the door to make sure Rose was gone. Charlie's instincts were always good.

The shivering wouldn't stop. Gross inefficiency, to

keep a hospital room so cold. Considering the price of the accommodations here, it would seem . . .

He was slipping, but he was only aware of it when the whirling sensation began.

Not yet. He wasn't ready to surrender yet.

He concentrated, bringing his mind into focus again, finding it a wrenching effort. Reaction; that was part of it. Reaction to a staggering realization.

His mind had already pieced this particular puzzle together, but on an unconscious level. It had correlated the facts, the juxtaposition of events, the anomalies, and produced an answer that seemed blind inspiration. And now he must repeat the process on a conscious level.

The truth was there; all he needed was an explanation.

But it was difficult to keep his thoughts in any kind of reasonable sequence, and reaction and illness weren't entirely responsible. There was an element of fear.

He felt a gentle touch against his forehead and opened his eyes abruptly. Not yet . . .

"Conan?"

"Yes, Nicky. I'm all right."

"No, you aren't, but I won't argue with you."

She went to the table at the end of the bed and brought a tray back to the bedside table. It was laden with a small, rubber-capped bottle and a hypodermic syringe. He frowned at it; he hadn't heard the nurse bring it in.

"Not yet," he said flatly.

"That isn't your decision."

He smiled faintly. "Perhaps. But I can make it hard for you. Please. Give me a few minutes with Charlie."

Duncan scowled at him. "Listen, Chief, there's always tomorrow."

"No. Tomorrow will be too late."

Charlie sighed and looked helplessly at Nicky. She studied Conan a moment; a scrutiny that was typically a paradoxical mixture of objective assessment and empathy. Finally, she smiled.

"Conan, if you aren't grateful for your usual good

health, I am. You're a damnably difficult patient. All right. Five minutes.'' She glanced at Duncan as she started for the door. "I'll be right outside.''

"Thanks, Doc." When the door closed behind her, he turned to Conan. "Okay, if you're feeling so talkative, maybe you'd like to explain that amnesia routine. You're damned lucky Nicky's so fast on the uptake.''

He laughed weakly. "And that she detests Rose so thoroughly.''

"So what's *your* excuse?''

"I . . . just don't want Rose involved." It was so hard to think; to stay with one line of reasoning and follow it through. "I don't trust him.''

"Well, that's understandable. Is that all?''

Conan hesitated. "For now, yes.''

"Okay. I'll let it ride—for now. Chief, you're running on nerve. What did you want to talk to me about?''

He frowned, resenting Duncan's words, finally realizing the resentment was for himself; for his own weakness. He concentrated, gathering his waning strength.

"I'm sorry to put so much on your shoulders, but I want you to check something at the shop tonight.''

"Sure. I brought a supply of uppers, just in case.''

"You may need them. But this won't take long. Look in the Anthropology section upstairs; the last room to the south. I put a third copy of *Crime and Punishment* there.''

"What should I do with it?''

"I just want to know if it's there.''

"Okay. What else is on your mind?''

Too much, he thought bitterly; too much to sort out.

"Call Miss Dobie. Tell her to be at the shop at eight tomorrow morning. That'll give us some leeway in case Rose decides to jump the gun. And tell her to keep the shop open all day tomorrow.''

"What do you mean—all day?''

"We usually close on Monday. The resort economy's sabbath.''

"Oh." Duncan smiled crookedly. "I'll tell her. You want me to stick around the shop tomorrow?"

"No, I'll be there."

He snorted. "Yeah, well, you might have a little argument with the Doc on that."

"No doubt." He pulled in a slow breath. Stupidity, to get himself confined to a hospital bed now; to find it so difficult to think, or even to speak. He had to be careful now to avoid slurring his words.

"Charlie, I'll have to call Steve Travers."

"Will he talk to me?"

He frowned slightly, the real question in his mind whether he was willing to surrender that task to Duncan. Finally, he nodded.

"Yes, he'll talk to you. He knows your name from past reminiscences."

Duncan raised an eyebrow. "I hope you had something good to say about me."

Conan looked up, giving him a sardonic smile.

"Nothing but the truth—always."

"Is that supposed to be encouraging?"

"Well, at least your name will be familiar. Tell him you're working on the Jeffries case, and give him everything we have. And I want some information from him."

Charlie nodded and took out his notebook.

"What kind of information?"

"First, who Mills was working for. If Steve still isn't talking, make it clear to him that we may have vital information." He felt himself tightening, and worked at systematically relaxing every muscle. "And give him the Major's license number, but don't tell him—"

"I know. You don't know who's driving the car."

"Yes. Ask him to put out an APB in this area on the car. I doubt it'll do any good, but it's worth a try."

Duncan glanced surreptitiously at his watch.

"Anything else?"

"Yes. See what he can dig up on Mrs. Leen. You have all the pertinent information." He paused, considering his next request. "There's someone else I'd like to know about."

"Anybody I know?"

"No. Anton Dominic."

"Who the hell is he?"

"I don't know if he has anything to do with this, but when Mills came into the shop, it was on Dominic's heels both times."

Duncan's eyes narrowed. "He was tailing him?"

"I can't be sure of that. It may be coincidence."

"Okay. But what can you give me besides a name?"

"He's a retired carpenter; about seventy. A Greek immigrant. He's been in Holliday Beach about two years."

"Well, that should be easy enough to check through Immigration."

"It should."

"What else?"

"That's all, Charlie. Tell Steve I'll . . . call him tomorrow."

Duncan put his notebook away, studying him in silence for a moment.

"Conan, are you holding out on me?"

The question was asked in a quiet tone that took him off guard. Conan closed his eyes, feeling his mind slipping out of focus again, and if he didn't tell Charlie all he knew—or assumed—it was only because the explanation would be too difficult. And because Charlie had enough to worry about tonight. If he understood, he wouldn't leave the hospital. The risk was probably slight at this point, but it existed.

Conan knew he'd been left on the floor in his office for dead. His survival wouldn't be considered desirable to some parties.

"Charlie, I . . . I'll talk to you about it tomorrow."

Duncan was obviously less than satisfied with this, but he had no opportunity to protest. Nicky Heideger came in at that point, her jaw set firmly.

"Gentlemen, it's time for lights out."

"All right, Doc." Charlie smiled faintly at Conan. "Tomorrow, Chief. Relax. Everything's under control."

Conan knew Duncan didn't believe that anymore than he did, but he nodded acceptance.

"Thanks, Charlie."

"Sure." He started for the door. "Good night, Doc. Oh—it's been nice meeting you."

CHAPTER 17

Charlie Duncan was standing at the bottom of the spiral staircase, dressed in a bathrobe, his red hair rumpled, his eyes ringed with dark shadows, and his expression an almost ludicrous combination of puzzlement and annoyance.

"What the hell are *you* doing here?"

Conan laughed, then crossed to the west wall and pulled the drapes with his left hand.

"Why shouldn't I be here? It's all I have to call home."

Duncan walked over to the windows, squinting miserably at the glare of sunlight.

"I mean how did you get past the Doc?"

"Past her? Charlie, Nicky brought me home." Then at Duncan's dubious expression, he added, "I'll admit it took a little fast talking."

"Yeah. At least. I never figured she'd fall for any of your Irish blarney."

"Ah, Charlie, me boy, never underestimate the golden tongue of a true son of the auld sod." He looked out at the breakers, smiling at the gossamer veils thrown back from the crests. "Actually, we made a bargain of sorts, and she found nothing out of the ordinary on the X rays."

"You mean the pictures of your head? Well, some things don't show up on X rays. So, what's your bargain?"

"I'm to check with her every day for the next week, and wear this damn thing"—he glanced down at the sling supporting his right arm—"and keep the arm immobile. Nicky is rather sensitive about her stitchery. Anyway, she gave me a bottle of pills for pain, with the comforting assurance that if it's sore now, it'll get worse, and sent me out into the world with her blessing."

Duncan finally laughed. "Blarney. That's all."

"Probably." He glanced at his watch, the anxiety closing in again, shadowing his eyes: 9:25. "Charlie, have you heard from Carl this morning?"

"Not since six. No action, Chief. He'd have called me if anything showed up."

"Did you get any sleep last night?"

"Yes. This morning, anyway. I relieved Carl until six, then I turned in. How're you feeling? I damned sure didn't think you'd be up this soon."

He laughed and looked out the window. He had no intention of elucidating on how he felt; every muscle in his body ached, aside from the dull throbbing in his shoulder and head.

"I'm all right, Charlie. Did you get through to Steve last night?"

"Sure. I gave him the whole story, and he said he'd do what he could for you. He wants you to call him as soon as you can."

"Anything about the Major's employers?"

"No. He says he still can't discuss it."

"Damn. All right, I'll call him in a few minutes. Look, why don't you put on some coffee and give Carl a call while I go up and change clothes?"

Duncan nodded and grinned as he eyed his shirt.

"Yeah, that rag isn't exactly up to your usual sartorial standards, Chief."

He laughed and started for the stairway.

"A donation from Nicky's personal Goodwill bag. My clothes were in bad shape."

"You need any help?"

"No. I'll manage."

Conan began to wonder about his ability to "manage" before he finished shaving and dressing. He found himself swearing under his breath at nearly every movement; the simplest task became a problem with the injured shoulder.

But by the time he came back downstairs, he'd learned a few tricks about "managing" with only limited use of his right arm.

Charlie was in the kitchen; Conan could see him through the pass-through, staring morosely at a sputtering skillet. He walked over to the pass-through, smiling faintly at Duncan's intent interest in his culinary task.

"Did you get hold of Carl?"

Duncan looked over at him and nodded. "Yeah. All quiet on that front. The old lady's still at home, and she hasn't made a move."

Conan frowned. "Nothing at all?"

"Well, Carl can't see through the walls, but she hasn't so much as opened her door since last night. You had breakfast yet?"

He sniffed the odor of cremated bacon and nodded with some relief.

"Yes. That comes with the seventy-five-dollar-a-day accommodations. Did you clear the bugs on the phones?"

"They're clean, and I didn't find any other bugs around."

"I'll call Steve, then."

Duncan nodded absently. "Okay. I'll be through here in a minute."

Conan crossed to the bar, settling himself on one of the stools, lit a cigarette, then picked up the receiver, finding left-handed dialing annoyingly awkward. He reached Travers after going through two receptionists.

"Conan, for God's sake, where are you? Still at the hospital?"

"No, I'm home."

"Already?"

"Well, I can be very persuasive, believe it or not, and anyway, Nicky found no cracks in my cranium."

"Then she's looking at the wrong cranium. Yours has been cracked for years."

Conan groaned. "I walked into that one. But we'd better get down to business. It's nearly ten, and I have to get to the bookshop."

"Okay. I hope you realize you've had me hopping half the night and all morning."

"Well, Steve, as Chief Rose told me just last night, criminals don't work eight-to-five shifts."

Travers made a few choice comments.

"I'll never understand," he concluded, "how Harvey Rose made chief in Holliday Beach. He's been kicked off, or asked to resign, from every force he's been on."

Conan puffed at his cigarette, his eyes narrowing.

"So I've heard. Steve, you just don't understand the local political situation. Some people feel more secure with a man like Harvey around."

"Sure. Anyway, I did some legwork for you—at the taxpayers' expense, you understand, which doesn't endear me to the powers that be around here."

"If you get any complaints, refer them to my tax returns. I'm definitely a taxpayer, and I'm entitled. Did you find that Chevrolet?"

Travers gave a short laugh. "You're going to love this. It'd already been picked up when I put out the APB—by the Holliday Beach Police Department, no less. They found it down on Front Street a couple of blocks from the bookshop. Deserted, they say."

"Damn. You can count on that car being clean as a whistle at this point."

"Conan, you don't have the proper respect for the local minions of the law."

"Oh, I have respect—of a sort. Did you get any information at all on the car?"

"It's registered to an agency of the federal government, and I'm not at liberty yet to say *what* agency."

"Oh, for God's sake, Steve, can't I get it through anyone's head—" He sighed and forced himself to relax. "All right, so I'm still a suspect—for crimes unknown. Has there been any sign of the Major's body?"

"No, but then nobody's been looking yet, as far as I know. I . . . uh, asked some questions about this Major."

"And?"

"Well, like I said, I'm not free to talk yet. But off the record, I got the impression he was working on something on his own. It didn't have anything to do with his assignment, and his boss wasn't too happy about it."

"Was his boss sure it had nothing to do with his assignment? Steve, this isn't Berlin. How many undercover operations do you think we'd have going in Holliday Beach?"

Travers sighed. "I don't know, and I'm just guessing, really. They haven't been exactly talkative around me, either. Maybe my good name's been tarnished by association with you."

"Well, I'm sorry about that. I'd like to know how *my* good name got so tarnished."

"Don't ask me. But I picked up a hint that this Major saw somebody he recognized in the bookshop a few days ago. I don't know if that was you or not."

Conan sent out a stream of smoke and tapped his cigarette impatiently against the ashtray.

"That still doesn't explain why I'm suddenly so untrustworthy. Did you tell them . . . about Mills?"

"You mean that he's dead? Yes, I told them."

"Do they believe it?"

"Well, last night, no. But this morning, after checking with his—I mean, finding out he hadn't shown up for his usual shift, they're beginning to worry."

"*Beginning* to worry? It's about time. And I know he had a partner here, so you don't need to pussyfoot around that. Steve, they should have someone down here checking, not sitting over there *worrying*."

"Checking *what*, Conan? They told me the Major had a habit of taking off on tangents of his own; they lost track of him for three days once. They also told me there's been no hint of trouble on his assignment. And they have nothing but your word for it that he's dead. Did anybody else see the body?"

"Yes."

"Who, for God's sake? Duncan said—"

"The man who killed him."

Travers loosed an exasperated sigh.

"Sure. That's a big help."

"It's certainly more than my word for it that someone put a bullet in *me* last night."

"I know. That's on the records as an attempted burglary. It's also on the records that the only witness to said burglary—namely you—suffered an attack of acute amnesia."

Conan's cheeks darkened, and the anger-generated tension sent a spasm of pain across his shoulder.

"If someone other than Harvey Rose was willing to listen to me, I might recover from that amnesia."

"Look, Conan, I'm doing my best, and, like I said, they aren't saying much to me, either."

He subsided, the tension sagging from his taut muscles.

"I know, Steve. It isn't your fault."

"Anyway, they'll probably have somebody down there to check things out soon, if they haven't already. But it seems they're a little shorthanded at the moment. There's kind of a delicate matter pending in Portland; something to do with about a million bucks' worth of heroin and the Cosa Nostra. That's pure scuttlebutt, by the way."

Conan's eyes narrowed. "Cosa Nostra. That probably means FBI, then."

"I told you it was scuttlebutt."

"It doesn't help right now, anyway. Did you get any results on those names Charlie gave you?"

Travers hesitated. "Well, it's funny, but I couldn't come up with anything on either one of them. I checked all the regular channels and scored a big fat zero. Immigration didn't even have anything on that Dominic. As far as official records go, those people just don't exist.''

"That's . . . quite interesting.''

"I'm glad you think so. I'll keep at it, but I doubt I'll turn up with anything.''

"The lack of information is informative in its own way. Anyway, thanks for the help, and try to get through to that federal agency, or I may get desperate and try on my own. I doubt they'd like that. I might inadvertently foul up some of their best laid plans in the process.''

"Now, look, Conan,'' Travers began hotly; then he sighed. "All right, I'll keep trying, but just hold off for a while. Please.''

"I will, Steve. As long as I can. Anyway, I'll keep you posted.''

"Sure. Thanks for the reassurance. And . . . good luck.''

Conan cradled the receiver and, for a moment, let his hand rest there, his fingers tapping against the plastic, his eyes fixed blindly on one of the jade prayer wheels in the case behind the bar.

"Well, what's the word?''

Duncan was putting two steaming cups on the table between the Barcelonas. Conan rose and crossed to the chairs, drawn by the welcome aroma of the coffee.

"The word is mixed; a little good and a lot bad.'' He eased himself carefully into one of the chairs. "Thanks for the coffee.''

Duncan nodded as he seated himself.

"What'd Steve have to say?''

Conan gave him the gist of the conversation, then waited silently for him to digest it. Charlie glowered into his cup for a while, then looked up at him.

"So they're not even admitting the Major's dead?''

"Consider the source—from their point of view.'' He paused to light a cigarette, another small task made difficult by the injury. "Apparently, they haven't much faith in my word. I assume they'll take me more seriously in time—when Mills doesn't show up at all."

"In time," he repeated glumly. "What the hell do you suppose his assignment was, anyway? You think Steve knows?"

"Probably, but I doubt he's been told very much."

"Well, Steve didn't help us much. He's too hogtied."

Conan raised his cup, savoring the coffee.

"He turned up one rather important item."

"What do you mean?"

"Dominic. I can understand the lack of information on Mrs. Leen, but Anton Dominic doesn't exist officially, either, and that's quite informative."

"You figure he's in this with Mrs. Leen?"

"I don't know. But before, I couldn't be sure Mills was tailing him; it might have been coincidence that they showed up in the shop at the same time twice in a row. It *still* might be coincidence, but the odds have dropped to nothing on that. Dominic isn't what he pretends to be."

"Maybe he's the hired man you keep talking about."

Conan's eyes were briefly opaque; stone black.

"No. He wouldn't be a match physically for Jeffries, much less the Major. And the Major put up a fight before he died."

Duncan shrugged. "Okay. How would he work out as the courier?"

"Not very well. He hasn't a car, for one thing."

"He might have access to one."

"Yes. But I know he wasn't in the shop Friday. He was ill, and Saturday was the first time he'd been in for two weeks. The book was undoubtedly delivered Friday. That's when Jeffries found it, and I can't imagine their leaving it on the shelf for any length of time."

"So where does Dominic fit in?"

"I don't know." He shook his head, feeling a vague sadness; regret. "I wish I didn't have to fit him in at all."

"Why not?"

"He's . . . a gentle man, Charlie. A man who lives on

ideas; who can get enthusiastic about Mu mesons and negative atomic particles and Einsteinian limits."

"So does that eliminate him as an enemy agent?"

"No."

"It's just that you happen to like the old guy, is that it?" Then at Conan's affirmative nod, "Yeah. Well, just don't put any blinders on. The way things are going around here, you better keep your eyes wide open."

Conan smiled faintly. "Sage advice, Charlie. I'll keep it in mind."

"You'd better. Anyway, I don't think Dominic's our main concern, if he's eliminated as the hired man. That's the one I'm worried about. He's leaving quite a trail of bodies behind him."

"He's a little heavy-handed. But at least I know who he is."

Duncan stared at him, then put his cup down with an impact that should have cracked it, and succeeded in dousing the table with coffee.

"Oh, hell." He pulled out a handkerchief and mopped up the coffee, scowling angrily. "All right, Chief, let's have that again. Slow."

Conan rose and went to the bar, then returned with a towel to help with Duncan's inept mopping.

"I said I know who the hired man is, but unfortunately I can't prove a damned thing. Here—that's good enough."

Duncan surrendered his sodden handkerchief to him, watching him balefully as he took it and the towel back to the bar.

"Conan, I'm not a jury. So who the hell is it? And when did you come up with this brainstorm of yours?"

He returned to his chair and picked up his cigarette.

"Harvey Rose. And the brainstorm hit last night."

"I should've known. I figured you were holding out on me. Look, if all you wanted was a legman, you could've hired somebody else and saved yourself some money."

Conan shook his head. "Charlie, I wasn't up to explaining it last night; I hadn't even thought it out. I wanted some time to think, and I'd already given you plenty to do. I . . . didn't want you distracted."

"Distracted? What do you mean?" He eyed Conan suspiciously, then finally nodded. "You figured Rose might come back to finish the job on you?"

"It was a possibility, but rather a remote one. His chances of getting caught were too high there, and I think he was partially convinced, at least, by the amnesia line."

"So, you didn't want me wasting time making sure he didn't come back to visit you—with malice aforethought?" He sagged back into his chair with a long sigh. "If I took time to comment on that, we'd be here all day. So, I'll let it pass. Now, if you don't think I'd be too *distracted*, maybe you'd care to tell me why the hell you homed in on Rose."

Conan hesitated, aware that his reasons might seem flimsy to Charlie; as flimsy as Nel Jeffries' reasons for believing her husband's death wasn't accidental.

"First, he's left-handed," he began. "I wasn't aware of that until last night. Jeffries was probably hit by a southpaw before he was drowned; the bruise was on the right side of the jaw. Secondly, Rose's face and the knuckles of his left hand were somewhat the worse for wear last night, and Mills put up a fight before he was shot."

"Maybe that wasn't the only fight in town last night."

"Probably not. I suppose what made me wonder, to begin with, was his remarkable attention to duty. Not only did he show up at the scene of a crime without being called, but he went to the trouble of going to the hospital at midnight to question me about it. Getting that kind of action from Rose is mind boggling. Usually, if he gets a call after hours, he either sends one of his rookies, or tells the caller to drop by the police station in the morning."

Duncan lit a cigarette, his brow lined with a thoughtful and still skeptical frown.

"Rose isn't exactly unique. I've run into plenty of his kind. The man in the big brass uniform with a tendency to blind spots when it pays. So his efficiency last night was a little odd. Is that all you're going on?"

Conan bit back an irritable rejoinder and nodded.

"In essence. The man was acting out of character—or so it would seem. But in fact, he wasn't; it's just that the reasons for his behavior weren't apparent. And it occurred to me that Rose would be a perfect candidate for the job of hired man and errand boy. He can be had, and he isn't bothered with trivia like ethics or conscience. He's in a position of authority and an excellent source of information on the activities of various law-enforcement agencies. Not only that, it would be easy to set up a communication system with him using radios; no one would think twice at seeing a policeman using a car radio, for instance. And another thing—Berg saw Rose drive past only a few minutes before the Major's car showed up. Any time after 5:00 P.M., you can usually find Harvey in one of the local bars, not cruising around in his car."

Duncan's initial skepticism was fading, but it wasn't entirely gone yet.

"Well, you may be on to something, but it's all just a little . . . vague."

"I know, and it doesn't get any less vague." He rose and went to the window, gazing up at the porcelain shadings of the sky. "I had another thought about Harvey Rose in relation to Captain Jeffries. Remember, I said no one would have any reason to assume Jeffries knew what was in that book unless he *told* someone. Well, who would he tell? Is it unreasonable that he'd tell a duly appointed officer of the law? Rose isn't held in the highest respect around here, but very few people know exactly how little respect he deserves." He paused, giving Duncan an oblique smile. "Brace yourself, Charlie, for another theory."

He shrugged. "I'm braced."

"All right. It goes like this. Rose had been ordered to watch Jeffries and get the book from him; he saw him walking down Front Street with the book. Rose was ostensibly out cruising the neighborhood, and he stopped to question him; after all, it was unusual for the Captain to be walking the streets alone at night. And this took place within less than a block of the beach access; Mrs. Crane said Jeffries was alone as far as Beach Street. So the ocean was all too handy. Rose probably asked if anything was wrong, and Jeffries, not looking past the uniform, told him everything. At least, enough to convince Rose that it was necessary to silence him. Someone else might have handled the situation with more finesse, and I doubt Mrs. Leen was too happy with Rose's solution. But he isn't known for his subtlety."

Duncan mulled this over for a while, then looked up at him speculatively.

"You know, Chief, it may be vague, but it makes sense. And Rose sure as hell was in a panic when he showed up at the bookshop last night. He kept asking if you'd said anything; really hammered at it."

Conan laughed. "I can understand his concern. My survival was undoubtedly a surprise to him. He was probably coming back to make sure of me after he disposed of the Major's body and his car."

"Okay. So you've got a working theory. Now, how the hell do we pin him?"

"Pin him? I can't even prove either of the murders were committed. All I can prove is that someone tried to kill me. But that doesn't help."

"Why not? If you could tie Rose in with—"

"Tie him how? For one thing, the incident at the shop has been officially written off as an attempted burglary. For another, I asked Nicky about the bullet she took out of my shoulder. Rose dutifully picked it up when he came to the hospital last night. Official evidence."

Duncan sighed disconsolately.

"Sure. It'll never see a ballistics lab."

"Harvey's in an excellent position for committing murders. The Major's car, for instance—'deserted.' And if he were foolish enough to leave any fingerprints at the shop last night, who'll handle that part of the investigation? If not Rose, then one of his men, and he'll have access to the reports."

"Checkmate, then."

"Only check, Charlie; it isn't mate yet."

"So, what's our next move?"

"I don't know. But Rose isn't our main concern; Mrs. Leen is. The crucial problem now is to figure out why she's here; what her mission is. And I don't think we have much time. She and her friends have been making some rather noticeable waves lately, and in this line of work you don't go around murdering people if you expect to stay and conduct business as usual."

Duncan frowned dubiously. "What do you mean about the old gal's mission? That's obvious, isn't it? She's middle man on an information exchange."

"No," he said flatly. "I thought so at first, but I can't buy it now. They've taken fantastic risks lately, but *not* to protect the system. They've risked exposure of the system. And why? To get at that book, or rather, whatever it contained; to get hold of that one particular message or piece of information. If it were a run-of-the-mill information exchange, they'd give up that one transmission and beat a strategic retreat before they'd risk exposing the system and the agents involved." He sighed and turned to look out the window. "And, Charlie, why set up an exchange *here*; why Holliday Beach? How would she get the information out of the country?"

"Well, by boat, maybe; radio transmissions."

"One of the largest fishing fleets on the coast works out of Holliday Bay, and there's also the Coast Guard station to contend with. The risks of discovery would be too high. They could find plenty of more remote spots along the coast that would be far safer. But an information exchange of some sort *does* exist here, and there must be a good reason. Mrs. Leen isn't here for the scenery."

"Then why the hell *is* she here?"

Conan laughed bitterly. "That's the question. But I'll give you odds she has one specific mission, and that book contained her instructions for the final phase of it. She isn't acting as if she intends to stay around Holliday Beach much longer." He was silent for a moment, focusing on the string of tiny dark spots along the horizon. "And don't forget the trawlers. Their arrival at this particular time is a little too coincidental.''

"Maybe she's setting up an escape route for herself.''

"Maybe.''

"Okay. So, where do we go from here?''

"We wait for Steve to get through to the FBI—if he can. We keep an eye on Mrs. Leen. Maybe we set another mouse trap. Did you check that third copy of the Dostoevsky?''

"What—oh. Yes. It's still there. Nobody had time to go through all those shelves, I guess.''

"No, and they weren't looking for another copy of the book.'' He glanced at his watch, then went to the table for his cigarettes; he put them in his pocket, then started for the hallway.

"Charlie, you stay here and get a couple of hours' rest. I doubt anything will break in that time.''

Duncan was on his feet, staring at him blankly.

"Where the hell are *you* going?''

"The bookshop.''

"What for?''

"For whatever turns up.''

CHAPTER 18

Conan drove the XK-E to the shop. The gear shift put a strain on the shoulder that would raise objections from Nicky, but he wanted a car handy today.

When he walked into the shop, Miss Dobie was behind the counter, gazing at him in open-mouthed amazement.

"Mr. Flagg, you shouldn't be here today!"

"It isn't as bad as it looks," he assured her.

"Well, I'm glad to hear that, because it *looks* awful. And if you don't mind my asking, what in the world happened last night?"

He turned up the palm of his free hand.

"I really don't know. Nicky calls it traumatic amnesia."

Her eyebrows went up. "Oh. Then you don't even know what hit you—or rather, *who* hit you?"

"No, and I'd like to find out so I could return the favor. But apparently, I walked in on a robbery."

"Apparently." She rested her chin on her hand, her eyes narrowed. "You know . . . it sure was a funny robbery. Nothing's missing. Except there was a book *you* put in the safe. I was looking for that 1929 edition of *The XIT*

Ranch yesterday. Saw an ad in *The Antiquarian* for it; dealer was offering seventy-five dollars. Anyway, I happened to notice that book, and I figured you must've put it in there, but it was gone this morning." She paused, watching him closely. "It was *Crime and Punishment*, wasn't it?"

Miss Dobie was sometimes too observant when it came to books. Conan glanced around the shop, relieved to see no one within earshot at the moment.

"Have you mentioned that book to anyone?"

"No, I thought maybe you took it out of the safe yourself later."

"Don't mention it, please, in case anyone asks."

"All right," she replied doubtfully. "If you say so."

"Did anyone from the police department show up this morning?"

"Oh, yes." She turned her eyes heavenward with a sigh of disgust. "That young cop—the new one. He fooled around for about half an hour, then he said I could clean up the place. The office was a real mess. I couldn't do much, but it's a little better."

"Thanks. How long have you been open?"

"Just since ten, but I got here at eight, like your friend Mr. Duncan told me. He's a nice guy; really pitched in last night."

"Yes, he is. We were in the Army together."

"That's what he told me." She paused again. "If you don't mind my asking something else—how come you're keeping the shop open today?"

"I just wanted someone around. Have there been many people in?"

"No, just a couple of locals and a few tourists."

"What locals?"

"Oh . . . let's see. Mrs. Hollis, and that Hanford boy."

"Has Rose been in yet?"

"No."

"He will be." He shifted his right arm in the sling, trying to find a more comfortable position. "Miss Dobie, has anyone asked for any particular books?"

"You mean like *Crime and Punishment*?"

"Yes," he replied tightly.

"No. Mr. Flagg, what's so—"

"Excuse me," he said, turning away abruptly. "I have to check something upstairs."

She loosed a sigh as he walked away. He hurried up the stairs, noting the dark stains on the floor at the bottom of the staircase, then went back to the Reference room and found the third copy of the Dostoevsky.

Downstairs, he passed Miss Dobie with only a casual nod on his way into the office. The book was tucked under his arm, and she took due note of it, but he closed the door before she could ask any more questions.

Miss Dobie had done a good job cleaning the office, but the Kerman carpet would have to be taken into Portland. He stared at the bloodstains, in his mind's eye seeing the Major's body there, and finding that image still incomprehensible. And equally incomprehensible that some of those stains were his own blood.

He looked around, assessing the damage, and realized he'd have to check for monitoring devices. One of Harvey Rose's men had spent a half hour here this morning.

He set to work, leaving the door slightly ajar. He begrudged the time and effort, but finally he was reasonably sure the room wasn't bugged. He still had reservations about the phone; it could be tapped somewhere else along the line.

At length, he took a final look around, then poured a cup of coffee and sank into his chair, taking a long, shaky breath. Nicky had warned him he'd be a little weak in the knees. He frowned irritably; she was, as usual, quite correct.

He swallowed one of the pills she'd given him, grimacing at the scalding temperature of the coffee, then glanced out at the counter—as he had every few minutes during his search—and watched as Miss Dobie rang up a sale for a young couple. Then he reached for the third copy of the Dostoevsky and studied it absently.

Finally, he took a new date card from his desk and

wrote across it: "First edition of this book available. Reasonable offers will be considered. CJF."

He pasted an envelope in the back cover, inserted the date card and closed the book, then leaned back, taking time to light a cigarette.

A better mousetrap. But he wasn't waiting for the world to beat a path to his door. All he wanted to catch with this trap was an answer.

He looked impatiently at his watch. He must wait now for the opportunity to set this particular trap. This would be another day of waiting. And hoping. The prospect did nothing for his temper.

He reached for the phone; at least there was one thing he could check himself. He dialed the Coast Guard station at Holliday Bay.

The opportunity to set his trap came sooner than he expected. It came within an hour of his arrival at the shop.

Conan had turned his chair to face the door, and he watched without moving as Harvey Rose's car came to a stop across the highway, and the Chief busied himself for a few seconds with his car radio.

Only when Rose left his car and crossed the highway to the shop, did Conan rise. He went to the door, but didn't open it, contenting himself with watching and listening, as Rose sauntered into the shop, his pale eyes shifting, scanning everything, particularly the office door. But Conan had left a scant quarter-inch opening that wouldn't be obvious except on close examination.

Rose finally focused on Beatrice Dobie.

"Good morning, Miss Dobie. I'm glad you're open today. Thought I'd better check again, see if anything's turned up here."

"You mean about the robbery?" She shrugged. "I don't know what would turn up that your man wouldn't find."

Rose walked over to the end of the counter and leaned on it, putting himself in profile to Conan.

"Well, I mean maybe you or Mr. Flagg might've

thought of something. I . . . uh, understand he's out of the hospital.''

She regarded him suspiciously. ''Yes, he is.''

''I hate to bother him. I mean, he probably isn't feeling too good. I thought maybe you could fill me in.'' He put a slight questioning inflection on the statement, but Miss Dobie ignored it.

''Well, I certainly hope you catch whoever's responsible. They nearly killed Mr. Flagg.'' She paused, frowning. ''But, you know, you'd think he could hold his own better than that. Unless there were two men, maybe.''

''He say there was more than one?'' Rose turned to look out the front entrance as if the answer were of no interest to him.

''Well, he didn't say. And something else I don't understand—those bloodstains at the foot of the stairs. There's even a few on the stairs themselves.''

''Oh? Was Mr. Flagg upstairs last night?''

''I suppose he might've been.''

''He see anybody up there?''

Miss Dobie frowned. ''Now, how could I answer that?''

''Oh . . . I just thought maybe he'd said something. Maybe last night when you were here.'' He gave her an oblique glance, then looked out toward the highway again.

''Well, he certainly wasn't saying anything last night.'' Rose shrugged. ''Sometimes people'll talk even when they're half out, you know.''

''He wasn't just *half* out.''

''Well, uh, I just thought—'' He seemed to become aware of the suspicion in her eyes and shifted the subject hurriedly. ''You find anything missing?''

''No,'' she said flatly.

''You're sure of that?''

''I checked very carefully.''

''Well, maybe there was something Mr. Flagg might know about.''

She glanced back at the office door and smiled faintly. Conan had opened the door, and was leaning against the jamb, the Dostoevsky in his left hand, the spine—and title—clearly visible.

She said casually, "Maybe you'd better ask Mr. Flagg yourself."

Rose turned, his face going red, then fading to a blotchy white as his gaze slid to the Dostoevsky.

"Good morning, Mr. Rose. I've been expecting you."

Rose focused on his face, swallowing hard.

"Uh . . . good morning."

"Any luck on the business here at the shop last night?"

"The . . . robbery. Well, no. We uh, don't have much to go on, you know." He cleared his throat, beginning to recover himself now. "I figure you must've scared the guy off. He's probably in Mexico by now."

"No doubt."

"Uh . . . by the way, how's that shoulder?"

Conan almost laughed at that show of concern.

"It'll be as good as new in a few weeks. Excuse me, I want to put this away while I'm thinking about it." He indicated the book in his hand. "It's a full-time job just keeping these books in order." He started toward the stairway, then paused. "Oh—if you have any more questions about the robbery, Miss Dobie will help you. Actually, she knows more about it than I do."

"Still don't remember anything?"

He shook his head. "It's still a complete blank. But if I ever get any faint stirrings, I'll let you know."

Rose's pale eyes strayed briefly to the book.

"Yeah. You do that." Then as Conan walked away, he turned to Miss Dobie. "You sure there's nothing missing?"

Conan didn't hear her response, but he trusted her; he'd asked her not to mention the Dostoevsky, and she wouldn't.

He went upstairs, glanced around the empty Fiction section, then put the book on the shelf, exactly where the other two copies had been.

This done, he crossed to the gable window on the east side of the room and looked out across the highway to

Rose's car. A few minutes later, the Chief hurried across the road to the car, taking time to make a radio call before he drove away. Conan smiled at that. It wouldn't be on any regular police frequency.

The trap was set. He had only to wait and see who would be attracted to the bait.

CHAPTER 19

The trap had a basic deficiency.

Conan paced the confines of his office, pausing at the window, then returned to his chair, studying a middle-aged couple as they came into the shop. Tourists; recently retired; probably the self-contained camper variety.

The deficiency was that the trap wasn't specific. He wouldn't be sure exactly who sprang it, unless he stood guard over the book upstairs, in which case, it was unlikely the trap would be sprung at all.

But it was his only hope, unless Steve came through with more information, or the Major's employers adopted a more cooperative attitude.

He let his head rest against the back of the chair, disciplining his mind to control the mounting tension and impatience. The trap hadn't been set a full hour yet.

The jingling of the door bells was a grating, jarring sound; one that intensified the ache in his shoulder with the inevitable reaction of tightening muscles.

Anton Dominic was coming into the shop.

He rose and moved to the office door to watch while Dominic and Miss Dobie exchanged greetings, the old man smiling ingenuously, diffidently. He made no mention of the robbery, and Miss Dobie didn't broach the subject.

Conan leaned against the wall, watching Dominic—a man who didn't exist officially. He listened to him as he chatted with Miss Dobie; listened closely and critically to his accent.

Conan had spent some time in Greece in the course of his personal pilgrimages, but that was several years ago. He couldn't be sure Dominic's accent wasn't typically Greek, yet it reminded him more of . . .

He tensed as the front door opened, and studied the man who entered.

There was nothing unusual about him; nothing to attract anyone's attention. Yet he held Conan's full attention. He was a stranger; a man in his late thirties, tall and athletically built, wearing dark glasses and informal clothing.

He nodded politely in response to Miss Dobie's greeting, then moved out of Conan's range of vision. To the paperback racks, no doubt.

Miss Dobie watched the man curiously for a moment, with a hint of a frown, as if she were trying to remember something about him. Then she resumed her conversation with Mr. Dominic, and Conan again focused his attention on the old man.

And an idea was taking shape in his mind. A test, of sorts, for a man who was more than he pretended to be.

When Dominic left the counter, Conan waited a full minute to give him time to make his way upstairs, then he opened the office door.

Miss Dobie looked around at him inquisitively, but he ignored the question in her eyes, keeping his voice low as he spoke, watching the man in the dark glasses. He was at one of the paperback racks.

"Miss Dobie, I want you to go upstairs to the Language section and bring me down a book in Russian—without attracting any attention."

Her eyebrows shot up. "Any particular book?"

"No, just so it's Russian."

She gazed at him in bewilderment, then sighed.

"All right. But I wish somebody would explain to me what's going on around here."

"I hope someday I *can*. Meanwhile, have faith."

"Oh, I do. It's all that's left to me."

When Beatrice Dobie returned a few minutes later, he took the book with a quick word of thanks and went to his desk, leaving the office door wide open.

He thumbed through the book, a basic grammar, and finally found what he was searching for: a long reading selection. When the book was open, the two pages showed nothing but small, regularly spaced print. He underlined a passage lightly with pencil, then settled back to wait.

It was fifteen minutes before Anton Dominic came back downstairs, shuffled up to the counter, and handed two books to Miss Dobie. Conan waved at him from behind his desk.

"Mr. Dominic, you're just the man I wanted to see."

The old man looked up in surprise, then smiled.

"Ah! Hello, Mr. Flack. You are want to see *me*?"

"Yes, I think you can help me with something, if you don't mind. Come on in."

Miss Dobie glanced around, but at Conan's warning look, turned away and continued checking out the books.

"I can be helping you?" Dominic moved hesitantly into the office, twisting his woolen cap in his birdlike hands. Then his eyes widened. "Ah—what iss be happen to your arm?"

"Just a little . . . accident. Nothing to worry about."

"I hope iss not be painful to you?"

"No, it's really nothing."

His smile returned at that assurance.

"Good. But what can I be helping you for?"

Conan leaned over the Russian book, a slight frown drawing his brows together.

"Well, you see, I'm working on a consultation project, and it involves some translation. My Greek isn't too good, and I'm having trouble with this one passage. I thought perhaps you could help me." He pushed the book closer to Dominic, pointing to the underlined paragraph. "Here—this is the passage that's giving me the trouble."

Dominic bent over the book, his head tilted back to focus the bifocal lenses of his glasses on the page, the traces of a pleased smile still clinging to his lips.

Conan turned his head—the old man's face was only inches from his own—concentrating on Dominic's eyes.

He was banking on the similarity between Greek and Russian characters; banking on the fact that it would be all but impossible for anyone *not* to read words set before them unexpectedly if the language were known. All he hoped for was a revealing eye movement; some faint hint of recognition. Nothing more.

Dominic's eyes went to the indicated passage, and for perhaps two seconds moved quite naturally, and unconsciously, across the lines of print.

Then realization struck him.

He straightened with an audible intake of breath and stared at Conan, his jaw slack, every trace of color draining from his face, leaving a sick pallor.

"N-no—no!" He pressed his hand against his chest, his voice a choked whisper. "No! I—I cannot help you. I . . . I do not know that—what language . . . I cannot help!"

Conan rose, baffled by the intensity of his reaction, alarmed at that hand-to-chest gesture, remembering the old man's heart condition.

"Mr. Dominic—"

"*No!*" He was backing out of the office, shaking his head frantically, feeling his way like a blind man. "I cannot help! I—I do not know what—"

"Wait! Mr. Dominic—please!"

But he turned in headlong flight, flung open the front door, and stumbled off down the sidewalk, leaving a taut silence broken only by the tuneless jangle of the bells.

"Mr. Flagg, what in the world happened?"

Miss Dobie was still holding Dominic's forgotten books. Conan glanced at her, then pulled in a deep breath, wondering what the real answer to that question was. He'd hoped for a reaction, but this went far beyond his expectations.

"I . . . I'm afraid he misunderstood me, Miss Dobie."

"Misunderstood you? About what?"

"It isn't important." He was watching the man in the dark glasses; watching him move to the door, looking neither to right nor left. "It was only a . . . language barrier."

"Well, I've never seen him in such a state. Why, he even went off without his books, and I know he wanted this one on the Berkeley cyclotron particularly."

"Miss Dobie—"

"What?"

The bells were still ringing in the wake of an unobtrusive exit; the man in the dark glasses.

"Do you know that man—the one who just left?"

She looked out the windows as the man crossed to a black Chevrolet. Then she frowned.

"Oh. That one. I didn't even hear him leave."

Conan's jaw tightened as he watched the car move off southward, but Miss Dobie could save him a fruitless errand if he were wrong about the man.

"Do you know him?"

"Well . . . you know, I was trying to figure out who he was when he came in. I'm sure I've seen him before."

"*Where*, Miss Dobie? Here at the shop?"

She thought the matter over for a while.

"Well, I think so, but with the dark glasses—"

"Was it recently? In the last few days?"

"Yes, I think maybe it was. Oh—wait a minute."

He sighed; he hadn't many minutes to spare.

"Oh, of course," she said finally, looking up at him. "*Now*, I remember."

"Who is he?"

"I suppose it was the uniform that threw me off." She laughed to herself. "I mean that coverall thing. He didn't have it on today. It's funny how you identify people by their clothes and never really—"

"Miss Dobie, *who is he*?"

"Oh." She looked at Conan, vaguely puzzled, then shrugged. "Well, it's only the new telephone man. You know, the one who came in Saturday to check—"

"Thanks."

He left her staring and went into the office for his jacket and keys, then paused to lock the door as he emerged.

"Miss Dobie, I'm going out for a few minutes. When I return, I want to know exactly who's been in the shop, what books are purchased or rented, and if you can find out without attracting any undue attention, by whom. Relay any phone calls not concerned with shop business to Mr. Duncan at my home. Don't use his name; just give them the number."

"Well, all right, Mr. Flagg, but—"

He didn't stay to answer her questions. He was out of the door and into the XK-E before she could get a full sentence out.

CHAPTER 20

When Conan returned to the shop, he was preoccupied with the task of getting the sling back into place, and distracted by the throbbing ache of the shoulder. But Miss Dobie's peculiarly distressed expression commanded his attention. She looked at him, then glanced uneasily toward the paperbacks.

He closed the door and followed the direction of her anxious gaze, a faint smile coming to his lips.

"Hello, Charlie."

Duncan eyed him with no trace of humor.

"I'd like a word with you, Chief. That is, if you aren't too *busy*."

Conan sighed; he should have called Duncan before he left the shop. He crossed the room and unlocked the office door.

"Go on in. I'll be with you in a minute."

Duncan made no response, but moved purposefully into the office and sat down in the chair opposite the desk.

"I'm sorry," Miss Dobie was saying, *sotto voce*. "He seemed so upset that you weren't here, but I didn't know—"

"It's all right. Were there any calls?"

"No. I mean, nothing except a couple of inquiries about books."

"What books?"

"Well . . . let's see. One call was from Mrs. Higgins asking if we had *Dollbaby* yet. The other was the McDill boy; he was looking for *Catcher in the Rye*."

"You kept track of the books you handled here?"

She smiled proudly and reached under the counter, then proffered a sheet of paper divided into columns with various notations in her bookkeeper's hand. He studied it with a little amazement, and finally laughed softly.

"Beautiful, Miss Dobie. Remarkable, in fact."

As he glanced over the sheet, he saw nothing that seemed unusual; definitely no entry concerning the Dostoevsky. He returned the sheet to her.

"Thank you. I need to talk to Charlie, and I'll have the door closed, so if you'll just continue with this . . ."

She nodded. "Yes, sir, I'll take care of it."

"And you *have* been keeping it out of sight?"

"Oh, yes." She gave him a conspiratorial smile. "I've been very careful."

"Miss Dobie, you're a rare gem. Thanks."

Conan closed the office door behind him, raising his hand to still Duncan's remonstrances.

"I know, I know. I should've called you."

Duncan scowled. "Yeah, well, I guess you aren't used to newfangled gadgets like phones out here in the sticks."

Conan went to the stereo, smiling crookedly, then picked a tape cartridge and inserted it.

"Actually, there wasn't time to call you, and I wasn't exactly sure where I was going."

He paused, listening with closed eyes to the measured and elegant harmonies of the opening bars of the *Swan of Tuonela*. Then he took a deep breath and went to his chair, sinking into the cushions gratefully.

Duncan's expression softened a little.

"How're you feeling, Conan?"

He gave a short laugh. "Lousy, but I'm still mobile."

"Okay. Now, would you mind filling me in? What sent you out of here in such a hurry? Miss Dobie said—"

"Miss Dobie gets easily excited." He lit a cigarette, pausing to take a long drag: "First, have you heard from Steve?"

"No. I haven't heard from anybody."

"Carl?"

"Oh, I checked with him before I came up here. Nothing. The old lady hasn't set foot out of her house."

"Damn. That bothers me. She hasn't even made the daily trek to the post office. What's she waiting for?"

"A word from on high, maybe. Now, what's been going on here?"

Conan leaned back, still frowning at the lack of news.

"Well, quite a lot, actually. I baited another mousetrap. The third copy of the Dostoevsky. I put a message on the date card suggesting that I have something to sell."

"The code?"

"Whatever it is Mrs. Leen lost last night. Rose obliged me by coming in to pump Miss Dobie. I let him have a good look at the book, and made it clear I was putting it upstairs. He made a radio call when he left the shop; reporting to Mrs. Leen, no doubt."

Duncan's eyes narrowed. "Maybe. And maybe to somebody else."

"It doesn't matter. I'm only hoping it will attract someone. It might even draw out our third man."

"Who's the third man?"

"The courier, probably. Someone, besides Rose, is involved with Mrs. Leen in this little conspiracy. I was wondering why Rose put the Dostoevsky back in the shop after he killed Jeffries, but put it in another hiding place last night—outside the shop. It occurred to me that Mrs. Leen would be familiar enough with the area to suggest another safe cache, but the courier wouldn't. Couriers are necessarily mobile, and it's unlikely he's a resident."

Charlie folded his arms and frowned questioningly.

"What're you saying? That Rose got his orders from the courier, and not Mrs. Leen?"

"Where Jeffries was concerned, yes. And I'm saying the courier is closely involved in Mrs. Leen's scheme."

"Couriers usually don't even know what they're carrying, Conan."

"Usually. I said this wasn't the *usual* information exchange."

"But if the courier gave the orders for Jeffries, how would the old lady know to come back to the shop for the book the next day?"

"He'd have to tell her, but it would only take a few words. Mrs. Leen was probably well aware of what had happened; Nel saw her upstairs Friday, looking for Dashiell Hammet in the D's, by the way."

Duncan regarded him with narrowed eyes.

"You holding out on me again? Any brainstorms about this third man?"

Conan hesitated. "There were too many people in the shop Friday, and the courier will be an outsider; probably not a total stranger to me, but relatively unfamiliar. Perhaps my mousetrap will flush him out—to mix a metaphor."

"What makes you think he's still around?"

"I can't be sure he is, but he was around last night. At least, someone besides Rose and Mrs. Leen was around. She wasn't calling Rose from the phone booth, and she'd be a fool to trust him with searching the shop. Whatever was lost, she values it highly. Harvey was probably told only that the *book* was important; I'm sure he didn't know why."

Duncan was silent for a moment, then he took a quick breath and ran a hand through his hair.

"Maybe. But you're taking off into theories again, and none of this tells me why you left here in such a hurry."

Conan laughed and leaned forward to tap the ash from his cigarette.

"No. Well, as I said, quite a lot went on this morning. Anton Dominic came in less than an hour after Rose."

"Dominic? That's interesting?"

"Yes, it was very interesting. First, I managed to find out he has at least a reading knowledge of Russian. But he doesn't want anyone to know about it." He paused, lost in remembrance, and the sick weight under his ribs had no physical origin.

" . . . bother you?"

He focused on Duncan with an effort. "What?"

"I asked why that seems to bother you."

"I'm not sure. Except that his reaction wasn't right somehow. Charlie, he was terrified."

"Maybe he figured you blew his cover."

"Maybe."

"But you don't buy it." Duncan sighed. "Listen, Chief, remember what I told you about putting on blinders. For all you know, he's the kingpin of this little operation. Just because Mrs. Leen picked up the book doesn't mean she's calling the shots."

"I know. Anyway, Dominic had an escort, and that was the reason for my abrupt departure."

"What kind of escort?"

"The telephone man. Major Mills's partner."

Duncan leaned forward intently. "You tailed him?"

"Yes. He's definitely keeping Dominic under surveillance—*full-time* surveillance. He's taken up residence in the house directly across the street from Dominic's, and I assume the Major was based there, too."

"They've set up a full-time house blind? Damn. Then I'd say this Dominic isn't exactly small fish."

Conan shrugged uneasily, immediately regretting the unconscious movement.

"I don't know what he is—except frightened. He went directly home from the shop, with the telephone man keeping him company at a discreet distance. Charlie, I want Berg to keep an eye on Dominic. I found a reasonably good vantage point; an empty house two doors west of Dominic's. It's on the same side of the street, which isn't so good, but at least it offers some cover."

"What about Mrs. Leen?"

"You'll have to take over there."

Duncan reached for the phone. "Okay, I'll call Carl."

"Charlie . . . maybe you'd better contact him by radio."

He hesitated, then glanced at the stereo.

"You worried about bugs?"

"Rose sent a cop down this morning. I checked the office again, but I'd like to stay on the safe side."

"You in a hurry to get Carl down there?"

"Not too much of a hurry. Dominic's under the eye of the FBI now, which won't help *us* any." He crushed his cigarette out impatiently, feeling the tension within him coalescing into anger. "Damn, I've half a mind to walk in on that bogus telephone man and—"

"Sure. I can see it now." Duncan laughed derisively. 'You just might end up in jail if you try pushing a—"

"I know. But damn it, we're running out of *time*."

"Maybe. Look, we don't even know enough about this thing to get in a panic yet."

The voice of pragmatism. But Conan found no reassurance in it now.

"Panic is a product of ignorance, Charlie, not of cognizance."

He rose and went to the window, watching a cluster of gulls spiraling seaward over the rooftops, He could see one corner of the roof and the chimney of Mrs. Leen's beachfront cottage, and on the hazy, sun-limned horizon, a line of tiny dark spots.

He tensed, his eyes moving from that faraway line to the chimney of Mrs. Leen's house, and he was wondering what he would do, in her place, if he had lost some vital piece of information pertaining to his mission; instructions of some sort, perhaps, or a rendezvous point or timetable . . .

"Conan, are you listening?"

He turned, looking blankly at Duncan. "What?"

"I said, since we're not—" He paused. "What is it? You've got that look on your face."

Conan laughed and returned to his chair.

"What look?"

"That an-idea-just-hit-me look. So give. What's going on in that uncracked cranium of yours?"

"I was just considering a couple of facts, Charlie."

Duncan sighed impatiently. "*What* facts?"

"Well, first, I checked with the Coast Guard this morning on the location of those trawlers."

"And?"

"For several days they've been moving steadily south, but yesterday they settled down due west of Holliday Beach, and they haven't moved since."

"What did the Coast Guard say about it?"

"Oh, that possibly they'd hit a good run of fish, or had mechanical problems. They don't know."

"Okay. So drop the other shoe."

"Well, I was thinking of the price of beachfront property"

Duncan stared at him. "For God's sake, at a time like this, you're worried about property values?"

He met Charlie's dismayed scowl with a wry grin.

"Runs in the family. How do you think my old man made all that money?"

"I don't give a damn about your old man. What the hell does the price of beachfront property have to do with this?"

"Charlie, when I bought my lot, beachfront property was selling for two hundred dollars a front foot."

"So?"

"I assume it's gone up since." He laughed bitterly. "I *know* it's gone up from my tax assessments. Anyway, all the front lots in Mrs. Leen's block are seventy-five feet wide. Now, the *house* she's living in isn't worth the powder to blow it up, which is probably why I never gave it much thought. But the *lot* is worth"—he did a little quick mental arithmetic—"at least fifteen thousand, and probably closer to eighteen thousand dollars."

Duncan gave a low whistle.

"That's not exactly small change."

"That's the point. And I know she had to pay cash. I

was distantly acquainted with the people she bought it from. The man had a serious illness, and they needed the money; they wouldn't settle for terms. Now, how many widows, supposedly living on Social Security, could afford the taxes on a lot like that, much less lay out the cash in a lump sum?''

Duncan frowned at him. "But I don't see—''

"I'm not sure it means anything, Charlie. I'm just wondering why she bought that particular house. There are always plenty of houses on the market around here, and once you get away from the beachfront, the prices drop about two-thirds. And spending that kind of money, while putting on a poor act, is the kind of thing that makes people ask questions in a small town. I'm wondering why she'd take that risk, not to mention the large expenditure of funds. I doubt her superiors would approve of her dishing out that much money just for the view.''

"Well, it's an interesting point,'' Duncan admitted, one eyebrow coming up. "But what does it mean?''

"I don't know.'' He paused, then, 'I was wondering what she'd do if the message in the book *did* have information vital to her mission, and she's lost it. She'd have to contact someone else connected with the mission.''

"Somebody on the trawlers, maybe?''

"That occurred to me.''

"But *how*, with the Coast Guard keeping tabs on them? Those boats will be monitored on every frequency.''

"True. It's highly unlikely any radio transmissions between Mrs. Leen and the trawlers would go undetected.'' He was silent for a while, then he straightened, glancing at his watch. "Charlie, you'd better get Berg on his way to Dominic's.'' He gave him the address and directions. "We'll continue this later. We might even get lucky and hear from Steve.''

"*That* would be a stroke of luck for sure. I feel like one of the blind men with the elephant.''

Conan nodded wearily. 'You aren't the only one feeling your way around.''

Duncan pulled himself to his feet, then paused, eyeing him suspiciously.

"You thinking of any more unannounced forays, by the way?"

Conan smiled briefly. "I *am* considering an expedition of sorts, but for now my plans are to stay here until closing time in case the message in the third copy of the Dostoevsky arouses any interest. I'll call you before I do anything rash."

Duncan considered this, with no indication of satisfaction, then reached into his jacket and pulled out a compact .32 automatic and handed it to him.

"I don't suppose you have such a mundane item as a gun in your possession."

Conan stared at the gun a moment, then with a quick sigh, reached out for it.

"No. I haven't found it necessary to own such a . . . mundane item."

"Yeah, well, I don't like the way Mrs. Leen and her friends play the game, so just humor me and keep that around. It might come in handy."

He nodded and put the gun in his desk drawer.

"All right. But what about you?"

"That's just the big firepower. I keep a smaller spare on hand." He started for the door, then turned. "And damn it, Chief, you let me know before you head out on any more independent excursions. Otherwise, I'll start charging you double time just for the extra worry."

CHAPTER 21

When Charlie left the shop, Conan went upstairs to check the *Crime and Punishment*, and found it still in place, his message still in the envelope.

He was frowning intently when he passed the counter on his way back to the office, and entirely unaware of Miss Dobie until she raised her voice.

"Mr. Flagg?"

He stopped and focused on her. "Oh—yes, Miss Dobie?"

"I realize you have a lot on your mind, and I hate to bother you, but I'm hungry."

He laughed and glanced at his watch; it was after two.

"I'm sorry, I didn't intend to leave you starving at your post. You go on over to the Chowder House, and I'll watch the counter."

She breathed a gusty sigh of relief.

"Thanks. Can I bring you something?"

He thought a moment; he'd been considering making a phone call, but he still had reservations about the shop phones, and this call was one he particularly didn't want

180

overheard. But Miss Dobie could use the telephone in the restaurant kitchen. . . .

"Mr. Flagg? Food?"

"Yes. Bring me—oh, anything. But there's something else I want you to do." He found a pen and a notepad on the counter and wrote a brief message, continuing his verbal instructions. "Use the kitchen extension; tell Lillian we're having trouble with our phones. There's plenty of noise in the kitchen; you won't be overheard. Call Sven. You'll have to look up the number." He handed her his scrawled note. "Make the arrangements for as close to this time as possible, and tell Sven price is no object. But, please, don't discuss this with anyone."

She looked at the note, her eyes widening.

" 'Curiouser and curiouser.' "

"Someday, Miss Dobie—"

"Yes, I know. Someday, you'll explain everything." She sighed. "Meanwhile, I'm beginning to wonder whether I'm showing symptoms of paranoia or just senile dementia."

"Of the two, it has to be paranoia." He grinned at her. "You're much too young for senile dementia."

She eyed him skeptically and laughed.

"Well, thanks for that, anyway."

Conan again found himself behind the counter, and if anything, it was even more unpleasant than it had been yesterday. For one thing, he was more uncomfortable.

In the first fifteen minutes, he had six customers, all local, and all of them asked about the robbery. He found the amnesia line useful in cutting off the inquiries, even if it was unsatisfactory to his questioners.

Then at a lull in the stream of customers, he lit another cigarette and leaned back against the wall, his eyes closed. But a few seconds later, they jerked open at the jingling of the bells.

Joe Zimmerman, the Dell salesman.

At Joe's side, her hand clasped familiarly in his, was Marty Hammill, a tall, Clairol blonde known among the local male population as "Big Yaller." The local women had other epithets for her, he was sure, but he'd never heard them.

Conan almost laughed. So this was Joe's girlfriend; this was what brought him to Holliday Beach on his vacation.

But then, Marty Hammill wasn't the run-of-the-mill call girl. She was an independent; attractive, sometimes capable of disarming honesty, and although few of her customers were aware of it, surprisingly well read.

It was Marty who spoke first.

"Hey, Conan, how the hell are you? Heard you had a little trouble up here last night."

He smiled wryly. "A little. Hello, Joe. Still on vacation?"

Zimmerman cast a heavy-lidded glance at Marty, then winked.

"Sure, Cone. The weather's been great."

Marty didn't miss the wink. Her dark eyes narrowed, then she laughed softly. But the laughter faded as she took in Conan's bruised forehead and the sling.

"Wow. Looks like you came out on the short end."

"You should've seen the *other* guy."

She laughed. "Sure, honey, I bet he was a mess."

Zimmerman leaned across the counter.

"What about the other guy, Cone? I mean, really—you get a look at him?"

"No," he replied coolly. "In fact, I haven't the slightest idea what happened. I was hit on the head during the melee, and I've drawn a total blank."

Marty shook her head, frowning.

"Looks like somebody got his licks in. I'm really sorry. I mean, you'd think in a small town you wouldn't have to worry about getting conked in your own shop."

"Marty, the world is full of nuts—present company excluded, of course. At least for the sake of courtesy."

She grinned at that, but the humor was lost on Zimmerman, who was still regarding him earnestly.

"You said a burglary. He get away with anything?"

"No. Apparently, the erstwhile burglar didn't know I keep nothing in the safe but rare books."

"Speaking of *nuts*," Marty interposed.

"It's all relative, Marty. Anyway, unless the burglar has sadistic tendencies, it was a total failure from his point of view." He stubbed out his cigarette and added quickly, "So much for my inept burglar. Now, what can I do for you today?"

Marty gave him a sidelong look and a slow smile.

"Well . . ." she began, her voice low and inviting, but edged with ironic laughter, "that all depends on what you have in mind, honey."

Zimmerman's head snapped around, and he glared at her. That hint of irony had escaped him.

"We were just fooling around town, Cone," he said slowly, his eyes still fixed on her.

She obviously heard the warning tone underlying his words, but his display of jealousy only amused her. She laughed, her oblique smile for Conan.

"Well, I'm all for . . . fooling around. Anytime."

Zimmerman's face went red, and his effort to mask the charged anger reflected in his eyes was futile. And Conan found himself tense, watching his face, wondering if Marty realized her little game might be dangerous.

"Look, doll," Joe said tightly. "I've just got a week's vacation—"

"That's *your* problem, Joey boy." She gave a quick sigh of disgust and glanced at Conan. "Good Lord, you meet a guy one night, and by the next day, he thinks he *owns* you."

Then she looked around at Zimmerman and finally seemed to recognize the thinly veiled rage in his features. She tilted her head back and smiled at him.

"Hey, Joe, I'm just kidding. Come on, don't get shook."

"Baby, you got a hell of a lot to learn," he said, and the chill in his tone made her smile falter. "You better keep that in mind."

There was a brief, taut silence; then Joe made an abrupt about-face. He grinned and reached for her hand.

"Come on, doll, let's take a look around."

Conan was aware of his own sudden release of tension, and saw the same reaction in Marty's smile.

"Okay, Joe, let's look."

"You'd never know it from the outside," Zimmerman went on, his anger apparently forgotten, "but this is really kind of an interesting old dump."

"Watch your language," Conan put in. "You're referring to the dump I love."

"No offense," he replied with a sly grin. "But you'll have to admit—"

"It's called 'charm,' Joe."

"Yeah. I'll have to remember that. Come on, doll. You'll have to see the upstairs; you'll never believe it."

Zimmerman and Marty had already left the shop when Miss Dobie returned, bearing a white paper sack which she surrendered to him as he pulled himself to his feet.

"Roast beef," she explained.

"Thanks. How was lunch?"

"The lunch special was salmon croquettes."

"Well, it could be worse."

She sighed. "I know. Tomorrow it's meatloaf. Oh, I took care of your call. It's arranged as you specified."

He smiled tightly. "Thank you, Miss Dobie."

"Shall I take over at the counter?"

"Yes, please."

"Okay. And the list? The books . . . etcetera?"

"You may as well continue with that, but don't—well, I mean, be discreet."

"Don't worry, Mr. Flagg. Mine is not to wonder why—"

"Miss Dobie—" He sighed. "Please. Just *do*, discreetly, and forget the 'or die' part."

Again, he left the office door open a few inches. He poured some coffee, then put a cartridge on the stereo, turning the volume low. He chose the *Brandenburg Concerti,* finding their reasonable forms particularly satisfying.

He sat down at the desk and consumed the sandwich Miss Dobie had brought him, his eyes straying constantly from the counter to his watch. He could feel the tension growing in him like the steady winding of a mainspring.

It was nearly three. Normal closing time was five; if the message in the Dostoevsky had aroused no reaction by then, there was no use staying longer.

Two hours.

Two long hours to wonder if he shouldn't be somewhere else, doing something else.

He finished the sandwich, wadded the napkins and threw them at the wastebasket; then he lit a cigarette and watched as a pair of middle-aged tourists came into the shop, and a few minutes later, a giggling covey of girls just off the school bus. Finally, as he gazed aimlessly around the room, his eyes rested on the File.

He pulled it toward him, and after a moment realized, even as he leafed through the cards, that it was only habit that motivated him. Whenever he was baffled by a consultation project, he always went to the File.

Almost any subject within the realm of human knowledge was represented here, as well as the recognized experts in every field.

But there was nothing—and no one—to help him now. This wasn't an ordinary consultation project.

He snapped the File shut abruptly and pushed it aside, then again looked at his watch. When he realized his hands were unconsciously balling into fists, he carefully relaxed them and turned his chair toward the door.

Settle down, he admonished himself. Patience. There was nothing to do but wait—and hope.

But at four-thirty, his patience ran out. He'd smoked a full pack of cigarettes during the long afternoon, and in the last hour and a half watched an intermittent procession of people moving in and out the front door. Many were familiar to him; regular customers. More were strangers, obviously tourists, just passing through.

But at no time did he see the small, red-jacketed *Crime and Punishment* crossing the counter. And a call to Charlie had similar negative results: neither Mrs. Leen, Anton Dominic, nor the Major's partner had made a move.

A call to Steve Travers had been equally fruitless. He was out of his office and couldn't be reached.

Conan looked at his watch again, then rose and went out to the counter. It was already beginning to get dark outside, and the shop was almost clear of customers.

"Well. Quiet day, Miss Dobie."

She shrugged. "I couldn't say, since I haven't the vaguest idea what's going on around here."

He ignored her mildly accusing tone.

"May I see that list you've been keeping?"

"Of course." She reached under the counter and handed him the sheet.

He studied it carefully, but found nothing on it that aroused his suspicions. And that was ironic; the name of the third man might be on that list, if he weren't a total stranger to both Miss Dobie and himself, and he considered that unlikely. Finally, he folded the sheet and put it in his back pocket.

"You may as well start closing up, Miss Dobie. I'll turn off the lights upstairs."

"I can do that. You look tired. Why don't you go on home and let me—?"

"*I'll* get the lights."

She shrugged and went to the front door to hang up the CLOSED sign, glancing at him with a little bewilderment as he moved purposefully toward the stairway.

Meg was at the top of the stairs, batting a hapless scrap of paper back and forth across the floor. He stopped long enough to give her a vigorous rub and a few words.

The only customer was a man in the Fiction section; a tourist; California, possibly. He was leaning against the sill of the gable window that overlooked the street, myopically engrossed in a Shellabarger historical novel.

Conan studied him closely for a moment, then sent him on his way with the announcement that it was closing time. Then he went to the Reference room and began turning off the lights as he worked his way back to the stairway.

The lone customer was gone when he returned to the Fiction section. He paused, listening to the scuffling sounds Meg made at her game, then crossed to the D's.

The Dostoevsky was still in place.

He pulled the book off the shelf and started to open it, then hesitated, feeling a prickling chill. He wondered at that premonitory sensation; wondered at the cause of it. Nerves, perhaps.

Still, he didn't open the book, but stared at it intently, as if it would provide an answer itself.

And in a sense, it did finally. There was nothing to explain that warning chill in its appearance; no marks, scratches, smudges—nothing.

The weight.

A perception born in his muscles and bones, translating itself into a wordless alarm. The weight. He'd handled this book and its twins too many times; his hands and arms recognized the difference, even if his mind didn't on a conscious level.

He stood silently, hefting the book. It was far too heavy; perhaps a full pound too heavy. And he wondered what gave this particular book that extra weight.

It wasn't hard to guess.

The office door was closed, but the quiet was more than the soundproofing. He'd sent Miss Dobie on her way fifteen minutes ago; the shop was closed, the silence that of solitude.

He leaned back in his chair, easing his right elbow onto the arm, and took a slow drag on his cigarette, studying the results of ten minutes of nerve-wracking and cautiously painstaking effort.

The book lay on the desk beside him, and he had opened it. But not in the usual sense. He'd opened it in a sort of surgical operation, with a narrow, sharply pointed knife, going through the front cover.

And now he surveyed the results of his surgery with a black rage closing in on him.

An exchange had been made sometime during the long afternoon. This wasn't the copy of *Crime and Punishment* he'd put on the shelf this morning; this one had been carefully prepared.

The pages had been cut out of the center of the book and the cavity filled with plastic explosive. A spring friction device was attached to it which would be activated by the opening of the book.

The rage was a part of the inevitable reaction, but at the moment it had little to do with the threat to his own life. Perhaps that would come later.

He'd set a mousetrap and had the favor returned—with interest. But this trap shared the deficiency of his own; it was nonspecific, and that was the cause of his rage.

The odds were high that he would be the only one to open this particular book, but there was still a chance that someone else might have inadvertently picked it up. Another innocent bystander might have paid with his life for an interest in Dostoevsky.

But this little bomb might still have achieved its purpose even in that event. The shop was an old building; the resulting explosion might have triggered its collapse, burying everyone inside in a pile of rubble—including its proprietor.

More innocent lives.

The rage dissipated; another luxury. He considered the implications of this particularly lethal mousetrap.

Some were obvious. For one, Mrs. Leen and her cohorts considered Conan Flagg a threat to themselves and their mission. It also implied that they didn't need what he supposedly had to sell, and this meant they'd found the lost message, or had another source for the information now.

And again, the almost desperate nature of this ploy implied a time limit.

There was another implication that was vague and nearly irrational; another subliminal perception, perhaps. It had to do with the character of a man who could set a trap that might snuff out innocent lives.

Conan knew who had set this trap; knew the identity of the third man—the courier. He could even produce some logical and reasonable facts to back up his conviction when he thought back over the last few days. But the conviction was rooted more in instinct than in logic.

But that wasn't the question that occupied his mind now. The important question still—the *only* important one—was Mrs. Leen's purpose. Why was she here, and what was the mission that drove her and her fellow conspirators to such desperate measures.

That it had been necessary to murder Jeffries and Mills might be attributable in part to bad luck, and to her hired man's lack of finesse and his tendency to panic.

But Rose hadn't planted this bomb. This came from the prime movers of the conspiracy, and it was carefully premeditated.

It seemed bitterly ironic that they considered him a threat to their mission. He was helpless to stop it—regarded with suspicion by the FBI, and totally ignorant of the purpose of the conspiracy. He wondered sickly if the FBI was actually aware of the existence of this conspiracy.

But he knew it existed, and perhaps Mrs. Leen and her friends were justified in considering him a threat; he wouldn't give up until he understood their purpose.

He crushed out his cigarette and picked up the phone.

"Hello, Charlie. Any action there?"

"Hell, no," Duncan responded irritably. "You heard from Steve yet?"

"No. What about Carl?"

"Nothing. I checked with him about ten minutes ago. What about your . . . uh, mousetrap? Anybody take the bait?"

Conan looked down at the book, his eyes going cold.

"Yes. Charlie, I'm going to call Steve's house and office

and leave your number, in case he should happen to have anything to say to us. I have a little expedition of sorts lined up, and I'll be out of touch for an hour or so."

"An expedition! Listen, Conan, if you—"

"Relax. I'll be there in ten minutes, and I'll tell you all about it. And I think you'll be interested in what I caught in my mousetrap."

"Okay. I'll be waiting."

Conan cleared the line, then dialed Steve Travers' home number, and while he waited for a response he opened the desk drawer and took out Charlie's .32.

It might, indeed, come in handy.

CHAPTER 22

As the clear light of a green-tinged sunset faded, the *Josephine* picked her way along the rocky coastline, riding dangerously close to the rough waters off Jefferson Heights. By the time she moved past the headland into the comparatively quiet waters off Holliday Beach, the sky was entirely dark except for a reddish glow on the horizon.

But the calm in the open waters was only comparative. Conan clung to the starboard railing, bracing himself against the slow roll of the long sea swells. Those swells that looked like trivial wrinkles when viewed from the shore, loomed large from the deck of a small fishing boat.

He shifted the strap of the binoculars case on his left shoulder, glancing toward the pilothouse, where Olaf Svensen was working intently at the wheel, his craggy features limned against the darkness by the glow of the binnacle light.

Conan moved toward the bow a few paces, his gaze shifting from the scattered glitter of lights on the shore, to the single chain of lights gleaming on the horizon. But even as one part of his mind concentrated on the lights, another part was occupied with Olaf Svensen.

Charlie had questioned him closely about Sven, in no way satisfied with the scant information Conan could offer. Duncan noted that a man with a fishing boat might be quite useful to Mrs. Leen, and he was particularly disturbed that Sven was another frequent visitor at the bookshop.

Svensen had listened patiently to Conan's instructions before they left the Bay, giving no indication that he thought it odd that Conan wanted to go out to sea at nightfall, staying as close to shore as possible, then stop at a certain point and wait with the lights and motor off. Sven's only reaction was to draw his bristling brows together and state a price for this unusual excursion. Conan paid him, and they left the Bay with no further words.

It was that apparent lack of curiosity that made Conan wonder now. But Sven had never been a man to ask questions.

He turned his full attention to the lights, assessing the *Josephine*'s position in relation to the shore lights and those on the horizon. At times, all of them disappeared as the boat dipped into the troughs.

He moved back to the pilothouse, glancing over Sven's shoulder at the compass. After a few more minutes, he made another visual check, then turned to Sven, raising his voice against the roar of the motor.

"All right, Sven. This looks about right."

The fisherman nodded, then shut off the engine, leaving the boat facing north, on a direct east-west line between the center of Holliday Beach and the trawlers. A few seconds later, the instrument panel went dark and the running lights blinked out.

The silence and darkness were profound, and Conan felt a momentary fear; a fear engendered by the black and omnipotent sea. He smiled at this atavistic sensation, then edged his way forward, stopping a few feet short of the bow. He took the binoculars from the case, braced his left elbow against the railing, and focused on the shore.

Before he left Holliday Beach, he'd stopped by his house and turned on certain lights. Now, he searched for that particular pattern of lighted windows, and at length found it, but only after three swells. The entire coastline disappeared every time the boat fell into a trough.

But once he homed in on the lights, he could keep the binoculars aligned with the spot fairly well between swells. Impatiently, he pulled his arm out of the sling; he needed both hands to keep the glasses steady. He waited for the boat to rise on another swell, then counted north from his house; the sixth set of lights belonged to Mrs. Edwina Leen's unassuming little beachfront cottage.

He heard the heavy thud of booted feet moving along the railing toward him, but Sven stopped a few feet away, maintaining the conversational hiatus that had existed between them during the whole of this voyage.

Assured that he could keep his objective in sight, he straightened and turned the binoculars toward the horizon.

It was a paradoxically beautiful sight, that scintillant chain, with the delicate, golden crescent of a new moon hovering above it. He located a cluster of lights near the center of the chain; the mother ship, seagoing factory and focus of the fleet's activities.

And as he lowered the binoculars, he was remembering the first time he'd seen the Berlin Wall. But there was no wall here; only an imaginary line called the three-mile limit.

Olaf Svensen's voice rumbled out of the darkness.

"Yust you look at them damn Rooskies," he muttered, his voice vibrating with rancor.

"Hell of a lot of them in this fleet," Conan commented.

Svensen lapsed into a few bitterly spoken words of Norwegian, then returned to English.

"Factories!" he pronounced with profound disgust. "That's all they be. Floatin' factories. They don' know what is, to be *fishermen*. And yust look how close they come in. They be runnin' right on the line."

"Are they running closer than usual?"

"You damn right, they closer!" Sven snorted. "They

figure maybe nobody watch at night. They t'ink they yust sneak in close, and nobody know.''

Conan made no response as Sven lapsed into mumbling Norwegian again. He turned and sighted in on Mrs. Leen's house, watching it through several swells. Then he took a deep breath, disciplining his mind to wait.

And it might be a long wait, he thought grimly. He might be too late, or in the wrong position, or the idea that brought him here might have no basis at all in fact.

A half hour later, he was still waiting. The moon had long ago slipped under the horizon, making the night even more oppressively black.

He longed for a cigarette, but wouldn't risk lighting one. He'd already stopped Sven from lighting his pipe. On the ocean, a small light could be seen a long way.

And that was one reason he was here, shivering in the dark, waiting for something that might never happen.

''Sven—''

Svensen was still leaning against the railing next to him. He responded with a mumbled, ''Ya?''

''Do me a favor; keep your eyes on those . . . Rooskies, and if you see anything unusual, let me know.''

''Okay. I keep my eyes open.''

Conan heard him moving across the deck to the opposite railing, and again felt a vague uneasiness. Sven still showed no apparent surprise at his unusual requests.

He braced his elbows against the railing and raised the binoculars, refocusing on Mrs. Leen's house. The process had become routine by now. A large swell lifted the *Josephine* and dropped her into a trough, and he swore under his breath as the shore lights disappeared.

When he had them in sight again, Edwina Leen's house had gone dark.

Conan tensed, unconsciously holding his breath.

Another swell, but a relatively small one; he maintained his visual lock on Mrs. Leen's house, oblivious to the tension-induced pain in his shoulder.

Then a tight smile of satisfaction crossed his lips.

From the darkened house, a tiny pinpoint of light appeared.

He controlled the impulse to shout his jubilation, concentrating on that white point of light. It had to be a powerful, extremely tight beam; a beam so tight, that had he been a short distance north or south, he'd have missed it entirely. Even now, he wondered if the boat shouldn't be a little farther north for him to catch the full brilliance of it.

"Sven," he called, "do you see anything over there?"

After a pause, Svensen answered, "No, not yet, Mr. Flagg. I see not'ing."

The light began to flash on and off, the irregular pulsation continuing for a full minute as Conan watched, desperately wishing for some means of recording those impulses. Then it blinked off, leaving nothing but darkness.

"Anything yet, Sven?"

"They yust sittin'—no . . . wait. I t'ink I see—"

Conan turned, looked intently toward the trawlers.

"What, Sven?"

"A light. Yust a little, blinkin' light. I can yust barely make it out."

Conan crossed the deck, stumbling on the cover of the hold, reaching out blindly for the railing.

"Where was the light coming from—the mother ship?"

"Ya, the mother ship. That damn floatin'—"

"I have it." He tightened his grip on the binoculars, fixing his intent gaze on one light among that glittering chain; one small, white, blinking light.

Mrs. Leen was desperate. Those signals were an admission of failure; failure to find the message that was hidden in the original copy of the Dostoevsky. No doubt she'd suffer for that failure, and for making this direct contact necessary.

But her ultimate fate was of little interest to him. She had her instructions now; those impulses carried the answers to her signaled questions.

He watched the flashing light, and wondered if somewhere in this long-distance visual conversation he was witnessing, his own name might not be mentioned.

On the way back to Holliday Bay, Svensen had been complaining about a strange noise in the engine. As soon as he tied up at the dock, he returned to the pilothouse, and descended the narrow hatchway into the hold to diagnose her mechanical ills. He didn't even seem to hear Conan's good-bye, or notice his quick departure.

Conan took the steps up to the street level two at a time, and as he reached the XK-E, looked back at the *Josephine*. Sven was nowhere to be seen, lost in the hold.

A man of little curiosity, perhaps; or a man who had long ago ceased to be surprised. Or—and the thought made him pause—a man who knew more than he was telling.

But there wasn't time to consider Olaf Svensen's character or motives.

He backed the XK-E out of the parking space, and gunned it past the Coast Guard station north of the docks, then turned left up a side street, skirting the Bay, to the highway.

He found himself flinching at every shift of gears, but resigned himself to the pain. Another of Nicky's pills would bring it under control.

A half mile from the Bay, he braked and pulled off the highway at a telephone booth. He left the motor running, glancing at his watch as he got of the car: 7:05. Mrs. Leen had had approximately thirty-five minutes since her exchange with the trawlers.

For a sick moment, he felt around in his pockets for a dime, wondering if he were in the classic position of utter helplessness, facing a pay phone without that magic silver disk. But to his relief, his pockets provided the necessary passkey to communication. He dialed the Alton house, fumbling in his haste.

Duncan answered after only one ring.

"Conan, is that you?"

"Yes, Charlie, what's—"

"Thank God! You okay? Where are you, anyway?"

"A phone booth, about half a mile south of the shop. Charlie, I hit paydirt. Mrs. Leen had a little tête-à-tête with the trawlers; light beams—very narrow and intense."

"I'll be damned. I'll never laugh again when you start running off about property values."

Conan couldn't muster so much as a smile.

"That was about six-thirty. Charlie, she has her instructions now. What's been going on there?"

Duncan's voice had an edge of tension in it.

"Maybe that explains a couple of things. Chief, the old lady had a bonfire. That would be about six forty-five."

"A bonfire? What do you mean?"

"I mean, she lit a fire in her fireplace, and it must've been a good one. Her chimney was spreading sparks all over the neighborhood. And in the last ten minutes, I've seen her look out her front window three times. Every time a car goes by."

"She's expecting someone, then."

"Yeah. And that fire makes sense now. She was probably getting rid of any incriminating evidence around the house. She must be ready to blow town. That's what that message to the trawlers must've been about."

Conan closed his eyes, concentrating.

"No. There's more to it, but that must be part of it. She's waiting for someone; a ride. She hasn't a car of her own; part of the poor act. What about Dominic?"

"I talked to Carl ten minutes ago, and he's getting some action down there, too, but I don't know what it means yet. He's waiting for instructions."

"Instructions?"

"Yeah, well, you see, he's been prowling around since it got dark; he didn't have a good enough view from that house he was in. Anyway, he says at about six-fifty, all the lights went out in the house across the street from Dominic's; that telephone man's blind."

"All the lights—"

"Oh—there's someone else. I guess the FBI sent a replacement for the Major; another guy showed up about six. The telephone man let him in; looked okay."

"But what about the lights?"

"I don't know what happened. Carl says the lights went out, so he slipped over to take a look. He couldn't hear a sound inside, and the shades were pulled, so he couldn't see anything. He went back across the street and checked Dominic, but he was still inside his house. Then he radioed me. He wasn't sure it was a good idea to bust in on a couple of FBI agents unannounced."

"He's sure Dominic didn't leave his house?" Conan leaned against the glass wall wearily, fighting to keep the tension under control.

"He's sure. You figure Dominic had something to do—?"

"I don't know. I still don't know where he fits into this thing."

"Well, he sure as hell fits *somewhere*. Anyway, Carl signed off in a hurry; he saw a couple of city police cars heading his way, and one of them was Harvey Rose's."

"Oh, God, did you warn him?"

"Yeah. I told him to watch out for Harv."

"This was—what? Ten minutes ago?"

"About. I'd better tell Carl what you want him to do." Conan was silent a moment, then he straightened.

"Nothing, except keep his eyes open. What about Steve?"

"Not word one. I haven't tried to phone him yet."

"I will. He has the authority to call in the Coast Guard, and those signals should give him something tangible to work with. Charlie, we must have Mrs. Leen; we can't lose her now. She has all the answers. We'll have to get her out of her house before her chauffeur arrives."

"I can get her out," Duncan said grimly.

"All right, but be careful. She may look like a sweet little old grandmother, but I have a feeling she can take care of herself."

"Listen, I've got that overweight Mata Hari pegged. Don't worry. What should I do with her?"

"The bookshop. I'll try to get through to Steve from here, then I'll go on to the shop and check it out. I'll meet you there in ten minutes. You'd better get the VW. You'll be an open target walking the streets with her.''

"Right. It'll only take a couple of minutes to pick up the car.''

"But hurry. We must get to her before she leaves—''

"Just relax. I'm on my way.''

The phone went dead, and Conan fumbled in his pockets for another dime, then dialed the operator. The only response was a busy signal. He left the booth, swearing inwardly. There were certain disadvantages to living in a small town, and one was having only two operators on the local switchboard at night.

He gunned the XK-E onto the highway, then reached into the glove compartment for Charlie's gun and thrust it under his belt. The tires screamed around a turn.

Time. How much was left before he reached the end of some unknown countdown? He didn't even know what was supposed to happen at the end of that countdown.

Edwina Leen knew.

The question now was how much would she tell?

He geared up to third, hitting the accelerator, and he was afraid he knew the answer to that particular question.

She would tell him nothing.

But she was his only hope now.

CHAPTER 23

"So. It's you. I *thought* you were one of them."

Mrs. Edwina Leen paused inside the office door, her puffy features set in an expression of injured dignity that would have been ludicrous under other circumstances.

Conan sat on the edge of the desk, resting his right arm on his upraised knee, and it was all he could do not to laugh. It was so incongruous, this pink-cheeked, myopic, white-haired, plump little old woman; this woman who should have been someone's chuckling, indulgent grandmother; this woman who was a professional spy, and judging by her survival to this ripe old age, undoubtedly highly skilled at her work.

"One of whom?" he asked.

She spat out the words viciously. "One of *them*—the FBI. Or is it another branch of your government's official network of spies?"

He laughed briefly, noting that she'd given up the pretense of deafness, and the stentorian tones and rural dialect that had successfully disguised a very slight accent.

He ignored both her question and her assumption, looking past her to Duncan, who was peering out through the one-way glass. A small .22 automatic rested easily in one hand; the other was wrapped around Mrs. Leen's arm.

"Any trouble, Charlie?"

"With her?" He shrugged. "No. She was expecting somebody; made her a little careless, I guess."

"Where's your car?"

"Around the corner by the grocery store."

"No sign of a tail?"

"No."

"It will do you no good!" Mrs. Leen burst out. "It's futile—all of this. It's too late!"

Duncan turned on her, raising the gun.

"Too late for *what*, Granny?" Then when she made no response, "It's sure as hell too late for you to catch your boat for home. Now, you just settle, and don't make any sudden moves."

She subsided into seething silence, a brief hint of fear in her eyes at the reminder that her escape route had been cut off.

"Charlie, keep an eye on the street," Conan said. "Someone will probably be around looking for her. Mrs. Leen, sit down."

She turned her resentful glare on him, then moved to the chair across the desk and seated herself, pulling her skirt down over her knees with a peculiarly fussy, old-maidish gesture.

Conan glanced at his watch, then focused his attention on her, keeping his voice level.

"Mrs. Leen, I want you to understand your position. You have no hope of making good your escape, nor completing your mission. It would be to your advantage to cooperate with us now."

"To cooperate?" Her eyes narrowed, and she studied him speculatively for a moment, then she smiled; a malign smile that was a travesty in that plump, pink face. "So. You need my *cooperation*. Well, you're in error, Mr. Flagg. Perhaps *I* won't escape, but you're too late to prevent the accomplishment of my mission!"

Then she began to laugh, a high-pitched cackling, and

Conan felt himself go pale and fought the urge to stop that triumphant laughter with his fist.

"What *is* your mission?" he demanded.

But she only laughed again. "You seem quite well informed about me. I should think you'd know all about—"

"Mrs. *Leen*—" He was on his feet, looking down at her, and what she read in his face silenced her. He said slowly, "Treason is considered a serious offense, in case you'd forgotten; it means life imprisonment—at the *least*."

The laughter had turned to sullen intransigence now.

"So. You think to frighten me? I'm an old woman. What does life imprisonment mean to me, or even execution? *No*. I have nothing to say to you. Nothing!"

"Damn it, don't you understand—"

"Conan—"

He turned at the urgency in Duncan's voice.

"What is it?"

"Company. Car slowing up; looks like it's about to stop. New-model Ford; maybe a rental."

"Probably. Come on, Mrs. Leen."

"What? What are you—let go of me!"

He started to pull her to her feet, but he was wearing the sling again, and she almost proved too much for him. Duncan stepped in, twisting her arm behind her back with no hint of respect for her years, stifling her protests with his big hand across her mouth.

"By the door, Charlie."

They escorted her, still struggling, to the door. Conan snapped off the light to avoid a telltale line of light under the door, then concentrated on the car inching along the street.

The car itself was of no interest to him; it wasn't familiar. But the lone driver was of immense interest. As he watched, the car came to a full stop outside the shop, and after a long hesitation the driver finally emerged.

And again, he felt an urge to laugh.

The man was wearing a belted trenchcoat, the collar turned up, and a hat with the brim pulled low over his face. He looked like a character out of a vintage 1940 movie. Even his posture and movements were Bogartish; the hands in the pockets, the tense, hunched set of the shoulders, the quick glances up and down the street.

Still, the costuming was effective in hiding his face; it was only a dark blur in the ambiguous shadows cast by the street lamps. But Conan didn't need to see his face.

Duncan asked quietly, "You know him, Chief?"

"The third man."

"The courier?"

"Yes."

The man approached the shop cautiously, looking in the windows, finally moving to the door, shading his eyes with one hand to block out the reflections on the glass.

Mrs. Leen had relaxed momentarily, but now she renewed her struggles, letting out frantic, muffled yelps, one foot shooting out and thudding against the door.

Conan wasn't concerned about her cries; the sound-proofing would silence them. But the kicks . . .

"Hold her, Charlie! Her legs—"

It was incredible that a fat old woman could muster such strength, but she was desperate, and it was all the two of them could do to control her.

Finally, Conan jerked the gun from his belt, aiming it not at her, but at the man outside the shop.

"Mrs. Leen, if your friend sets foot inside that door, he's dead!"

Her struggles ceased, and in the silence that followed her fast-paced, wheezing breathing seemed loud.

Duncan sighed with relief, cautiously taking his hand from her mouth.

"Well, Granny, that shows real consideration for your friend."

"Not for him," Conan said. "For her mission. She has someone else to do her dirty work for her—as usual."

He watched the courier, looking for any indication that he'd heard her kick the door. But he was turning away now, pausing to look up at the upstairs windows.

"Charlie, as soon as he leaves, follow him."

"Okay, but he'll have a hell of a start on me by the time I get to the car."

"I know, but you'll have to try. What about Dominic? Did you talk to Carl?"

He felt Mrs. Leen tense at Dominic's name.

"No, I couldn't raise him," Charlie replied. "But he won't get out of reach of his radio for long. I'll give him another try from the car. What about Steve?"

The man was stepping into the Ford now, looking back over his shoulder toward the shop.

"No luck. I didn't have time to try him from this phone."

The car emitted a pale cloud of smoke, then surged forward, the lights flashing on as it turned onto the highway, heading south. Charlie reached for the doorknob, while Conan pulled Mrs. Leen back out of his way.

"Wish me luck, Chief—and watch that old biddy!"

He was gone before Conan had time to wish him anything. The bells marked his exit with a shattering clangor.

There was another possibility now, if Charlie didn't lose the courier. A large *if*. The countdown was still ticking, and it would be as long as the third man was free.

Conan switched on the light, raising the gun as he guided Mrs. Leen back to her chair. But she offered no resistance, only glaring at him balefully once she was seated.

"Your man won't find him," she insisted truculently. "It's too late!"

"Is it?" he demanded. "Then why is your accomplice still around?"

"He was coming for *me*! That's all. He was—"

"Of course. I believe that; but I also know your accomplice to be a man of many talents, and I'm sure he's serving this mission as something more than a chauffeur for you. Mrs. Leen, I'll ask again—*what is your mission*?"

"And I'll tell you again," she hissed, "I have nothing to say to you. *Nothing!* You'll find out what my mission is, Mr. Flagg; you'll find out when it's accomplished!"

He didn't trust himself to speak, or even to move for a moment. Then he reached for the phone and began dialing, trying to control the anger that set his hands trembling. As he listened to the drawn-out burrs on the phone, he looked at his watch again: 7:30. And Mrs. Leen might claim a victory in truth before he even found out what it was he was trying to stop.

"Oregon State Police. May I—?"

"Steve Travers, please—and hurry."

There was a clicking, a brief hesitation, then the crisp, feminine voice again.

"I'm sorry, sir, but Mr. Travers cannot be reached—"

"This is an emergency. I must talk to him."

"I'm sorry, sir, but he cannot be reached at this time. May I connect you with somebody else?"

"Is he at home?"

"No, sir. Perhaps someone else could—"

"No."

He slammed the receiver down, grimacing at the spasm of pain engendered by the movement, then leaned across the desk toward Mrs. Leen. She drew back slightly.

"I *will* have an answer," he said tautly, "one way or another. Now, how many more are going to die for your damned mission? Or does it matter to you? Does it matter that two innocent—" He straightened abruptly, his mouth twisted with disgust, and the image in his mind was Major Mills lying almost exactly where she was sitting now. And the sullen defiance in her puffy features was a goad to his frustration. She had the answers, but even if *she* were within his reach, those answers weren't.

"No, of course not," he said bitterly. "I'd be a fool to appeal to you in the name of mercy or conscience."

"Yes, you would," she retorted, drawing herself up. "There are some things which transcend individual lives; matters of principle; treachery which cannot be allowed—" she stopped abruptly, her thin lips compressed.

"Treachery? What are you talking about?"

But she only lifted her chin and glared at him, and Conan felt the rage closing in again.

"Treachery! You have the gall to speak of treachery—and *principle*. You're neck deep in murder and treason, and you can mouth smug, self-righteous nonsense about principle?"

He paused, aware that he was trembling again; it was getting out of control, the frustration and tension, the clock ticking inexorably in his mind.

Finally, he said softly, "I won't appeal to your conscience, Mrs. Leen; certainly, I won't threaten you with bodily harm. But I will point out—again—that you're in a hopeless position, whether the mission succeeds or not. And you can't yet be sure of its success. No court will be impressed with your so-called principles, but they might be impressed with a little cooperation at this point. Your *life* may be at stake here, either figuratively or literally. Don't you understand that?"

She pulled in a deep breath, her flaccid features jelling into numbed, stoic resignation, and he recognized in this something of true dignity, and even of courage. He felt a palling, stifling weariness that made even breathing an effort; he knew its source: defeat.

"I'm well aware of my position," she said slowly, the words devoid of inflection. "I know exactly how much I have at stake. Your contempt doesn't move me. I've made my decision on the basis of my own beliefs and—even if the word offends you—my own principles."

She paused, a faint sigh escaping her, her eyes seemingly focused on nothing, and Conan gazed at her hopelessly. He could laugh at her matronly indignation, regard her rationalizations with contempt, but he could feel only numb despair at this calm, resigned acceptance.

She would give him no answers. The clock would tick itself down to zero, and he would still be helplessly ignorant of her mission.

She said dully, "So. You have me, and no doubt your courts will convict me. But you'll have to be satisfied with that; you'll have no more." She smiled pensively, as if she were looking back to the memories of some vanished time. "I'm an old woman. It's a fair enough exchange."

* * *

He stared at her, the word reverberating in his mind, and it was like suddenly surfacing after a dive too deep, reaching out for the sweet, clear air and finding it there.

Exchange.

His mind seized the word, working at it, searching desperately for the key.

Exchange.

That word *was* the key, and yet it was some time before he could fit it into the lock that let him grasp the truth behind that closed door.

She'd given him the key, and if there were any justice in the whims of destiny, it would be in his using that key as a tool, a weapon to destroy her conspiracy.

And perhaps she recognized that possibility in what she read in his face now. Her round cheeks had a gray, dry look, her mouth sagged open, but there were no words; she only watched him intently, her rheumy, staring eyes magnified by the thick lenses of her glasses.

Exchange.

"Oh, dear God—"

The words were his own, but he wasn't aware of them, and no more aware of Edwina Leen. He sank into his chair and pulled the File toward him. And he wasn't even aware that his hands were no longer trembling.

The heading was "Physics, nuclear." He pulled out all the cards in that section and shuffled through them, tossing them onto the desk one after another. Then he stopped, holding one card, pushing the others aside, his eyes moving across the neatly typed lines.

DEMETRIEV, DR. ALEXEI, specializing in
particle behavior
Chairman, Nuclear Physics Research Institute
Leningrad, USSR

But the last two lines had been crossed out, and a brief notation scrawled across the card; the handwriting was his own: "Defected—present address unknown."

And now he remembered the headline that had prompted him to make that notation. PROMINENT RED SCIENTIST DEFECTS AT NOBEL CEREMONIES.

He remembered the subsequent furor that defection had evoked, occurring as it had at such a highly publicized and public event; remembered the charges and counter-charges; the volleys of diplomatic protests, vitriolic exchanges on the highest political levels; the endless meaningless television commentaries and interviews—in none of which Demetriev himself had appeared. He was hospitalized with a heart attack, and that had seemed only a glib excuse at the time.

The American government had seized this spectacular defection as a propaganda bonanza, and it was that. It was to the same degree a source of resounding embarrassment to the Soviet government, as well as a source of anxiety on a military level; Demetriev had been active in the development of their atomic weapons program.

Conan closed his eyes wearily, and he wanted to weep.

A gentle old man whose life's blood was ideas and concepts beyond the grasp of most men; a frail man with birdlike hands, grateful for every small consideration; a frightened, sick man, trembling in abject terror at revealing comprehension of his mother tongue. This man had been catapulted into world renown, a political plum, or a political disaster; a pawn in games he would never understand.

Conan looked across the desk at Edwina Leen, regarding her with a certain detachment.

Alexei Demetriev was a traitor in her eyes, who could redeem himself only by returning to his homeland and making a public repudiation of his treason.

And he would make that repudiation if he returned—one way or another. If he lived that long.

He said softly, "Alexei Demetriev."

She stiffened, her eyes briefly reflecting something more than resignation. Fear. And in that was full confirmation.

He came to his feet abruptly, crossed the room to the percolator and jerked out the cord. She made no protest when he tied her hands behind her and anchored the cord around the chair legs; she seemed incapable of any reaction at all.

He went to the desk and found a scratch pad, looking at his watch as he opened the drawer and grabbed a pen. 7:35.

There wasn't time to try to call Steve again, or to wait for Charlie. With luck, if Duncan hadn't lost the courier, they would be heading for the same destination. But if Charlie wasn't successful and returned to the shop . . .

He scrawled the words hastily, finding it an effort to make them legible or logical.

"See file card—Demetriev is Dominic. Abduction. Call Steve to alert Coast Guard—trawlers. Going to Dominic's house—CJF."

7:35.

When was the kidnapping to take place, or was it already accomplished? And the rendezvous—there would be a boat to take them to the trawlers. How much time, if any, was left him?

He looked down at Edwina Leen, knowing she had the answers, and knowing she wouldn't give them to him.

But she'd given him enough.

He thrust the .32 under his belt and started for the door. She watched him, her pouched eyes glazed and lifeless, but before he closed the door, she found her voice; the voice of a harpy, shrill, quivering.

"It's too late! Too late—"

CHAPTER 24

He hit the turn onto Dominic's street too fast, and nearly grazed a telephone pole, but his foot slammed down on the accelerator a moment later when he had the car under control.

There wasn't time to speculate on Charlie's success in pursuing the third man, but he saw neither the VW nor the courier's Ford near Dominic's house.

Nor was there time to worry about finding Carl Berg; he could only hope Berg would recognize him or his car, and offer assistance if he needed it. And there wasn't time to check the house across the street where the windows were still ominously dark.

There were lights in Dominic's windows, but the hope in those lights was dimmed by the awareness that if the old man was still inside, he wasn't alone. Harvey Rose's car was parked in front of the cottage.

There wasn't time for reconnoitering, or for caution, or even common sense. He went in by the front door, reaching it by a sprint across open ground well lighted by the street lamps; he approached the door without knowing if it would be locked, or what he could expect behind it.

The .32 was in his hand, the sling hanging loose. He vaulted the porch steps, reaching out for the doorknob, and nearly lost his balance as the door swung open. He dropped to the floor, and Harvey Rose's shot went over his head.

Conan fired from his knees, the bullet sending a shower of plaster from the ceiling above Rose's head. It wasn't bad marksmanship; it was a warning shot, and it served its purpose.

The policeman froze, staring at him as if he were an apparition.

"What the hell—?"

"Drop the gun, Rose."

Conan came to his feet, his gaze never shifting from Rose, who still seemed to find him incomprehensible; but he let the .38 police special slip out of his hand and fall to the floor with a startling crash.

Only then did Conan allow himself a split-second glance at Dominic, who was slumped in an armchair a few paces to Rose's left. The old man was bundled up in his heavy, oversize topcoat, gazing at Conan in a paralysis of alarm, his breath coming in short, painful gasps, his arms twisted awkwardly behind him. Tied.

Conan focused his full attention on Rose, approaching him warily, the gun raised.

"Turn around, Rose."

"Now—now, wait a minute." He was crouching, his eyes glazed, the pale irises circled with white.

"Back up—now!"

Rose's gun was on the floor perhaps six feet away, and Conan moved in closer.

"*No!*" Rose bellowed. "I ain't takin' the rap for—"

He didn't finish the sentence; he was lunging for the gun. An insensate cry of rage as Conan kicked it out of reach, then a hurtling charge.

Conan side-stepped, but not fast enough to avoid one flailing, grasping hand. He spun around, letting Rose's momentum throw him off balance, then pulled his knee up hard. Rose doubled over with a strangled cry of pain, and Conan brought the gun down on the back of his head with every ounce of strength he could muster, feeling a savage sense of satisfaction as Rose dropped to the floor dead weight.

But the exertion brought him to his knees, teeth clenched against the pain. He held his right arm against his body, fighting for breath, his eyes squeezed shut.

"Mr. Flack—Mr. Flack, are you be . . . all right?"

Dominic, still in the chair, regarded him anxiously. Conan nodded, bringing his eyes into focus on Rose. He was collapsed in an ungainly heap, out cold.

"Yes," he said finally, easing his arm into the sling. "I'm all right."

But Dominic—no. *Demetriev* . . .

Conan's head was clearing now, and the sense of urgency returned with a rush verging on panic. He picked up the .32 and pulled himself to his feet, then moved to Demetriev's chair and knelt beside him.

The old man's breathing was labored, much too fast, his face deathly pale. And if everything about Anton Dominic had been a protective subterfuge, his heart condition wasn't a part of it; it was entirely real.

"Dr. Demetriev, are you—?"

The old man gasped, staring at him fearfully.

"How . . . how are you know—?" Then some of the fear faded. "Are you also be with FBI?"

Conan reached around behind Demetriev's back, frowning as he encountered the cold metal of handcuffs. The key. Rose must have the key.

"No, I'm not with the FBI," he replied absently, "but I'm—what's wrong?"

The fear was in his eyes again; fear that was nothing less than terror. But his gaze was focused beyond Conan, on the front door.

Conan's jaw went tight, the self-contempt constricting his throat.

Fool—damned fool . . .

A hoary Western adage ignored: keep your back to the wall.

A light footstep and the click of the door closing.

"Just freeze—both of you!"

There was a gun behind that voice; he didn't have to see it to know it was there. And he had a gun in his own hand; a gun the man behind him couldn't see.

He looked into Alexei Demetriev's terror-pale face.

To attempt to use his gun now couldn't be regarded as even a remote possibility. Not when Demetriev might be caught in the cross fire.

But the gun . . .

Conan moved quickly, without taking time to think it out. He thrust the .32 into the pocket of Demetriev's overcoat. It was a heavy material, and . . .

"I said *freeze*!" The voice was closer, and it had a cold bite to it. "Just move back from the old man, nice and slow. And get your hands up where I can see them."

Conan rose slowly, bringing his left hand up at his side, and backed away from Demetriev.

"Mind if I make that just one hand, Joe?"

A low, grating laugh that made every muscle in his body tighten.

"Sure, ol' buddy. I hear you're having a little trouble with your arm lately." Then as Conan started to turn, "No, you don't. Not yet."

He felt the barrel of the gun against his back and waited as he as searched, looking down at Demetriev, feeling a sick despair at the fear in his eyes, and the hopelessness. And more than that; pain.

"Okay—over against the wall."

He complied, turning as he reached the wall to find himself looking into the muzzle of a .45 automatic. He could have predicted it would be a .45. The man behind the gun would find that kind of firepower satisfying.

Joe Zimmerman, the All-American Failure.

The third man.

* * *

Zimmerman's mouth twisted into a sardonic grin.

"How about that, Cone? Your ol' buddy, Joe Zimmerman. Surprise."

"Not really, Joe."

Zimmerman's lips curled. "Yeah? The old lady clue you in? I thought I lost you a while back. Or was that you tailing me?"

Conan didn't answer, too chilled with the quenching of that hope—that Charlie might still be on Joe's trail. But Charlie would go back to the shop; the note was there. But how long . . . ?

And Berg. Where was Carl Berg?

"Should've known the old lady'd talk," Joe muttered. "Can't trust a woman for this kind of work; a little pressure and they fall apart. Okay, Cone, where's your gun? Pull your arm out of that sling."

He obeyed, letting Zimmerman satisfy himself that nothing was hidden there, and even that small movement renewed the aching.

Joe searched him again, his hands moving jerkily, then he pushed him back against the wall with his hand at his throat.

"Listen, buddy, don't try holding out on me!"

"Joe, I didn't even own a gun."

"Yeah? So who put Rose out of commission? You, with one bare hand?"

"You don't think that's possible?"

Zimmerman hesitated, glancing contemptuously at Rose, who still showed no sign of regaining consciousness.

"Knowing ol' Harv, maybe it is, at that." He released Conan, then reached into his coat pocket, his features drawn and tense.

"Please—" Demetriev's querulous voice. "Do not be hurting Mr. Flack. I . . . I will go with you, but please—"

"You'll go with me, all right," Joe snapped. "Now,

shut up and don't move, if you don't want your friend hurt."

Demetriev gazed at Conan in mute appeal.

"Joe, for God's sake, he needs a doctor."

"He'll get a doctor—in due time," he responded indifferently, pulling a length of nylon rope from his pocket.

"Damn it, in due time may be too late."

Zimmerman tensed and the gun came up.

"If you're so damned worried, just be quiet and play along with me. You give me any trouble, it'll only slow us down that much more."

Us.

Conan was silent, trying to make sense of that word, wondering if he were included in that *us*; wondering now why Joe hadn't already used that gun.

Joe said curtly, "Put your hands out—wrists crossed. And *slow*. Seeing as how you're having a little trouble with your arm, I'll just tie your hands in front. I don't figure you'll be doing much—"

The rope. Zimmerman intended to take him, too.

The reaction was almost instinctive, his left hand knotting into a fist, smashing up toward that mouth that was still curled in a faint, contemptuous smile.

Joe ducked, the blow glancing off his cheek, his face suddenly red with rage. His left hand shot out, closing on Conan's shoulder, shoving him hard against the wall.

Conan groaned, and he couldn't react fast enough to avoid the quick slash of the gun barrel. It smashed against his jaw, and he felt the floor tilting under him, found himself slipping helplessly, the shrieking blackness closing in.

He heard the dry movement of air in his throat, and a silence all around him, except for someone else's breathing close by; quick, shallow breaths.

His hands. A fumbling and jerking, ropes tightening around his wrists. It had only been a matter of seconds. He was slumped on the floor, his back against the wall, the left side of his face throbbing, a warm, seeping dampness under the bandages on his shoulder, the sling hanging loose and useless.

Demetriev . . .

He moved, his eyes flashing open, and Zimmerman reacted suddenly, jamming the gun into his stomach.

"Just keep it up!" he snapped, his voice tight and vicious, too much nerve in it. "Come on—give me an excuse! I'll blow you wide open, ol' buddy. Don't think I won't. It's not *my* idea to bring you along." He paused, then brought his face close to Conan's, grinning with malicious relish. "The KGB is interested in you, Cone. They want to have a little talk with you; they figure maybe the two of you have a lot in common."

Conan absorbed this in silence, and after the initial shock he closed his eyes wearily and laughed, wondering how the proprietor of a small, out-of-the-way village bookshop had become an object of suspicion in the eyes of the two major world powers.

"Listen, ol' buddy, you won't think it's so damned funny later on. Now, on your feet!"

Zimmerman helped him up with no pretense of kindness. Conan leaned against the wall, waiting until the dizziness passed, looking down at Demetriev, who apparently hadn't moved, and seemed incapable of moving. He wondered if Demetriev was even aware of the gun in his pocket.

Conan turned his bound wrists to look at his watch: 7:50. And the countdown was still ticking.

Zimmerman jerked Demetriev to his feet, unconcerned at his choked moan, and turned on Conan.

"I've got something to say to you, Cone, and you'd damn well better listen, and listen *good*. I got one aim in life right now—to get Demetriev on his way home. And I got nothing to lose. If the FBI picks me up, I've had it. I'll die before I give up, and I'll see both of you dead before *I* die. And the old man goes *first*. That clear?"

Conan nodded mutely, then Joe snapped his wrist up and looked at his watch, his features settling into taut, determined lines; but there was a hint of desperation, too, and that offered Conan no encouragement.

The .45 came up.

"Okay, you two, we're going for a little ride, and neither one of you better give me any trouble. And, Cone— remember what I said. The old man goes first."

CHAPTER 25

Conan looked around the deserted dock desperately. The quiet slapping of water and the creaking of wood were the only sounds. Two dim lights cast exaggerated shadows of masts and rigging across the planking; shadows that moved as the boats rocked with the waves, giving the illusion of movement to the planks themselves, and the fluid quality of a dream to the whole scene.

But he could hear Zimmerman's and Demetriev's footsteps only a few paces behind him, and he thought of the .45 pressed against the physicist's side.

There was nothing dreamlike about that gun.

He looked north toward the Coast Guard station. In a fenced area on one side of the building, a helicopter rested like a monstrous, sleeping dragonfly. At the small dock below the station, the Coast Guard cutter was moored, rocking placidly, silent and unmanned. There were lights in the station; a crew was always on duty. But if anyone there noticed the three men walking along the dock, there was no indication of it.

Only a few boats were moored at the dock. On the south side, he noted the familiar outlines of the *Josephine*, but he saw no sign of life aboard her. Probably Sven had cured her mechanical ills and gone home long ago.

"Okay, Cone—hold it right there!"

Conan stopped and waited as Zimmerman, with Demetriev in tow, moved up ahead of him. To their right, a small, ill-kept fishing boat was moored; on the stern were the words "*Sea Queen*, Crescent City."

He could barely see the dial of his watch in the dim light: 8:03. His hands curled into fists, and he found himself surprised at the slow passage of time. It had been only half an hour since he left the bookshop.

And yet the time was slipping by too fast.

Charlie. He must have found the note by now. . . .

A wiry, dark man in faded dungarees and a stained sweat shirt moved out of the *Sea Queen*'s pilothouse.

"You're late," he observed sourly.

Joe responded curtly, "Listen, Harrison, you think I can't tell time? Get the engine started."

"They told me just one passenger." Harrison squinted dubiously at Conan. "And where's the woman?"

Zimmerman glanced toward the Coast Guard station.

"There's been a change in plans, and forget the woman. She'll just have to fend for herself."

Conan caught a movement out of the corner of his eye, and looked up, past Zimmerman, and saw a shadowy figure emerge from the *Josephine*'s pilothouse, then hesitate and draw back. Harrison was still arguing with Joe, but Conan wasn't listening.

Sven.

If he could make him understand . . .

But the light was dim, and he couldn't be sure Sven would recognize him, or even if he did, that he'd realize anything was wrong. Sven was a curiously incurious man.

Zimmerman's voice had taken on a sharp edge in his short and heated dialogue with the pilot. Conan looked from one to the other; neither had apparently noticed the movement aboard the *Josephine*. Joe had his back to the boat, and Harrison's view was blocked by the *Sea Queen*'s pilothouse.

"Damn it, Harrison, they won't wait much longer. Now, get this tub started and let's get the hell out of here. Conan, you—"

"Listen, I got my orders," Harrison interrupted testily. "And I ain't—" He stopped abruptly as Joe brought his gun out and aimed it directly at him.

"I said start the engine, you stupid—"

"Okay! Okay!" He threw up his hands helplessly and turned toward the pilothouse. "But I *still* don't like it."

"You don't have to like it. Just do what you're told and you won't get hurt." He glanced fleetingly at the Coast Guard station again, then focused on Conan as the boat's motor throbbed into life, shouting over the roar.

"Come on, get in—and hurry up!"

Conan risked one look at the *Josephine* and saw Sven through the windows of the pilothouse. He stepped backward, glaring at Joe, watching him closely, calculating the risk.

"This is as far as I go, Zimmerman!" The roar of the motor gave him an excuse to raise his voice to a shout he hoped Sven could hear.

Joe's face went red, and he snapped the gun up against Demetriev's head.

"One last warning, Flagg! You just keep pushing me and see where you end up—*both* of you!"

Demetriev moaned, his eyes rolling around toward the gun, and Conan stood a moment, as if undecided, gazing at him. Finally, he let his shoulders sag, then turned and stepped over the railing into the *Sea Queen*, fighting for balance as Zimmerman hurried him on his way with a hard shove.

"Into the stern, Cone, and stay down. Okay, Doctor, you're next. Up by the pilothouse. I'll get the anchor ropes, Harrison. You just tend to the wheel and get this damned tub headed out!"

Conan sank against the stern with the hectic roar of the engine rising to a vibrating crescendo as Joe leaped aboard, and the boat lurched away from the dock.

He had one last glimpse of Olaf Svensen before he lowered himself to the deck. The old fisherman was still watching from the shadows of the *Josephine*'s pilothouse.

Conan closed his eyes, hoping that the man of little curiosity would find something in what he'd just seen to wonder about.

Beyond the narrow channel of Holliday Bay, the *Sea Queen* moved into a tangible, oppressive darkness. There was a faint glow from the running lights atop the pilothouse; red on the port side, green on the starboard, but they were shielded at the back. The white mast light made a weaving beacon against the stars, but it was too high to cast any light into the boat.

Inside the pilothouse, a three-walled affair, open at the back, there was a faint glow from the binnacle light. Conan could see Zimmerman standing next to Demetriev, holding the handrail along the side wall to brace himself and the old man against the rising and falling of the waves.

Demetriev seemed oblivious to everything. His head rested against the wall, rolling back and forth with the motion of the boat. And Conan wondered exactly how bad his heart was; how much longer he could hold out.

And he was wondering how long it would take the *Sea Queen* to reach the trawlers. Fifteen minutes, perhaps; twenty at the most.

It didn't matter. It wasn't enough.

He'd felt some hope on seeing Sven; embraced the hope blindly. But now it was crumbling into helpless despair. He was intensely aware of the leaden pounding of his heartbeat in every artery, and a kind of static change running along the nerves under his skin.

He squeezed his eyes shut, concentrating on bringing himself under control, reining the rising panic.

He still had a few high cards left in his game. Charlie, of course—Charlie was his ace; and there was the gun in Demetriev's pocket; and the slight advantage of having his hands tied in front of him rather than behind his back; and Sven.

But as the *Sea Queen* moved on into the darkness, the

chances of any of these factors turning the game in his favor were becoming more remote with every passing minute.

There were too many square miles of ocean between the Bay and the trawlers. Even if Charlie reached Travers and the Coast Guard was alerted, finding one small fishing boat on a moonless night wouldn't be easy; not in the short span of time left to them.

And the gun; with Joe so close to Demetriev, there was little hope of getting at the gun. The slight advantage of having his hands tied in front was offset by the weakness of the shoulder. It ached constantly, and he could still feel the warm dampness under the bandages.

And Sven—Conan almost laughed. Sven had probably watched Zimmerman push him and Demetriev into the boat, shrugged his shoulders, and gone home.

Zimmerman was holding all the high cards now.

He became aware of the burning in his wrists; he'd been pulling at the ropes. And that was futile; they were a light, tough nylon cord, and he'd only succeeded in tightening the knots.

He felt the anger and frustration—and the fear—eating like acid, corrosive and bitter; his nerves seemed to be disintegrating with that mordant infusion. His muscles tightened, caught in an uncontrolled, unconscious tetany between the mental signals that shouted *act*, and the conflicting signals that recognized the futility of action.

But he would not wait passively, hoping for the *deus ex machina*. He *would* act, whatever the risk to Demetriev— or himself. In the end, the results would probably be the same. Any action was better than . . .

His head came up, and for a long while he was motionless, not even breathing, his senses straining. A sound. A drawn-out, mournful moan repeating itself at regular intervals.

It was faint against the rumble of the engine, but still, that desolate, sighing sound amplified itself in his awareness, carrying with it chilling clarity.

The marker buoy.

That buoy was anchored at the three-mile limit; the borderline between United States and international waters.

CHAPTER 26

"For God's sake, will you at least *try*?" Charlie Duncan was shouting into the phone, staring across Conan's desk into the mocking face of Mrs. Edwina Leen.

The feminine voice at the other end of the line was cold.

"I'm sorry, sir, but Mr. Travers gave me strict orders that he would accept no calls. He's in conference."

Duncan glared at Mrs. Leen, choking back his frustration as he looked down at his watch: 8:10. And where the hell was Conan? *And* Carl?

"Look, this is an emergency. Tell Travers—"

"If it's an emergency, sir, I suggest you call—"

"Will you shut up and listen!" Mrs. Leen laughed softly, and Duncan snapped, "Look, Granny, you're just lucky I never hit a woman when she's tied down."

The secretary made a choked sound. "*Really*, sir!"

"I wasn't talking to you, lady. Now, get Travers on the line and tell him—"

"Sir, I'm sorry," she interrupted, with no hint of apology in her tone, "but I can't do that. I'm *only* acting under orders."

He pulled in a deep breath, controlling his voice with an effort, staring down at the file card on the desk. Demetriev. If Conan was right . . .

"Yes, ma'am, I understand. But this particular emergency concerns Mr. Travers. Tell him I'm calling about Conan Flagg."

"Well, I can't just—"

"Listen, damn it! Did you get that name?"

There was a slight pause, then, "Did you say *Flagg*? Conan Flagg?"

"Yes, ma'am. That's exactly what I said."

Duncan was taken entirely off guard by the short, uneasy laugh that followed.

"Oh, well, why didn't you say so to begin with?"

"Lady, I've been trying—"

"Just a moment, sir. Of course, I'll connect you with Mr. Travers."

The line clicked to hold, and Duncan braced the phone against his shoulder as he lit a cigarette, too relieved to be annoyed. And now, he could meet Mrs. Leen's eye and watch her growing anxiety with some relish.

But something was drastically wrong, and Mrs. Leen's anxiety offered little reassurance. Carl Berg was too good an operative to get out of reach of his radio for more than a few minutes, and Duncan had tried to contact him four times in the last half hour. He'd even attempted to telephone Dominic's house, but the line was out of order. And that damned courier—Duncan blew out an impatient stream of smoke. He had to give the man credit; he was quick, and he knew all the tricks for shaking a tail.

"Hello. Conan, is that—?"

Charlie straightened. "No, Steve, this is Duncan."

"What's the problem, Charlie? My secretary said—"

"You can tell your secretary to—never mind. Steve, I need help. Can you get hold of somebody with some authority fast? Conan may be in trouble, and I've got a man down there with a two-way radio, but I haven't been able to raise him. You'd better—"

"Wait a minute. Just slow down a little. What's going on?"

Duncan sighed. It would take so long to explain.

"Get hold of the FBI and see if the name Alexei Demetriev rings any bells."

Travers paused. "Hold on a minute."

It was only a matter of seconds. The next voice was unfamiliar.

"Mr. Duncan, I'm Inspector David West, FBI. Mr. Travers and I were just discussing—"

"Thank God." Duncan breathed a long sigh of relief. "Inspector, I haven't got time to be polite. Will you tell Travers to get a patrol car to Demetriev's house—*now*."

A brief hesitation, then, "Yes, just a moment."

Duncan waited again, watching Mrs. Leen. She'd turned noticeably paler at the word *Inspector*.

"All right, Mr. Duncan, he's taking care of it."

"Good. By the way, I have somebody here at the bookshop for you. Mrs. Edwina Leen."

"We checked the name, but—"

"It doesn't matter. It's probably an alias, and she'll keep. I'm worried about Conan. He left here alone, headed for Demetriev's place about—"

"How did he know about Demetriev?"

"I don't know. All I have is a note and a file card. Do you guys have any idea what's going on down here?"

West said sharply, "Mr. Duncan, we *do* have agents keeping Dr. Demetriev under full-time surveillance. I sent another man down this morning when Mills didn't check in, and there are more on their way now. In fact, they should be arriving within a few minutes."

"That's encouraging. But when did you last hear from your agents in the house blind?"

"The house—well, they're supposed to report at eight. I haven't checked the Portland office to—"

"I can save you some trouble. There was no eight o'clock report from them."

"But, what—?"

"Inspector, somebody's about to walk off with your prize defector."

"Are you sure? How do you know?"

"Maybe Conan's wrong, but I don't think so. I had a man working surveillance on Demetriev. Is Steve there?"

"Yes, Charlie," Travers replied. "We have a conference phone; I'm listening."

"Okay. I couldn't raise Carl, and he wouldn't get away from his radio for half an hour when he knew I might be calling. And if something's happened to him, Conan's on his own in very unfriendly territory. I even tried calling Demetriev's house. The phone's dead."

West's voice betrayed his chagrin at that.

"The phone's dead? Mr. Duncan, perhaps you should call the local police until our agents—"

"*No*, for God's sake, not the local police."

"What do you mean?"

Travers cut in, "I'll explain that to him, Charlie. Look, I checked and we have a couple of patrol cars in the area. I sent them to Demetriev's."

"Good." Duncan crushed out his cigarette hastily. "You better send one of them to the Bay, and alert the Coast Guard to check out any boats leaving the dock. Mrs. Leen's tied down here at the shop. I'm heading for Demetriev's."

"*Wait*," West put in. "What about the Bay?"

Duncan thrust his gun in his belt holster, glancing impatiently at his watch.

"Conan took a little fishing trip earlier this evening and caught a signal light between Mrs. Leen's house and those Russian trawlers. You figure it. Now, you two can sit there and ponder this thing if you want; I'm going to Demetriev's and find out what the hell's going on."

"Charlie, hold on," Travers said. "How long ago did Conan leave?"

"Maybe half an hour ago. I don't know exactly. Oh— put out an APB on a tan Ford, license number ETM581."

"Okay, but who—?"

"No time to explain now. Where can I reach you?"

"Here. I'll keep the line open for you."

"That's a relief. I might not have time to work through your secretary again. Thanks. And good-bye."

"Charlie—"

But anything Travers had to add was cut off as he slammed the receiver down and started for the door. He didn't even glance at Edwina Leen.

CHAPTER 27

The ticking of his pulse, metronomic, and paradoxically regular, parceled out the time.

Conan listened, body and mind locked in numb paralysis, to the lonely, baleful moaning of the marker buoy. Then abruptly, the metronomic beat of his pulse quickened, and he raised his bound wrists, his hands cramped into fists, pulling at the ropes in helpless rage and frustration.

It was the pain that finally subdued the panic; the pain radiating from his shoulder until it impressed itself upon his consciousness, acting as a sort of cauterizing agent.

He forced himself to relax, letting his balled fists uncurl, loosening the tension on the ropes. Panic was another luxury; he couldn't afford it now. He had to think.

The ropes. He had to find some kind of instrument, some sharp edge. But he wasn't familiar enough with fishing boats to know what might be available that would serve his purpose.

He was tightening again, moving to the edge of panic, and again, he forced himself to relax—and to think.

The marker buoy formed a counterpoint to his pulse,

meting out the passing time. Think. The ropes weren't his primary problem. The gun. There wasn't time to worry about the ropes. The gun in Demetriev's pocket.

The high cards; the gun and his hands tied in front. Perhaps that would be enough. It had to be. And another high card he hadn't taken into consideration—darkness.

Zimmerman couldn't see into the back of the boat, and he was intent on the trawlers. And the roar of the motor; another high card.

Perhaps on some level he was aware of the hopeless odds against reaching that gun alive, but he wouldn't allow himself to recognize them now. He couldn't, unless he was willing to surrender himself to despair.

He began to slide to his left toward the port railing. Demetriev and Zimmerman were on the left side of the pilothouse. If he could get close enough without being seen, and if Demetriev was alert enough to react at the right time . . .

He reached the railing, his breath coming fast and hard, and he was still capable of awareness of pain; but it was a peripheral awareness. His mind was too intently concentrated on his objective, and on Zimmerman.

Then he froze as both Zimmerman and the pilot turned and looked back.

But after a moment, he realized they weren't looking at him, but at something beyond the boat. He heard their voices in a brief exchange that was unintelligible against the roar of the motor.

But if the words were unintelligible, something in their tone still came through; an urgency, even anxiety. And it was in their posture and gestures, too. He watched intently as Harrison again turned to look backward, then leaned closer to Joe for hurried consultation.

At length, Conan risked a look over the stern, pushing himself up cautiously and twisting around. Behind them, in the darkness between the *Sea Queen* and the scatter of shore lights, he saw two closer lights; red and green. Running lights.

He slid back down against the stern, unconsciously

holding his breath as he looked up toward the pilothouse. But Joe was still staring back at the second boat, his body tense and rigid.

Conan's breath came out in a long, tremulous sigh. Perhaps the odds were turning in his favor; one of his high cards might be about to pay off.

Perhaps.

But whether that card paid off or not, the other boat offered a distraction. The gun. That was the only card that counted now.

He reached up for the railing to pull himself into a crouching position, but again froze at a shout from Zimmerman.

And again, it wasn't directed at him. It was a command to Harrison, and without further warning, the pilot turned the wheel abruptly to the right, and gunned the engine to full speed.

The *Sea Queen* heeled over, sending Conan sliding across the deck, then she seemed to leap forward, trembling under the full power of the motor.

She was quartering the swells, rocking sickeningly from side to side, her curved flanks cutting under the waves, sending cascades of icy water washing across the deck. The motor roared and spluttered irregularly, sounding eerily like the hoarse panting of a fleeing animal.

Conan flailed helplessly in the darkness, chilled by floods of sea water, and finally managed to grasp the port railing again. He clung desperately to the wet metal, wondering what had precipitated this full-throttle flight—and wondering if the *Sea Queen* was equal to the battering quartering swells and the tearing vibrations of the engine.

But for the moment, he could only cling to the railing, gasping at the periodic onslaughts of water as the boat smashed into the oncoming waves.

He closed his eyes against another flood of frigid water as the boat heeled into a swell. But he was only dimly aware of the cold and the pain.

For the first time since the *Sea Queen* left Holliday Bay, he was beginning to feel some real hope.

* * *

For what seemed an interminable length of time, the *Sea Queen* plunged ahead, full speed, with Harrison fighting the wheel all the way.

Then, as suddenly as it began, the breakneck flight ended. Silence and darkness descended abruptly as the motor ceased its roaring, and a few seconds later all the lights went off.

In the echoing quiet, the boat swooped down the back of a swell into the trough, the water washing against the hull in a silken rush.

Then softly in the distance, the bleak call of the marker buoy sounded, and from the opposite direction—somewhere behind them—the faint rumble of a motor.

But the motor was a long way off now.

Conan crouched against the railing, trying to adjust his senses to the sudden absence of sound and light, remembering his equally silent and lightless vigil aboard the *Josephine*. And he had no doubt Zimmerman's purpose was the same as his had been: to escape detection.

Harrison had taken a quartering tack northwest, and the blackness wasn't entirely devoid of light. The trawlers. Conan looked over the railing, feeling a fleeting dizziness. That chain of lights wasn't so distant now; it seemed to bead the entire horizon, to fill his span of vision.

The gun.

He had to get to Demetriev.

But he might as well have been blind in the darkness; now he couldn't even be sure where the old man was. He could only assume he was still in the pilothouse, as he could only assume Zimmerman and Harrison were still there.

Voices. He tensed, his eyes focusing unconsciously, and uselessly, in the direction of the pilothouse.

Harrison was speaking, his voice low and indistinct, as if he were intimidated by the overwhelming silence and darkness. Conan could understand only a few words, but he caught the last of Zimmerman's equally low-pitched response.

" . . . wait and see if he's following us. Now, relax, damn it."

The pilot's reply was lost, but from his edgy tone, it was obvious he wasn't close to relaxation.

Conan waited a few seconds longer until Harrison and Zimmerman resumed their conversation, then began edging his way along the railing toward the pilothouse, crouching low, remembering that the shore lights were behind him.

He made slow progress, waiting through the silences, and even as he concentrated on that intermittent exchange, he was listening to the rumble of the boat behind them. And it seemed to be getting louder.

There was still no sound to help him locate Demetriev, but he had no doubt he'd be close to Zimmerman.

The pilot's voice knifed through the quiet.

"Listen, I don't give a damn what you say, I ain't just sittin' here! That boat's closin' *in*!"

"Shut up!" Zimmerman snapped, his voice rising in volume with Harrison's. "Can you tell if it's the Coast Guard cutter?"

A brief silence, then, "No . . . I don't think so. Lights are too high in the water. But it's gettin' closer—"

"Don't panic. It's just another fishing boat."

"Leavin' the Bay this time of night?"

Conan listened intently. He'd covered well over half the distance to the pilothouse, and the voices were uncomfortably close, and getting closer with every hesitant, cautious step.

Zimmerman said irritably, "You just calm down. He can't do a damn thing if he does see us. If you just sit tight, he'll probably go on past us."

"Yeah, and he might not." There was a movement and a few shuffling footsteps. "Hey! Damn it, look at them trawlers!"

"What's wrong?"

"They're takin' off! They're gonna leave us here holdin' the bag! The dirty—"

"You damned fool, they're just scattering. It'll make it harder for anybody to find us. Now, shut up!"

"They're leavin', damn it! And that boat. I ain't waitin' any—"

"Harrison, I said shut up, or so help me, I'll blow your brains out and run this leaky tub myself!" A short silence, cadenced with the sound of heavy breathing. "You settle down. I'm going back and check on Flagg; it's been too damned quiet back there. Where's that flashlight?"

A few seconds later, Conan heard heavy footsteps moving along the opposite railing and recognized a golden opportunity—or a last chance. If Demetriev was still by the side wall of the pilothouse . . .

Harrison's voice was shrill with panic.

"I ain't waitin'! I ain't waitin' for nothin'!"

"Harrison, what the hell—?"

But Zimmerman's voice was drowned in a roar as the *Sea Queen*'s engine burst into life again, and the boat plunged sideways into an oncoming swell.

Conan careened against the railing, struggling to keep his footing against the wall of water pouring over the deck. He was dimly aware of a muffled, choked cry from the stern, then he staggered as a heavy body crashed into him.

"Help—help me!"

Demetriev.

He reached out for the physicist's hurtling body, but with his bound hands, only managed to catch his arm, then as the *Sea Queen* pitched again, they both sprawled to the deck.

But even before the boat began to right herself, Conan was groping for Demetriev's pocket. He almost had his fingers on the gun, when the boat heeled again.

"Harrison!" Zimmerman's voice, screaming against the throb of the motor. "Damn you—*stop!*"

Conan's fumbling fingers closed on the gun.

"Doctor, are you all right?"

He leaned down to hear Demetriev's weak reply, at the same time taking advantage of a brief lull in the pitching of the boat to pull himself and the old man upright.

"I . . . I am all right. Do not worry—"

"Harrison, you damned fool!" Zimmerman again. Conan listened intently, trying to locate the sound of that voice. The opposite railing. He was moving toward the pilothouse.

"Doctor, get back in the stern. And keep down."

The motor roared as the *Sea Queen* crashed into another swell, and Conan lost Demetriev. He could only hope he was capable of working his way back to the stern; it was all he could do to keep himself on his feet. At least Joe would be having the same problem.

The pilot—he had to stop Harrison. He clung to the railing with his left hand, the gun gripped in his right. His hands were numb; the ropes.

A beam of light streaked across the pilothouse, momentarily, revealing Harrison hunched over the wheel.

Flashlight. Zimmerman's flashlight.

Conan dropped to the deck as the beam focused on him, the rush of air from the bullet coming simultaneously with a sharp cracking sound.

The *Sea Queen* groaned as she swooped into another deep trough, spinning at the bottom and meeting the next swell broadside. The crest of the wave broke over the railing, sweeping across the deck.

"*Flagg!*" Another shot smashed into the planks.

He fought his way to the railing and pulled himself up, then fell up to the deck again as the flashlight homed in on him. He rolled sideways, then brought his arms up, steadying the gun.

At his second shot, the flashlight exploded into darkness. He heard a cry of pain, but didn't take time to assess the damage. He made it to his feet before the boat heeled into the next trough, and clung to the railing as another wave flooded the deck. And he knew his disequilibrium was more than the movement of the boat now. Dizziness. But he had to hold on.

He was vaguely aware of a new sound—a strange whirring, beating sound—but he wasted no time trying to iden-

tify it. He lunged for the pilothouse, falling against the
side wall as the boat heeled again.

"Harrison, stop the engine!"

The pilot didn't seem to hear that shout. He was losing
control of the boat, fighting the wheel, all the while babbling incoherently. Conan braced himself and jammed the
gun against his side.

"Stop her, Harrison! You'll sink this damned—"

"No—no—don't shoot!" The wheel began spinning un-
controllably. "Don't kill me! Don't—"

"Harrison, for God's sake, the engine—turn off the engine!"

Conan reached out and caught the wheel with his left
hand, grimacing at the effort, almost losing his grip on the
gun. The ropes cut into his wrists, and he was chilled with
a new assault of dizziness at the pain in his shoulder.

"Harrison—"

The pilot was still stammering, fumbling for the ignition switch. The boat angled into another wave, and together they fought to control the wheel.

When the motor ceased its wracking vibration, Conan
sagged back against the wall, letting Harrison take over,
waiting for the dizziness to pass.

The sound. That beating whir . . .

For a moment, he thought it was in his head, but a wind
moved around him that wasn't a sea wind, and almost
directly overhead, flashing red lights. . . .

The helicopter.

It had to be the Coast Guard helicopter. And behind the
Sea Queen, toward the shore, running lights; two sets—

The flash of light and sharp crack came from the starboard railing, and the window of the pilothouse exploded.
Joe Zimmerman wasn't out of the game yet.

Conan dropped to the deck, then took cover behind the
side wall of the pilothouse as another bullet slammed into
the instrument panel.

"Flagg! Damn you—where are you?"

He looked out from behind the wall, his eyes straining
into the darkness where he heard Zimmerman's thick,

slurred voice. Then a scuffling movement in front of him, another gunshot and a yelp of pain.

"Don't shoot! Don't—it's *me*! Don't—"

"Harrison?" Joe's voice was closer now. "Damn it, get out of the way! Where's the old man?"

"I—I don't know! Don't shoot me!"

Conan looked up, shivering in the wind of the 'copter's rotors, directing an urgent, wordless plea to the men in that roaring mantis machine—*hurry*. . . .

"Flagg!"

A series of shots erupted from the starboard railing, staccato pulse beats of light and sound, aimless and random, expressions of rage.

Conan watched that explosion of frustration, but his gaze kept shifting to the helicopter. It was slowly descending, and now a new sound was added to the cacophony of beating rotors: the wail of a siren.

And the wail was echoed in Zimmerman's long-drawn howl of stymied rage as the darkness vanished in a cold glare of spotlights from the 'copter.

The light was a sensory shock. Conan recoiled, reeling with a sensation near vertigo as the light threw everything around him into sharp, surrealistic relief. He heard a voice blaring from a loudspeaker, but he was incapable of assimilating the words.

The intensity of the light drowned all color. Every detail was limned in harsh blacks and whites: Harrison cringing on the deck only a few feet away, clutching a bleeding arm; Demetriev crouched against the stern, looking somehow broken, like a wounded bird; and across the boat, Zimmerman, almost unrecognizable in his vengeful frenzy, backed against the railing like an animal at bay, the left side of his face smeared with blood.

Conan pulled himself to his feet and moved out from behind the pilothouse.

"Joe!" He heard the amplified voice from the helicopter, urgent and demanding, but still could make no sense of the words, and he knew Zimmerman was beyond hearing them. "Joe—it's all over!"

Zimmerman's gaze shifted and the full intensity of his berserk rage was focused on Conan; he raised his hand, the gun coming up, aimed directly at his heart.

But he didn't fire.

With a shutter-click flick, he seemed to assess and dismiss him, then turn with inevitable purpose toward the stern—to Demetriev.

And without a split-second's warning, his gun came around, aligned with Demetriev's frozen face, and Conan saw his finger tightening on the trigger.

He reacted, reflexes impelling nerves and muscles without a conscious decision. There was no time.

His hands came up, the gun aimed and fired—straight at Zimmerman—all in half the blinking of an eye.

The .32 seemed to explode in his hand.

And that explosion went on and on—not echoing, but caught in a sensory time lapse; an intensely heightened awareness of the finest detail of every passing millisecond.

He saw Zimmerman's body jerk spasmodically even as his finger closed on the trigger of the .45. And the gun recoiled, leaping from his hand, the bullet smashed into the stern, a foot from Demetriev's head.

Zimmerman falling, toppling, And he turned in that endless descent and stared at Conan, his mouth open and moving as if he were trying to speak. Then his jaw went slack, and his body crumpled with the impact of collision against the unyielding surface of the deck.

CHAPTER 28

He had known, even as Zimmerman fell, that he was dead. Still, he searched for some faint beat of life. Finally, when it was obvious there was no trace of a pulse, he reached across the body with his left hand and gripped the railing, sinking under the weight of a sudden, debilitating weakness.

He wondered vaguely why he should feel anything for killing this man. And he wondered, too, how human beings ever inured themselves to killing other human beings.

He looked across the deck toward Demetriev. Two Coast Guardsmen were bending over him, one administering oxygen. The helicopter still hovered overhead, a rope ladder dangling, swaying in the wind of the rotors. That aural assault was still numbing, but mercifully the sirens had stopped.

He was aware of movements around him, crisp orders, terse questions and responses, and somewhere, Harrison's meaningless babbling. Beyond the railing, he saw the cutter approaching, and another boat standing off a little distance. He smiled weakly as he read the name on her side. The *Josephine*.

"Sir . . . can I help you?"

He couldn't seem to make sense of the simplest words. He looked around at the Guardsman, his eyes going out of focus. The pain and weariness he hadn't allowed himself to feel in the grim necessity of crisis were coming home to him now, and his lips were numbed as he tried to speak.

"Dem-Demetriev—the old man . . . is he all right?"

"I think so. There's a doctor and an ambulance standing by at the dock." A brief hesitation, then, "Sir, are you—should I call the medic?"

Conan looked over at the anxious group clustered around Demetriev.

"Not now. He has his hands full. Later—"

He tightened his grip on the railing, and finally, feeling some return of strength, pulled himself to his feet. He knew he could hold out a while longer, but he was still grudgingly thankful for the Guardsman's supporting hand.

Someone had cut the ropes from his wrists. He wondered when; he hadn't been aware of it. And he noted absently that Nicky's beautiful job of stitching hadn't been up to the rigors of the evening. Dark threads of blood were moving down the back of his hand.

The movement of the boat was becoming intolerable.

He turned away; turned from that mute, lifeless form at his feet, and felt his way along the railing toward the bow.

Charlie Duncan pushed through the crowd gathering on the dock. A signal from one of the FBI agents opened the way for him when he reached the *Sea Queen*, but he'd have boarded her, one way or another, without the official sanction, in spite of the cordon of policemen and Guardsmen.

He surveyed the crowded deck, a frown drawing his brows together. Demetriev, in the stern, was enclosed by Guardsmen, policemen, white-garbed ambulance attendants, and FBI agents, whose conservative business suits seemed as much like uniforms as the other, more straightforward uniforms in evidence here.

He spoke briefly with Inspector West, who was part of

the cluster gathered around Demetriev. Nicky Heideger was there, too, but she was too busy to look up.

Then he stepped aside as a sheet-covered stretcher was carried off the boat. Harry Morton. The courier. Duncan scanned the deck again, his mouth tightening irritably at the noise and confusion.

Finally, he walked around the pilothouse and into an area of relative quiet. Conan was sitting against the starboard railing near the bow, entirely alone; Alexei Demetriev was the center of attention now. He sat with a certain stoic patience, cross-legged, with a blanket wrapped around him, and Duncan almost laughed. Chief Joseph.

But he suspected the stoicism reflected a physical state more than a philosophical attitude. He walked over and knelt beside him.

"Hey, Chief."

Conan looked up, bringing his eyes into focus; his field of vision was rather narrow, but at the moment it didn't bother him. Very little bothered him. He smiled faintly.

"Hello, Charlie. Thanks for sending the Marines."

"Yeah, well, I'm sorry it took so long for them to land. How're you feeling—or . . . maybe you better not try to answer that."

Conan laughed at Duncan's uncertain frown. There was no cause for concern; he wasn't feeling much of anything now.

"I'm all right. I think I'm . . . a little seasick. Funny. I've never had any trouble with it before."

"Sure. Well, hold on awhile. Nicky'll be here. She's busy with Demetriev now."

"How is he?"

"All I know is he's still alive. She'll fill you in."

Conan nodded. "Charlie, what happened to Berg? Is he—?"

Duncan laughed and settled himself on the deck, cross-legged like Conan.

"Well, he's okay, but it's a long story."

"Just give me the high points, then. Do you have a cigarette? Mine are rather wet."

"Like the rest of you." He reached into his jacket pocket for his cigarettes and lit one for Conan, noting that he was using his left hand exclusively. "What the hell did you do—jump in?"

Conan took a long drag on the cigarette, savoring it, letting his eyes close briefly.

"No, but I might as well have. What about Carl?"

"Well, you remember I told you he'd sighted a couple of city police cars right before he signed off." He paused to light a cigarette for himself, the flare of the match momentarily lighting his tense features. "I don't know where the tip came from. Maybe a neighbor. But somebody reported Carl sneaking around Demetriev's house. Anyway, Harvey Rose picked him up. Suspicion of intent to burgle, or something. He sent Carl down to your local emporium of justice with the second cop."

"He *what*? Good God, but—"

"Yeah, I know. Of course, Carl didn't want to say much around Rose, so he went along, figuring he'd call me when he got to the jail. But it seems the local fuzz hasn't heard about some of those inalienable constitutional rights. He never got a chance to make that call."

"Of course not. Is he all right?"

"I talked to him by phone a little while ago. The FBI gave the local boys the word, so he's out now."

Conan inhaled on his cigarette, looking up at the crowded dock, wondering if there was any real purpose behind all that activity. It kept merging into a vague, meaningless blur, haloed in spotlights and blinking emergency lights.

"When did the Marines hit Holliday Beach?"

"You mean the FBI? Too late. Fortunately, some of them were already on their way down from Portland to check out the Major's 'disappearance.' And you. You really had them in a sweat. But, Conan, they didn't have the faintest idea what was going on here—I mean, with Demetriev. The timing was damned good. Like the two watchdogs in the house across the street. They weren't due to report in until eight o'clock. The Portland office had no way of knowing what had happened to them. And by eight, Demetriev was already on his way home.''

"And what *did* happen to them?''

"Well, that's still a little hazy at this point, except one has a concussion, and they were both tied and gagged.''

Conan frowned. "But why didn't the FBI know what was happening? What about the Major? He must've known—''

"Nothing. Chief. Maybe he was getting some ideas, but he . . . didn't have time to follow through on them. He was sent here to help keep an eye on Demetriev. That's all. And, of course, he was new on the assignment; he'd only been in town a few days. Anyway, he happened to see Harry Morton walk out of your shop Friday, and recognized him. He had a run-in with Morton in San Francisco a few years back.''

Conan said numbly, "Morton was . . . Zimmerman.''

"Yeah. Anyway, the Major knew he was a courier and strong-arm man for the Party, so he got to wondering what he was up to.''

"And he started investigating on his own?''

"Not entirely on his own. The Bureau dug up some information for him, but I gather they weren't too happy about him neglecting his duties for something they figured had nothing to do with Demetriev. Besides, they weren't even sure it was really Morton he'd seen until today. They finally tracked down his latest alias and found out he was working as a book salesman, and his route included your shop.'' Duncan paused, loosing a sigh of disgust. "Anyway, they sent a replacement down this morning, and one guess where he spent the day.''

"The bookshop.'' He smiled faintly, remembering the lone "tourist'' he'd found upstairs as he was closing; the one standing at the gable window where he'd have a good view of the street and anyone coming into the shop.

"Yeah. He saw Morton there, and you really confused the issue with the old man and that Russian gimmick. You scared hell out of Demetriev, and the FBI figured you were trying to check his identity.''

"I was." He felt a mordant regret; a regret for the unexpected success of that little test.

"Anyway, they were beginning to wonder what was going on. They had four guys on the way down to check things out. They hit town about eight-fifteen."

Conan laughed. "Excellent timing."

"Sure. The timing was just as excellent all down the line." He made a sour grimace. "First, I lost Morton, then missed you when I went back to the shop. I finally got hold of Travers, and he sent a state patrolman down to Demetriev's, and all he turned up was Harvey Rose. And when Steve notified the Coast Guard, they said a couple of fishing boats left the Bay maybe five minutes before they got the call. If it hadn't been for that old Norsky tagging along behind you, they'd have had a hell of a time finding you." He laughed softly, shaking his head. "Funny, you know, the old guy had it figured pretty close. I mean, he figured you were being carted off to the trawlers. He didn't know why."

Conan smiled at that. "Well, Sven never trusted those Rooskies. What about Rose? Has he said anything yet?"

"I don't know. I've been a little busy trying to keep track of you and answer questions for the FBI. But my bet is he'll sing like a bird."

"If he thinks it'll help him."

"He needs all the help he can get, especially if they find the Major's body and run a ballistics check on the bullet. Rose's gun is safely in custody, by the way."

"They'll find the body," Conan said grimly, "when the tides are right."

Duncan nodded, taking a drag on his cigarette, then he gave Conan an oblique smile.

"You really busted ol' Harv a good one. He was still out when they found him."

He smiled, his eyes cold.

"It was quite satisfactory."

"Yeah, I can believe it. He owed you."

"He owed a few other people, too."

"Well, he'll never pay for all of it, but one man can

only pay so much. I mean, like Jeffries. They'll never tie that one on him."

"No. It's amazing that a man so inept could manage to commit a perfect crime." He let his head rest against the railing, wondering vaguely what time it was, but not caring enough to look at his watch. "It doesn't matter. He'll pay all he's capable of paying, and I've met my commitment, as well as satisfying myself."

"What do you mean—commitment?"

"To Nel Jeffries."

"Nel . . . oh, yeah." He gave a brief laugh. "The lady who got you into this mess. I almost forgot about her."

"The lady—yes." He smiled, thinking that Steve Travers owed an apology to that particular lady. Then he looked over at Duncan. "How's Mrs. Leen, by the way?"

"Speaking of ladies?"

"Well, I don't think I'd go that far."

"Mrs. Leen is *quiet*. Damn, I'd like to be the one to tell her Demetriev's home free." He eyed Conan suspiciously. "Did she tell you about him? And where'd that card come from?"

"The File." Then, at Duncan's puzzled expression, he explained, "I use it in my consultation business; an index of the top experts in almost any field. Demetriev was certainly one of the top men in physics; it isn't surprising his name was there. And it was there all the time, if I'd known what to look for." He paused, then, "You're in the File, too, incidentally."

"Among all those top experts?" His eyes narrowed. "Well, I'm glad somebody recognizes my true worth."

"Of course, you're the only private investigator I happen to know, but—"

"Yeah, I thought so. Thanks a lot, Chief."

Conan laughed. "My father used to tell me, always give a man his due."

"I'll get my due—when I make out your bill. Now, what about Mrs. Leen? She say anything about Demetriev?"

He shook his head slowly. "No. She'd never have purposely divulged anything, under any pressure. But she let a vital word slip. She's an extraordinary woman, Charlie.''

''Sure. I'm impressed. But what was this vital word she slipped?''

''She called her arrest a fair enough *exchange*. It finally came through to me that Demetriev wasn't a part of her conspiracy, he was the *object* of it. And I knew his interests; it wasn't hard to guess his forte was physics. Once I saw the card, I remembered his defection, and it all began to make sense.'' He took a quick puff on his cigarette, surprised to find his hand trembling. ''Damn, I'm sorry about that ploy with the Russian book. He was already frightened enough.''

Duncan shrugged. ''Sure, but when you were looking for physicists in that card catalog of yours, you had a good idea your man was Russian, didn't you? And it tied with the Russian trawlers.''

''Yes, I suppose so. What about the trawlers?''

''Well, last I heard, they were heading south—at a fast clip.''

''No doubt.''

''They can't touch them, Conan; you know that.''

''I know.'' He recoiled at a flash of light from the dock, every muscle tightening spasmodically. ''What the hell was that?''

''Some damn reporter. Just a flashbulb.''

He frowned, vainly attempting to focus on the flurry of movement, shivering with a passing chill.

''I . . . must be getting shell shock.''

Duncan frowned. ''Maybe. Look, I'm going to get Nicky.''

''No. She knows I'm here, and Demetriev's in worse shape than I am.''

Duncan hesitated, then breathed a sign of resignation.

''Yeah, I guess so. Well, anyway, it's been quite a night.''

''So it has.''

''You know, the old lady almost pulled it off, even with

you breathing down her neck. Her and that . . . third man. And with Rose, she had an in to everything the FBI was doing. They couldn't run full-time surveillance like that without cooperation from the local cops." He took a long breath. "The whole thing was too damned close. Too bad you didn't get any brainstorms about Morton—or Zimmerman."

Conan closed his eyes. "Yes. Too bad."

He made no attempt to explain that he *did* have a brainstorm about Zimmerman; it would be too much of an effort, and Charlie wouldn't be impressed with the real reasons behind that brainstorm.

He could feel an echo of that black rage, remembering the results of his careful surgery on the book; the surgery that revealed a crude bomb intended for Conan Flagg.

He knew then that Joe had put that book on the shelf for him.

When he baited his own little trap, Conan was well aware that the third man might be a total stranger; but if he were also the courier, then it was far more likely that he wouldn't be entirely unfamiliar. The information system had been in operation for over a year, assuming it was set up on Mrs. Leen's arrival, and the courier must have made numerous appearances in the shop during that time.

Of the people who came into the shop after Conan baited his own trap, only two were serious suspects in his mind—Joe and Demetriev. And Joe was suspect only in the sense that certain anomalies in his behavior were vaguely disturbing.

But the bomb had changed his mind. In spite of Charlie's warnings about putting on blinders, he couldn't believe that gentle, timid old man could plant a bomb that might kill innocent people.

But Joe Zimmerman was a man with a strong but tender ego, and he would be capable of that. He would also be capable of bolstering his ego with a secret life playing henchman and courier for the Party.

And Joe had been in the shop Friday, and at the counter when Harold Jeffries checked out *Crime and Punishment*.

He'd also made an unprecedented unscheduled visit to the shop Sunday—after Mrs. Leen found the book missing Saturday morning. And she had returned for the copy of the book a few hours after Joe's appearance Sunday afternoon.

A vacation. Yet Joe had said nothing about a vacation on his regular visit Friday. He'd also given the impression he was in town seeing a girlfriend, and that it was a relationship of long standing. But the "girlfriend" had exposed that lie this morning.

. . . you meet a guy one night, and by the next morning he thinks he owns you. . . .

Joe's unstinting regularity on his rounds began to make sense, too. It would facilitate the exchanges. Mrs. Leen would know she could always find him in the bookshop in the early afternoon of the second Friday of every month. And Zimmerman always spent at least a few minutes upstairs on his visits, and occasionally purchased a book. Special books, no doubt. And his curiosity today about the "robbery," particularly about whether Conan might have seen the burglar or . . .

"Conan?"

He opened his eyes, then raised his cigarette to his lips, but it had gone out. He tossed it over the railing and pulled the blanket around him. The numbness was like a blanket; he might not be thinking too clearly, but neither was he feeling too clearly.

"Yes, Charlie?"

Duncan was craning his neck to look around the pilot-house.

"I think they're taking Demetriev off."

He asked dully, "Where will they take him?"

"Portland; the University Hospital. There's a helicopter standing by to transport him. Maybe now somebody'll get around to—yeah, I figured as much."

Two men in neat business suits were approaching. Conan studied them disinterestedly, thinking how incongruous those suits seemed in this context. One of the men stopped by the pilothouse while the older of the pair walked over toward them.

Charlie didn't rise, but there was a hint of respect in his tone.

"Hello, Inspector."

"Mr. Duncan." He knelt, bringing himself on a level with them, and studied Conan a moment, then extended his hand. "Mr. Flagg, I'm Inspector David West."

Conan mustered a courteous smile, responding to that offered hand with his left hand.

"Sorry, Inspector, but—"

"Yes, I know. I thought you'd already been taken to the hospital."

"I'm waiting for my own doctor."

West smiled at that. "Dr. Heideger? She's seeing Demetriev to the helicopter."

"What about Demetriev? How is he?"

"Well, he's in rather serious condition; his heart, you know. But I understand he'll pull through, barring any unforeseen complications."

His breath came out in a long sigh. "Thank God."

West nodded soberly. "But a great deal of the thanks for his survival goes to you, Mr. Flagg. We're all grateful for your tenacity and . . . well, your good reflexes."

Conan tensed, and he was becoming aware of pain again. He was silent as West went on, hearing that interminable explosion in his hand, seeing the endless descent of Zimmerman's body. . . .

" . . . with Morton. He had a reputation as a man who'd stop at nothing once he—"

"Inspector—" His voice was tight. "Not . . . now."

David West hesitated, then averted his eyes uneasily.

"Yes, of course. I'm sorry."

Conan knew he *was* sorry; he'd been there.

"Inspector, can you tell me why . . . why Major Mills was so suspicious of me?"

West sighed, regret shadowing his eyes at the Major's name.

"Only because he saw Morton leaving your shop and

knew he was a courier. And, of course, he knew you'd have some experience in espionage." He paused, his gaze direct. "He was a careful man, if not always a cautious one. He only wanted to be sure of you. If it's any comfort, I don't think he ever really doubted you. He just had to be sure."

"Thanks." He pulled the blanket closer around him. "What will happen to Demetriev? I suppose you'll have to find another place for him to hide; another identity."

"Yes, but we hope it won't be necessary for him to hide indefinitely. We'll see that this kidnapping attempt gets plenty of publicity, especially in the foreign press; that will make further attempts less inviting. After this, if he returns to his homeland, it might seem a little suspicious; it wouldn't be so effective from a propaganda standpoint. And maybe in time, he won't be such a big issue; people will forget about him. We have a couple of universities lined up where he could probably get back into his work without attracting too much attention."

Conan nodded, thinking of the man he'd known as Anton Dominic, recognizing the vague sadness he felt as a sense of loss.

"Would it be possible for me to write to him, or—?"

"No, I'm afraid not. I'm sorry."

"I . . . had some books ordered for him."

West smiled. "He'll be convalescing for quite a while before we can move him. I'll see that he gets them."

"Thank you."

"Of course. Mr. Flagg, I'll have some questions for you, but they can wait. However, I would like to have your permission to look around the bookshop tomorrow."

He frowned, finding it an effort to keep his eyes in focus at all now.

"The shop? But . . . why?"

"We still have some loose ends to tie."

"Yes. I'll call Miss Dobie."

Duncan put in, "I'll take care of that, Conan."

"All right. Thanks, Charlie."

"There's one loose end we're particularly interested in,

Mr. Flagg." West shifted into a more comfortable position, frowning slightly. "Mr. Duncan told us about the *Crime and Punishment*, and your theory that it contained a message of some sort which was lost before Mrs. Leen acquired the book."

"It was the only theory that explained the facts."

West nodded absently. "Yes, and I'm sure it's essentially correct. You can understand we're anxious to find that missing item. It was undoubtedly coded, and even though the information may be of no value now, the code itself could help us in breaking related ones. We're checking Mrs. Leen's house, but I doubt we'll find anything."

"You won't find that message, at least. She never had it."

"Probably not." He regarded Conan intently. "Mr. Flagg, you were the only one—with the possible exception of this Captain Jeffries Mr. Duncan mentioned—who saw that book. Have you any idea what might have been contained in it, or in what form?"

Conan frowned in annoyance, not at West, but at the unanswered and unanswerable question he'd raised.

"No. Inspector, I examined that book as closely as possible without actually tearing it apart, but I found nothing. Of course, the missing item may not have been in the book when I found it. I'm sure Rose wasn't told what was so important about the book, and he wouldn't know if something were missing. Perhaps Jeffries removed it—whatever it was."

"Well, we'll check Jeffries' house and his clothing, but it's probably too late for that. I suppose the house has been cleaned and the clothing disposed of by now."

"Possibly, but I'm sure Nel will cooperate in any way she can." He smiled faintly. "She'll be all too happy to find an attentive official ear. Of course, it's also possible Major Mills found something I'd overlooked the night he was killed."

West nodded with no enthusiasm. "Yes, well, we'll just have to do what we can."

"If you *do* find it, I'd appreciate knowing where—and *what*."

Charlie laughed. "Don't mind him, Inspector. He has a little problem with curiosity."

"In this case, I can understand it. If we should be fortunate enough to find anything, Mr. Flagg, I'll tell you as much as I'm free to tell."

"Thanks. I appreciate that—very much."

"Well, we owe you—" He stopped, then came to his feet at the sound of approaching footsteps. "Ah, here's Dr. Heideger."

Nicky wasn't alone. Two attendants were on her heels carrying an empty stretcher, but Conan was only vaguely aware of them, or the stretcher, or West's leave-taking. Nicky's arrival seemed to act as a signal for his body, and all his defenses were slipping.

Charlie rose for Nicky. "Hello, Doc."

"Hello, Mr. Duncan. I'm beginning to think you're a jinx. Every time I run into you, it's at the scene of a disaster."

"*I'm* not the jinx. I just hang out with bad company."

"Like your friend with the long nose, here?"

She put her medical bag down and knelt at Conan's side, frowning as she pushed the blanket aside and saw the red streaks on his hand.

"Conan, I told you to be careful with those stitches."

He laughed at that, but found it painful. The numbness was leaving him now that she was here.

"I'm sorry, Nicky, about your stitchery."

"Sure." She pressed her fingers against his wrist. "Well, I charge double for the second time around. Besides, it'll hurt you more than it will me."

"Charlie, that's called a proper bedside manner."

"Yeah, well, I say, always give a man his due. Maybe you've got it coming."

Nicky pressed her hand to his forehead, studying him clinically.

"He'll get his due. Conan, I'm taking you to the hospital so I can get a good look at what you've done to my sutures."

"Wait, Nicky, what about Demetriev?"

She smiled. "Demetriev. He's still Dominic to me. Don't worry about him; that old man has grit. Oh—he asked me to give you a message."

"A message? What?"

"Well, he wasn't too coherent, and he has a hard time with English anyway, but the gist of it was—thanks."

He nodded silently, finding no words appropriate, then tensed as Nicky signaled the attendants, and he became fully aware of the stretcher.

"You aren't taking me out on *that*."

She looked at him levelly. "You want to bet?"

He sighed. "All right, but do me one favor, Nicky."

"That all depends."

"Just one."

"Well . . . okay. What is it?"

"When you get me to that damned hospital, put me on a no-visitors status."

She laughed softly. "Consider it done."

CHAPTER 29

Beatrice Dobie was at the entrance of the bookshop, leaning against the doorjamb, enjoying the warmth of the winter sun.

"Well, good morning, Mr. Flagg—and welcome back!"

"Good morning, indeed, Miss Dobie." Conan laughed, impulsively throwing his good arm around her shoulders and giving her a quick peck on the cheek. "It's a glorious morning. Coffee on?"

She was flushing at his unaccustomed display of affection as she followed him into the office.

"Of course. That's always the first order of business. Here"—she hurried to the percolator—"let me pour you a cup. You'll have to be careful with that shoulder."

He smiled at her solicitude, but didn't argue. He sat down at the desk and surveyed the two large stacks of mail that had accumulated in his three-day absence.

"Good God, what a waste of paper," he commented sourly. "You could save a tree a year on what crosses this desk, and most of it pure and unadulterated nonsense. Oh—thanks." He took the cup she handed him and watched her as she settled into the chair across the desk.

"Well, Miss Dobie, and how are you?"

She was smiling contentedly. "Oh, I'm just fine. I've been basking in reflected glory these last few days."

"Oh?"

"Well, you weren't available," she explained, gingerly sipping at her coffee, "so all the newspaper and magazine reporters, and those TV people were coming to me to get the inside dope on your epic adventure."

Conan laughed. "I hope you gave them a good story."

"I did my best, and it was colorful enough, anyway. Of course, Inspector West cramped my style a bit; he told me exactly how much I should say. But at least I had some of my own questions answered along the way. It was all very exciting. Too bad you missed it."

"You mean it's all over? I don't get to bask in my own glory?"

"Afraid not. By this time, it's old stuff." She loosed a great sigh. *"Sic transit gloria."*

He shrugged. "Well, so be it. And it's just as well. I'm not too anxious to push my career as a detective, anyway. It gets a little strenuous at times."

She peered at him thoughtfully over the rim of her cup.

"Speaking of your career as a detective, I think my feelings are hurt."

"You think?"

"Well . . . it sort of hurt, I guess, that I had to find out you're a genuine private detective from an *Oregonian* reporter."

"I'm sorry about that, but don't take it personally. And you weren't the only one whose feelings were hurt." He smiled to himself, remembering Charlie Duncan's very expressive response to that piece of news. "Actually, I didn't intend for *anyone* to know about it. I have Inspector West to thank for that. Now, I'll be besieged with nuts and paranoic spouses. I may have to officially retire."

"Well, you know, that might not be so easy. No telling what you've gotten yourself into, now that the word is out."

He raised an eyebrow. "I know what your problem is.

You had a taste of all that reflected glory, and it's gone to your head.''

"That may be, but—oh!'' She turned toward the door as Meg skidded around the corner and into the office with a frantic scrabbling of claws, playing a crumpled bit of paper like a hockey puck.

"Meg!'' Conan laughed as he watched her right herself after her careening turn. "How are you, Duchess?''

She picked up her paper puck, then looked up at him, her sapphire eyes wide, reflecting red glints.

"Come on,'' he said, patting his knee. "Come see me.''

For a moment, she seemed to consider whether she wished to give up her game. Then, deciding on a compromise, she kept the paper firmly clasped between her teeth and leaped into his lap.

"I missed you, Duchess,'' he said, running his hand along her back, feeling the vibrations of her purring under his fingers. "I hope you got to bask in some of that reflected glory.''

"Of course, she did,'' Miss Dobie put in. "That cat could upstage Helen Hayes. They had her on TV day before yesterday.''

He laughed, looking down at Meg and her expression of oblivious bliss.

"The star. But of course, you knew that all along, didn't . . . you—?'' He stopped abruptly.

It was the crumpled paper Meg held between her teeth that caught his attention.

"Here—let me have that.''

She objected with a low, deep-throated growl as he pried it out of her mouth, but he quieted her protests with another scrap of paper taken hurriedly from the desk. She leaped after it as he tossed it on the floor, apparently satisfied with the exchange.

Conan unfolded the paper he'd taken from her, flattening it against the desk. It was a date card from one of the rental books.

"Anything important?'' Miss Dobie asked. Then she

raised an eyebrow and shot Meg a disapproving look. "This is getting ridiculous. Now she's pulling the date cards out of the books. She likes that stiff paper, you know. I suppose it got dropped on the floor sometime."

But Conan wasn't listening. He was studying the card, a prickling chill running along his skin.

He recognized it.

He recognized the charred edge at the bottom and the inept attempt at repair with transparent tape. It was so crumpled, chewed, smudged, and so liberally punctured with tooth-marks, the dates were almost illegible. But he managed to decipher the last one.

November 12. Friday.

This was the date from the original copy of *Crime and Punishment*; the book that cost Harold Jeffries his life.

And now he knew why.

"Mr. Flagg? Is something wrong?"

He waved her to silence without looking up."

The tape hadn't been put there purposes of repair, but for preservation of sorts; something characteristic of a meticulous and fussy man like Harold Jeffries. It had been put there to preserve something he'd discovered accidentally when he let that card slip out of his hand and into the fireplace.

The fire had acted as an unwitting agent in that discovery, but apparently moisture, accompanied by bending and crumpling, worked just as well, and Meg's chewing and pouncing had not only loosened the tape, but exposed the special qualities of this card on two of the other corners.

It was laminated.

And the adhesive had given way to both fire and Meg's mangling. It was particularly apparent on the charred bottom edge. Where the tape had been dislodged, the card was split into three layers. He carefully pried the top layer back, but only a scant half inch. The adhesive still held toward the center.

But it was enough to see what Harold Jeffries must have seen. The center layer was a thin film, covered with unintelligible symbols.

Symbols. Words, to the initiate.

Words were only composites of symbols whose meaning was agreed upon by the people who spoke, or wrote, or read them.

This language would have few initiates, but Mrs. Edwina Leen had been one of them.

"Oh, no—" His voice was little more than a whisper.

"Mr. Flagg, for Heaven's sake, what's wrong?"

Miss Dobie was looking at him anxiously, alarmed at his expression, but he hardly heard her. He was still staring at the card.

"Mr. Flagg?"

At length, he looked up at her, then at Meg, who was busily playing tiger games on the floor. He closed his eyes briefly, and finally began to laugh.

Beatrice Dobie stared at him, nonplussed.

"Mr. Flagg, *what's wrong?*"

"I'm sorry, it's just that it's so damned"—he paused, the laughter fading—"ironic, I suppose."

"*What* is? What's on that card?"

He studied it, feeling no desire to laugh now, then handed it to her.

"That's the date card from the copy of *Crime and Punishment* Captain Jeffries checked out Friday. I'm sure of that; I examined the book rather carefully when I found it Saturday, and I recognized the charring at the bottom."

A slight pallor touched her cheeks.

"This is from . . . the book that—"

"Yes."

She frowned at the layered bottom edge and pulled the top layer back gingerly, then looked up at him blankly.

'But, what's all this?"

"A message—in code."

"You mean this is—"

"That's the missing item Mrs. Leen was so anxious to acquire."

She looked down at the card again.

"I wonder what all those little squiggles mean."

He leaned back, gazing absently at the card.

"I'm assuming those little squiggles include the time-table and rendezvous instructions for Demetriev's abduction. It probably told her Harrison's name, the name of his boat, and when and where he'd arrive to take Demetriev—and herself and Joe, of course—to the trawlers. She was utterly helpless without that information; the timing was particularly important on this little operation."

Miss Dobie scrutinized the card, pursing her lips in apparent dissatisfaction.

"I thought she got her instructions from the trawlers. I mean, those signals you saw."

"She did, but only when she couldn't find that card. It was extremely risky to make direct contact with the trawlers by any means. That particular means was set up from the beginning—from her arrival in Holliday Beach—but it was too dangerous to be anything but an emergency measure." His eyes narrowed, briefly cold. "I'm sure she was very reluctant to use it, not only because of the risk, but because it meant admitting that she'd let a vital piece of information slip through her fingers."

Miss Dobie still seemed less than satisfied.

"But how did *Meg* get hold of this card?"

Conan shrugged. "Probably on the night Mills was killed. He put up a struggle before Rose shot him; in the melee, the card might have fallen from the book. Or Mills may have actually handled the book; he knew the title from monitoring my phone conversations. He might have removed the card himself. Perhaps Rose beat a strategic retreat in the middle of his own search, and didn't attack the Major until after he'd had a chance to look at the book. I don't know. Obviously, the card was separated from the book, and Rose didn't know how important it was. By the time Joe came around to search the shop, I suppose Meg had already claimed it."

"And those FBI men went over this place with a fine-toothed comb."

"It would take more than a fine-toothed comb to get at Meg's hiding places."

She was silent for a while, watching Meg at her predatory antics. Finally, she breathed a profound sigh.

"Well . . . I guess it turned out to be a blessing in disguise." Conan winced at the platitude, but made no comment. "Otherwise, you might never have found out about Dr. Demetriev."

"Possibly. Or perhaps I—or someone else—might have found out *sooner*." He straightened, squaring his shoulders decisively. "Anyway, you can send that card to Inspector West with my compliments. And Meg's."

He reached for the File and began leafing through the cards while Miss Dobie watched curiously. Finally, he pulled out the Luigi Benevento card, and his features relaxed into a quiet smile.

"You know, Miss Dobie, you're absolutely right."

"I am?"

"Didn't you say the best way to get a lead on that Fabrizi project was to see Benevento in Florence?"

"Oh. Did I say that?"

"Of course you did." He grinned at her. "And I always take your advice."

She laughed at that. "Oh, yes. Always. I can think of at least . . . well, let's see, at least *two* occasions in the last seven years when you've taken my advice."

"That isn't a bad record." He reached for the phone. "Now, if you'll excuse me—"

She smiled knowingly, and as he dialed gathered up her coffee cup and Meg, and started for the door.

"Give my regards to Miss Hartford," she said as she closed the door behind her.

He nodded, then turned his attention to the phone.

"Trans-World Travel Agency. May I help you?"

"May I speak to Miss Hartford, please?"

When the connection was made, he smiled and leaned back with a luxurious sense of anticipation.

"This is Miss Hartford, may I—"

"Lisa, this is Conan Flagg."

"Conan! It's been months. I thought maybe you'd found a cure for itchy feet."

He laughed. "Never."

"That's a good news. What can I do for you?"

He closed his eyes, smiling at a warm-toned image of the Duomo; the wide piazza with the flapping, cooing clouds of pigeons; the soaring campanile. . . .

"Lisa, you can book me on the first flight available—to Florence."